GULLAH SECRETS

ALSO BY SUSAN GABRIEL

Fiction

Temple Secret Series:
Temple Secrets
Gullah Secrets

The Wildflower Trilogy:
The Secret Sense of Wildflower
(a Best Book of 2012 – Kirkus Reviews)
Lily's Song
Daisy's Fortune

Trueluck Summer
Grace, Grits and Ghosts: Southern Short Stories
Seeking Sara Summers
Circle of the Ancestors
Quentin & the Cave Boy

Nonfiction

Fearless Writing for Women:
Extreme Encouragement & Writing Inspiration

GULLAH SECRETS

SEQUEL TO TEMPLE SECRETS

SUSAN GABRIEL

WILD LILY ARTS

ISBN: 978-0-9981050-1-7

Cover design by Lizzie Gardiner, lizziegardiner.co.uk

Wild Lily Arts

Printed in the United States of America

In memory of
Peg Hall

CHAPTER ONE

Old Sally

Old Sally sits overlooking the Atlantic Ocean, the sunrise stretching toward her like a golden path between this world and the next. At 102 years of age, Old Sally has been teaching her granddaughter Violet the art of Gullah folk magic to ensure their traditions stay alive.

Plenty of troubles in this world are from people forgetting their ancestors' wisdom, she thinks.

Swells of an ocean at high tide slap against the South Carolina shore as pelicans dive in quest of their morning meal. Dolphin Island is on the other side of the Georgia state line, close enough to Savannah that her family always worked there. Old Sally and Violet often meet on the front porch in the early mornings and sit in their favorite rocking chairs while Violet writes what she learns in a hardback notebook. At one time, Old Sally's root doctoring was known all over the Southeast, but nowadays most people take a pill to make their symptoms go away instead of using a root cure.

Even with a household full of people underfoot, Old Sally takes time to ponder things. According to Old Sally's grandmother, Sadie, who taught her everything she knows about Gullah folk magic, silence is where wisdom is found. Over her long life, Old Sally has made a friend of silence. She looks over at Violet, who is mixed race and a lighter shade than Old Sally with her leathered, dark skin. Violet is still as beautiful in her forties as she was when she was young.

"A penny for your thoughts," Violet says.

"Those will cost you a quarter," Old Sally says with a smile.

She laughs when Violet pulls a coin from her pocket and places it on the porch railing in front of them. Their playfulness pleases Old Sally. Often, her memories are from when she was a girl, the end of life circling back around to the beginning.

To the Gullah people, like their African ancestors, time is eternal and continually renews itself like an unbroken circle. Past, present, and future are one. In the Gullah concept of time, the dead still have an impact on the community of the living. While their bodies go into the ground and their souls to God, their presence is still felt as long as they are remembered.

It always touched Old Sally that her Gullah ancestors were buried with their heads turned toward the east. A sacred ritual, her grandmother told her, that signifies the circle of life that rises and sets with the sun. East is also the direction of their beloved homeland. The place her ancestors lived before they were forced onto ships and brought here to the South Carolina and Georgia coasts to be slaves for white landowners.

Remembering their transaction, Old Sally picks up the quarter and puts it in the pocket of her cotton dress.

"I be thinking about my grandmother," Old Sally begins. "She lived with my family the entire time I was growing up. It be my grandmother who always had time for me and who explained things I didn't understand. Before I was born, she had been a slave," Old Sally continues. "The stories she told from those days always made me cry. But she also taught me what it meant to be free, and how to think for myself."

Old Sally pauses, remembering how her grandmother insisted that she learn to read. Before her grandmother's death, Sally taught her how to read and write in return.

"Your great-grandmother was very gifted with folk magic," Old Sally begins again. "She made me look like a beginner. Like I've told you before, you be gifted, too, Violet. You have the family sensitivity."

Violet looks out over the sea as if pondering the responsibility of this gift.

The Gullah women of their family all have different talents. Violet sees spirits and has a shoulder that predicts when something terrible is about to happen. Old Sally's youngest daughter, Queenie, offers laughter as a potion. Her long-gone daughter, Maya, had been an expert at reading tea leaves. Besides root doctoring and spells, Old Sally also helps people transition from this world into the next.

Old Sally pushes the quarter toward Violet, who looks up with a smile. If the light catches her just right, Sally can see Queenie in her, Violet's mother.

"For some reason, I was thinking about Miss Temple and how hard she was on Queenie," Violet says. "Ghosts don't relocate, do they?"

"Not that I know of," Old Sally says, although she must admit to herself she has wondered the same thing.

Old Sally's family and the Temples have a shared history that goes back several generations. Old Sally's grandmother was a slave for the elite Temple family in Savannah before she was finally freed. Then Old Sally worked for Iris Temple in the same mansion for sixty years, even before "Old" was added to her name. When she got too old and tired to work there anymore, her granddaughter Violet took over as housekeeper and cook, and her daughter Queenie became Iris's companion.

Like two trees that have grown together and intermingled roots, the two families sometimes share parentage, which complicates matters even more. Sally's grandmother Sadie gave birth to a baby boy named Adam, who was half Temple and taken from her at the age of ten, sent to a plantation in Charleston. For that evil deed, Sadie was the first of Sally's ancestors to put a Gullah curse on the Temples. Two generations later, Old Sally had Queenie by Edward Temple, Iris's father, making Queenie and Iris half sisters. Then Queenie had Violet by Mister Oscar, Iris's husband. For two hundred years, black servants and lily-white rich folks in Savannah mixed and mingled in all sorts of ways that weren't the least bit socially acceptable.

Of course, Iris's last will and testament changed everything when she left the Temple mansion to Violet, who was not only the housekeeper but also Mister Oscar's daughter. All because of Iris's fear of going against deathbed requests. And not just any deathbed request, but one from her dead husband, who still haunted the Temple mansion.

Old Sally sighs. The spirit world feels so close it's hard to imagine some people never give it a thought.

After the Temple mansion burned to the ground over two years ago—a fire Edward Temple accidentally started in which he also lost his life—no one heard anything else from the ghostly Temples. Old Sally hopes they have finally been laid to rest. But maybe not.

Those Temples are a stubborn bunch, she thinks. *Wouldn't be like them to just fade away.*

Just in case, Old Sally keeps a bowl filled with water in the front room to run the ghosts off like her grandmother taught her, and she continues the protection spells like she always has.

"If we were having the wedding at the mansion today, Miss Temple would try to ruin it for Queenie," Violet says.

Old Sally agrees, thinking that maybe the Temple ghosts are haunting Violet today, too. "We are lucky to have it here at the beach," Sally says.

Doing battle with Iris Temple, dead or alive, is not something anyone would want to do. Especially not Old Sally. She had her fill of Iris a long time ago.

The sky is a deep blue. The breeze, gentle and warm, with no hints of anything that might ruin the day. But before they get ready for the wedding, Old Sally must think of a Gullah story for Violet to put in her notebook. Lately, she has been sharing the Gullah legends she grew up hearing.

"Perhaps it's time to tell you about the mermaid storm," Old Sally says. "It was my grandmother's favorite story to tell my brothers and me whenever she wanted to mesmerize us, as well as scare us to death."

Violet opens her book, ready to take notes.

"It was October of 1893," Old Sally begins. "Common knowledge to the Gullah people at that time was that whenever a mermaid was captured, a storm brewed." She pauses like her grandmother always did, to pull her listeners in. "Well, a white man on the island did indeed capture a mermaid one day, and he was hiding her in his shed behind his family's beach cottage. He refused to release the mermaid," she continues, "and a few days later a rare hurricane struck the island. It was a horrible storm. The ocean rose and rose until it finally got so high that the captive mermaid was washed back to sea. However, as punishment for the man's misdeeds, his entire family was drowned in the tidal surge."

Violet stops writing. "Well, that story would scare me, too."

"My grandmother always ended the tale with 'Let's just hope no white folks have captured any mermaids lately.'" Old Sally chuckles, remembering her grandmother's laughter.

A bluebird lands on the arm of an empty rocking chair by the front door, surprising them both. A rare shade of indigo blue, the bird's beauty is otherworldly. She watches them as though noting their plainness in comparison to her exquisiteness and chirps a tune before flying away.

"A songbird singing on a doorstep means company's coming," Old Sally says.

"Really?" Violet writes this down.

"And if somebody accidentally drops a dishrag in the kitchen, that means they're coming soon."

Violet jots this in her notebook, too.

The scent of melancholy rides in on the breeze. Sometimes the loneliness of missing all the family and friends who have gone on before her takes Old Sally's breath away. Most notably, her grandmother is on her mind today.

"How did I get to be this old, Violet?"

"Just lucky, I guess," Violet says, still writing. She doesn't realize the significance of Old Sally's comment. "I wish I'd seen all the change you've seen in your lifetime," she adds, looking up from her notebook. "It must be fascinating."

"Overwhelming is the word I'd use," Old Sally says. "To live in the twenty-first century is like holding onto the tail of a comet."

"Well, I'm very grateful that you're here." Violet closes her notebook and looks at her watch. She stands and leans over to kiss Old Sally's cheek.

"I've got to get busy. It's a big day."

Old Sally agrees.

Alone again, she smiles, happy to pass on the Gullah secrets to her granddaughter, just like her grandmother did to her. Not that they are secrets exactly, but they might as well be since so few people know their traditions. Someday soon Old Sally will return to her ancestors, a fact that doesn't scare her in the least. However, she is not ready to go home just yet. She still has unfinished business. Memories of the past must be sorted through, and the last of the Gullah traditions must be passed on to Violet. Not to mention, there is a wedding later today that she doesn't want to miss.

CHAPTER TWO

Queenie

Queenie Temple studies her reflection in her bedroom's full-length mirror, sucking in her ample waistline to no avail. The white plus-size wedding gown she and Rose found in Savannah a few weeks ago is not cooperating. In her sixties, Queenie is not a typical bride, although she is having a traditional June wedding.

"How do women fit into these things?" Queenie says to her daughter, Violet, who inches the zipper upward on the back of her dress.

"It would help if you stood still," Violet says, coaxing the fabric to loosen. "When it comes to squirming, you're worse than when Tia and Leisha were little girls."

Queenie smiles. "I do feel like a youngster these days." The sigh that follows is unexpected. "But the truth is, I'm not a spring chicken anymore, Vi. Hell, I'm not even a *fall* chicken." She cackles. "Is my intended here yet?"

"He got here an hour ago," Violet says. "He's pacing and wearing a path into the kitchen floor."

"Oh heavens, do you think he's having second thoughts?" Queenie's newly tweezed eyebrows float above the glasses she has begun to need.

Violet tugs at Queenie's dress. "I think he's more nervous that *you'll* have second thoughts," she says. "He's wearing a new bow tie, by the way. Wait till you see it."

"That man," Queenie clucks. "Did I tell you about the time he came to bed wearing nothing but a bow tie?"

Violet tugs at the back of Queenie's dress again. "That's what the girls would call TMI," she says. "Too Much Information."

Queenie laughs again. "Maybe you should sew up the back and then cut me out of it later."

"It's bad luck to mend a garment someone is wearing," Violet says. "I imagine that goes for sewing someone into a wedding dress, too."

"Is that another Gullah saying?"

"Yes," Violet admits. "I hope it doesn't bother you, it helps me remember them."

"No problem." Queenie wipes a thin layer of sweat from above her upper lip. "I can't believe how nervous I am. You'd think I'd never been married before."

"You haven't," Violet says, playing deadpan to Queenie's humor.

Queenie cackles again. The more nervous she gets, the more she laughs. She has been this way her entire life. If given a choice between laughter or tears, laughter is the winner every time. Crying is usually reserved for sacred moments, the last time being when Spud proposed. Her eyes mist with the memory. They were eating at their favorite seafood restaurant in Hilton Head—The Spicy Sturgeon. Halfway through the meal, Queenie bit into the best crab cake she had ever tasted and nearly cracked a crown. Wearing a lobster bib, Spud quickly dropped to one knee. Then he spoke the words Queenie had waited forty years to hear, even though she and Spud had only dated for one of those years: *I'd be greatly honored, Queenie Temple, if you would agree to become my wife.*

Leave it to Spud to hide an engagement ring inside a crab cake. In the moments that followed, Queenie cried an ocean of tears. Grateful tears. Relieved tears. Tears she had been holding in for decades. She cried for so long Spud's knee gave out, and two waiters had to help him stand again.

Now, six months later, Queenie and Spud will exchange their vows on the beach in front of the house this very day. Old Sally will be officiating, along with the young priest who buried Iris, Queenie's half sister. Iris was a Savannah matriarch known for being difficult, and Queenie served as her personal assistant for thirty-five years. The priest's signature on the marriage license will make their marriage official in matters of the law, and her mother's blessing—whom Queenie calls Old Sally like everybody else—will make it official everywhere else. Heaven included.

"Did you do the things I suggested?" Violet continues to fiddle with the vexing zipper.

Queenie thinks for a minute. "You mean about wishing on a new moon? Yes, I did that a few days ago. I also said 'rabbit' first thing before getting out of bed on the first day of the month. I'll take all the good luck I can get."

"You didn't happen to dream of gray horses last night, did you?" Violet asks. "That's supposed to be good luck, too."

"Not that I remember," Queenie says. "I think I dreamed I was at the Kentucky Fried Chicken drive-thru in Savannah.

The one Iris went to. In the dream, I drove up to that little window and picked up a live chicken instead of a cooked one."

Violet laughs before stepping back to take another look at Queenie's dress. "Not to worry. As far as I know, dreaming of live chickens is not bad luck."

Queenie's cheeks flush hot thinking of how she denied herself and Violet the relationship they could have had for all those years when Queenie was hiding the fact that she was Violet's mother. It is easily the biggest regret of her life. They have always been close. But being mother and daughter feels different from being an aunt and niece. Looking back on it, she realizes now that if she could do it over, she would have told the truth, no matter how angry Oscar might have been or how much she might have feared the outcome. As Iris's husband and Queenie's employer, Oscar had a lot of power over her and took advantage of it.

Thankfully, Queenie no longer has a need for secret-keeping. She wants to shout to the world her love for the one man she's waited her entire life to find: Spud Grainger. A retired butcher from the Piggly Wiggly. Retired thanks to Iris's surprising generosity in her will. Denzel Washington he is not. For one thing, he is about ten shades lighter than Denzel. In other words, he is white to Queenie's black. But life seldom works out as planned.

The zipper finally closed, Queenie and Violet share a mother-daughter sigh of relief. When Queenie turns to the mirror to have a look, her mood shifts like the weather vane on the back porch when a storm is coming in.

"Oh, Violet, who am I kidding by wearing white? It's not like a person can revert back to virgin-hood, even if it was thirty years between dates."

"You look beautiful," Violet reassures her.

They stand at the mirror as if taking in the family resemblance.

"Sometimes I feel like I don't deserve happiness like this." Queenie lowers her head.

"Don't say things like that," Violet says. "You deserve happiness as much as anybody. Maybe more, given you put up with Iris Temple for thirty-five years. For that, you probably deserve lifelong happiness *and* a medal."

Queenie walks to the front window, Violet following, and then delivers another sigh as she looks out over the ocean from the second floor. "Maybe Iris was my penance for not being truthful while you were growing up."

"Listen to me." Violet looks into her eyes. "You have waited a long time to be happy, Queenie Temple, and I will not let anyone take this moment away from you. Especially not you. I know you don't think you deserve anything like this, but you do," she continues. "Spud makes you happy. In fact, this last year is the happiest I've ever seen you."

Queenie wipes away a plump tear before giving Violet a hug.

"Thank you for that," Queenie says. "Everybody needs a good talking-to now and again." Queenie stands taller, grateful that Violet feels she can be honest with her.

"I can't believe you went to the Piggly Wiggly with Miss Temple all those years and never even noticed Spud," Violet says.

"Well, he was Iris's old flame, and nobody in their right mind messed with Iris."

They exchange a knowing look.

"Well, I bet wherever Miss Temple is, she's happy for you, too," Violet says.

Queenie turns to look at the overhead light and waits on the ghost of Iris Temple to disagree like she did in the old mansion when her spirit shook the chandeliers. Blissful silence answers her. Queenie has not missed her half sister's haunting presence one bit. Or any of the other ghosts in the Temple mansion, for that matter, who for years gave her the shivers in cold hallways and various rooms of that old house. But it is quite a stretch to imagine Iris happy for her. Iris was notably the most stubborn, controlling matriarch in Savannah, if not the entire Southeast.

"Everything is going too well, Vi. I'm worried something will happen to ruin this day."

"Relax," Violet says. "Nothing is going to go wrong."

"But what if the Temple ghosts find out I'm marrying Spud?"

"Don't be silly," Violet says. "Those ghosts are long gone." But she doesn't look entirely convinced.

If Queenie had to imagine the worst news she could receive on her wedding day, it would be that the one ghost in Savannah she had hoped to sweet Jesus she had rid herself of had returned. A ghost by the name of Iris. A ghost who was once in love with Queenie's intended.

For years Queenie accompanied Iris to the meat section of the Piggly Wiggly, watching her practically marinate all over Spud while at the same time rejecting him. Queenie wasn't sure what game Iris was playing, but it didn't seem fair to Spud. A man Queenie didn't give a second look back then is now a different story.

Queenie begins to pace, imagining every catastrophe that can befall two people getting married.

"Have you and Mama put a protection spell on the wedding?"

"We did spells earlier in the week," Violet says, giving the dress another tug to test its hold.

In the last year, Queenie has found Violet and her mama conjuring up all sorts of awful-smelling things on the kitchen stove. Concoctions that could ward off anything bad within a hundred miles by smell alone. But at this moment Queenie is glad her family tradition includes folk magic and getting rid of any unwanted evil. If that isn't a description of Iris, she isn't sure what is.

After Old Sally passes from this world, Violet will be the keeper of the Gullah secrets. Secrets Queenie has never had any desire to know. The family sensitivity skipped a generation, and Queenie is okay with that. The truth is, she has neither the temperament nor desire to deal with mysterious forces.

Queenie glances at the clock on her bedside table. Guests will arrive in less than an hour. In the meantime, everything has been planned and is in the process of being executed. Old Sally will be the one to give Queenie away and walk with her down the aisle. For months Queenie worried that her mama might not get to attend the wedding. When someone is a centenarian, you figure their days are numbered. But for weeks now Queenie has shoved that thought to the back of her mind with all the other worst-case scenarios.

"In one hour, you will be Mrs. Spud Grainger," Violet says.

"Maybe people should call me Mrs. Potato Head since I'm marrying a Spud." Queenie's laughter tests the strength of her zipper.

Violet laughs, too, something Queenie has seen her do more often these last few months. Ever since she opened her tea shop, Violet has possessed a level of contentment that

Queenie has never seen before. It is as if Violet has finally stepped into the role she was meant to play.

Queenie scrutinizes herself in the mirror once again. "There's something off," she says.

"I told you, you look beautiful," Violet says.

Queenie pauses, taking in her reflection until her eyes widen. "I've got it," she says. "There isn't an ounce of color in this whole outfit. Wearing all this white, I look like a milk chocolate Disney princess. That will not do."

Violet insists this isn't true, which only prompts another angst-filled sigh before Queenie begins to pace again, unconvinced.

"Why am I trying to look all traditional? I've never been traditional a day in my life. I don't look one bit like myself," Queenie says, thinking, *Oprah would not approve.* Seeing all this white in the mirror makes her feel like one of Rose's bare-white canvases.

"You're just a little nervous," Violet says.

Queenie pauses. "I need a dash of color," she says.

"A dash of color?" Violet's brows raise as if she thinks that a *dash* of anything would never be enough for Queenie. If Sam's Club sold color in bulk, Queenie would bring it home by the truckload.

Queenie steps into her walk-in closet, her billowing white gown refusing to clear the door. When she breaches the doorway, she nearly falls headfirst into her shoes. When they were designing this addition, she gave up bathroom footage to add more room for storage. The Temple mansion in Savannah, where she used to live, had absurdly tiny closets for such a prominent home.

"Almost there," she says to Violet, who holds Queenie's dress out behind her to keep it from getting wrinkled.

Inside her closet, Queenie ties a bright yellow silk scarf around her neck. Then she trades out her white sequined dressy flats for a pair of purple pumps. Yet, there is still something missing. Queenie sifts through her closet until she finds a large round box containing a hat she has never dared to wear. And for Queenie that is saying a lot. It is bold and big and red. Is now the time to debut it? Or in this case, add it to the veil she already intends to wear? It is a silly notion, she admits, but Queenie is desperate for some color.

For months Queenie planned a traditional wedding like the ones in those wedding magazines. An event meant to finally make her acceptable, in her own eyes and others. Now she is considering wearing a hat that would make even the characters in *Steel Magnolias* balk. The color of fire engines and emergency exits, the wide drooping brim makes her look like a deeply suntanned southern belle.

With Violet's help, Queenie successfully breaches the closet door again, and carefully positions the hat on her head while looking in the mirror.

"Perfect," she says, beaming a smile at Violet.

Violet's initial shock appears to soften. Queenie is now adorned in color.

To calm her nervousness, Queenie takes a deep breath followed by a slow exhale. In less than an hour, she will marry Spud Grainger, the only man in her six decades of life that she has ever truly loved. Nobody and nothing will prevent her destiny.

CHAPTER THREE

Rose

Coming home to Savannah, where she grew up, and now living on Dolphin Island with her chosen family has been good for Rose. She hadn't realized how much she missed shade and moisture until she returned from living in Wyoming. Growing up as a Temple meant Rose grew up facing a lot of expectations. She wasn't anything like her mother—the great and formidable Iris Temple—and every day of her life Rose was aware of how disappointed her mother was in her. But with her mother gone, life seems easier here.

Rose and Violet were up most of the night with preparations for Queenie and Spud's wedding reception. Rose coordinated the event: invitations, flowers, rentals, and helping Queenie find a gown. After Queenie finally decided what kind of ceremony she wanted—a decision process that took months—Rose had only six weeks to get everything arranged. Now Violet is helping Queenie with her dress.

Arranging a wedding is what she had hoped she and her

daughter Katie might do together someday. But it seems that isn't meant to be. Though it has entered a new millennium, the world needs to do a lot of changing for Katie and her girl-friend Angela to get married. Rose doesn't have that level of faith in humanity. Not after the events of last year on September 11.

To stop Spud Grainger's hand-wringing and pacing, Rose gives him a dozen lemons to cut for fresh lemonade. He stands at the granite kitchen counter in front of the cutting board, wearing a purple suit. It never occurred to her that he might need some direction on appropriate wedding attire, but she imagines Queenie will love it.

"Have you talked to Queenie today?" Rose asks Spud.

"She has forbidden it," Spud says, a smile upon his mustached lips.

Rose imagines a romantic relationship with Queenie would require a certain amount of willingness to take orders.

Good for him, she thinks. *Now if only Max could learn that, too.*

The cordless telephone rings in the kitchen. Considering the household living situation, Rose never knows how to answer. Lately, she identifies herself and then hopes the caller knows who to ask for.

"Rose, this is Regina. Edward's wife."

Her missing fingertip throbs in recognition upon hearing her brother's name.

Rose has only talked to Regina once on the telephone since they met last summer at the Temple Garden, a park created by the city where her family's mansion once stood. For decades, Edward kept Regina a secret from their family. A fact that seems poignant to Rose. Has Regina somehow found out about Queenie's wedding and wants to know the whereabouts of her invitation?

They exchange pleasantries, and then Regina's tone grows more serious. "I called to warn you about something," she says.

"Warn me?" Rose sits on a nearby stool, ready for bad news. The room filled with the puckering smell of cut lemons, Spud has overheard and looks at Rose.

Everything has gone so well with the wedding preparations, Rose has anticipated a giant shoe poised to drop. From the sound of Regina's voice, this call might be it.

"I had an unexpected visitor last night," Regina says. "A young woman." She pauses.

Is her brother's widow the type to dangle a disaster in her face? Perhaps she is more like Edward than Rose initially thought.

"The young woman claims to be Edward's daughter," Regina says.

In her imagination, Rose hears a shoe drop with a thud onto the slate kitchen floor. Somehow, Rose knew her brother would find a way to mess with her life even from the grave.

"Edward has a daughter?" Rose asks.

"It seems so." Regina exhales as though smoking a cigarette. She doesn't seem the type to smoke. Rose has an easier time imagining her at the gym seven days a week. Maybe both things are true.

When Rose asks Regina for details, she obliges. The young woman, whose name is Heather, showed up at Edward's penthouse in Atlanta, where Regina still lives, and announced she was looking for her father.

"It's hard to imagine Edward a father," Rose says.

Regina's laugh is short and unexpected. "I know what you mean. It always surprised me that he could keep an orchid alive."

Orchids? Rose can't envision her brother tending to

anything except maybe the stock market. Of course, he didn't seem the type to marry an African-American woman, either. The truth is, she doubts she even knew her brother at all.

Regina pauses and exhales again. Rose can almost smell the burning tobacco.

"It seems Heather's mother was an employee of his for a brief time," Regina begins again. "Twenty-two years ago, Edward gave the mother enough money to get rid of her, as well as abort the baby. But it seems she decided to keep it and raised the child by herself," she continues. "The mother died recently, and the daughter is now looking for her biological father. Namely, guess who?"

"Did you tell her he died in a fire two years ago?" Rose asks.

"She didn't seem surprised by the news," Regina says.

Rose pauses. Why would the young woman go looking for Edward if she knew about the fire? Something doesn't make sense.

"She kept her father's last name?" Rose asks.

"Yes," Regina says. "Her mother was smart enough to list Edward's name on the birth certificate. Heather has a copy with her, but who knows if the thing is real. There are all sorts of cons out there these days, you know." Regina exhales again.

Could Edward have had a secret daughter? He certainly had a secret wife that nobody knew about. The Temple family is steeped in secrets. Not only do they have their own fair share, but they have collected them for over two hundred years to blackmail the citizens of Savannah whenever they needed to boost their influence. There are two ledgers full of secrets, it turns out, though Rose hasn't made time to explore the second.

Phone in hand, Rose walks over to the sunroom and Old Sally's table filled with all the objects that represent the people she watches over, Rose being one of them. The key to the second safe-deposit box is right where she left it.

Perhaps it's time to go see what's in that second book, Rose tells herself.

At the very least, she can see what it contains before destroying it. Somehow the world would seem better off if someone finally laid all those secrets to rest. But first, she needs to get through Queenie's wedding.

Regina is silent like a fisherman slowly moving bait through the water to fool the fish into thinking it doesn't have a hook. But Rose refuses to bite.

"Thank you for warning me," she says, "but I need to get busy here. We're—"

"Wait," Regina says, "there's more."

"More?" Rose doesn't have time for more. She also doesn't have time to figure out Regina's motives.

"Heather visited again this morning," Regina says. "I gave her your address. She left here about fifteen minutes ago, heading in your direction."

"You gave her my address?" Rose returns to the kitchen, where Spud is up to his elbows in lemons. "Why would you do that without asking me first?"

"Is there a problem?" Regina's voice reveals a slight lift. Is she smiling?

"We've got a lot happening here today," Rose says, thinking this is the understatement of the century. A short century so far, since it is only 2002.

"I thought I'd give you a head's up," Regina says, before offering a quick goodbye.

It seems Edward's widow has enjoyed dropping this latest family secret in Rose's lap.

A surprise relative showing up is the last thing she

expected, and she doesn't want anything to take away from Queenie's day. The wedding is scheduled to start in less than an hour. Rose pauses, unsure of what to do with this news. A young woman, claiming to be her brother's daughter, is driving from Atlanta to their island today. A trip of just under 300 miles that usually takes about four and a half hours to drive. At this rate, she will miss the wedding, but the party afterward might still be going on.

When she looks up, her daughter Katie—petite, tan, and very pregnant—is staring at her.

"What is it, Mom? Your face has gone all white."

"Nothing," Rose says when what she wants to say is, *Everything*.

Katie drops the dishrag she was using to clean off the counters. When she can't bend over to retrieve it, Rose picks it up. Didn't Violet tell her earlier that dropping a dishrag means company is coming?

Rose will be a grandmother soon. Katie's first attempt at artificial insemination ended in a miscarriage last August. A hard moment for all of them. But the second try worked. Something that Katie attributes to taking Old Sally's root medicines. Rose imagines the rewards of grandmotherhood will quickly outweigh her insecurities of feeling ancient. Katie is two weeks from her due date and looks like she should have given birth a month ago.

But first, a thousand details need to be attended to in the next hour, including keeping the groom from collapsing into a nervous heap. And now a stranger named Heather is driving in from Atlanta?

Katie opens the refrigerator and devours a vanilla yogurt in six bites before excusing herself to go to the bathroom. Both are familiar scenes these days. Katie's small white terrier,

Harpo, follows her everywhere, his nails clicking softly on the wooden and slate floors. Only Rose and Spud remain in the kitchen.

"What was that phone call about?" Spud washes the cutting board in the sink.

"We have an unexpected guest arriving later this afternoon," Rose says. His suit reminds her of an eggplant parmesan recipe she hasn't made for a while and needs to find again.

"Well, as my beloved future wife would say, the more the merrier." Spud pets his mustache thoughtfully as if struck with the realization that he will soon have a wife.

But Rose doesn't feel merry. She feels stressed. She wants a smooth send-off to celebrate Spud and Queenie's life together. No complications. How rare is it for two people who have never married before to say vows in their sixties? And these are two people she loves.

In the meantime, Regina's phone call now has Rose angry. Why did Regina give Edward's supposed daughter Rose's address if she felt uncomfortable around her? Was this merely the next logical step, or was her intention more devious?

After glancing at her watch, Rose turns her attention to what she has left to do for the wedding. The rented white tent is already in place on the beach, and Max and Jack are setting up folding chairs. For weeks she questioned the wisdom of a beach wedding, given all the rain they have this time of year, but it is a sunny June day.

Angela, Katie's girlfriend, enters the kitchen carrying flowers she picked from Old Sally's garden in back. Daisies, irises, and lilies. The flowers are to go in large vases throughout the house. While Rose arranges the plates and silver for the reception, Angela cuts the stems and places them in four different jars for Violet to do the final arranging.

Angela has proven to be the most surprising addition to their nontraditional family. An author and tattooed feminist, Angela is also quick to help in any situation, with the added bonus of having a way of managing Katie that allows Rose to relax.

When Rose and Angela first met at her mother's funeral, Angela came across as thorny. A northerner with issues. But once Rose got to know her, Angela's brusqueness fell away. Perhaps Angela should answer the door when the young stranger arrives from Atlanta. She could ascertain what the stranger wants and maybe even scare her away. In the meantime, how can she be confident that the young woman really is Edward's child?

When Katie returns, Angela pats Katie's stomach to say hello to the baby. Their relationship was hard for Rose at first, though she pretended it wasn't. If given a choice, Rose would want a more mainstream lifestyle for her daughter, and therefore perhaps a safer lifestyle. But after 9/11 she wonders if anyone is truly safe, no matter what lifestyle they choose. Rose also thought she would have to give up her dream of being a grandmother someday. But it is incredible the medical procedures they can do these days that allow sperm donors—in this case, one of Angela's male friends—and potential mothers to unite.

"I wish you'd tell me what's wrong," Katie says to Rose.

"Everything's fine," Rose says, not wanting to worry her daughter, who worries way too much for someone in her twenties. But as an only child, she has always seemed older and more responsible than most people her age.

In the meantime, something about the stranger coming has Rose on edge. Spud turns up the volume on the small television sitting on the counter in the kitchen. The latest weather forecast reveals clear, sunny skies for today—perfect weather for a wedding—and a tropical storm has formed in the Caribbean. Rose sighs with relief that it won't rain on Queenie's wedding.

Seconds later the weatherman pauses for breaking news, explaining that a tropical storm becomes a hurricane when the wind speed reaches 74 miles per hour. He goes on to explain that every year the National Weather Service starts the naming of storms with the letter *A*, and since it has already been an active storm year, they are already up to the letter *I*.

Upon hearing the name of the hurricane, Rose gasps, and Spud looks like he might faint. Is the universe playing a joke on them? A joke that her dead mother somehow fashioned?

In an ironic—if not uncanny—turn of events, a hurricane named Iris has materialized and is spinning out in the Atlantic, as though she is late for Queenie and Spud's wedding.

CHAPTER FOUR

Violet

Violet returns to the kitchen to find Spud beset with citrus and Rose looking worried. While they spent decades apart, Violet's best friend from her childhood is back. When they were young and Old Sally brought Rose to the beach, she had Rose and Violet do a Gullah charm of washing their hands together in the kitchen sink. This supposedly ensured that they would be best friends forever. For further assurance, Old Sally burned onion peelings on the stove to strengthen the bond. It was a time when little black girls and little white girls—one poor and one rich—weren't allowed to be friends at all, and most certainly not best friends. But that didn't stop them. It seems the Gullah charm is still working.

Over the last few months, Violet has evolved from feeling like an orphan to being part of a large, extended family. To have this many people living together has taken some getting used to. But the house they designed to expand on Old Sally's has two stories and plenty of room, with large porches and floor-to-ceiling windows, as well as a cottage out back for Rose and Max. She has moments when, surprisingly, she misses working for Miss Temple and having time alone, but otherwise, this living arrangement makes her feel more alive. Whole. Useful.

For the first time, Violet notices Spud's purple suit. Perhaps this confirms he and Queenie are meant for each other. At the same time, she wonders briefly if Queenie can be trusted to be left alone. If she adds any more color, she will look like she's leading a gay pride parade. Yet, it appears there are other concerns.

"What's going on?" Violet asks. "Why is everybody looking so strange? We've got a wedding soon."

Rose's pale complexion is even more pale. Come to think of it, Spud looks whiter than usual, too.

"Someone may be crashing the party," Spud says, his eyebrows raised.

"Who?" Violet asks.

"Iris."

Spud loosens his bow tie as though Iris's delicate fingers are choking him from the grave.

"I don't understand." Violet didn't get enough sleep last night and her morning started at dawn with Old Sally. Grouchiness is next if she isn't careful.

Meanwhile, the color returns to Rose's face, and there is a hint of magic in her eyes. "It seems Mother's ghost has finally found us," she says to Violet. "She's hitched a ride on a hurricane!"

Violet smiles, her irritation gone in an instant. However, her confusion is gaining ground. The last time Violet felt this clueless was at the reading of Miss Temple's will two years ago. The day she found out that Queenie wasn't her aunt, but her mother, who had been threatened and sworn to secrecy by her father, Mister Oscar, Miss Temple's husband. Violet isn't in the mood for surprises. At least not until this wedding is over.

For over a week, the spirit of Miss Temple has felt somehow close. After the fire, Violet wasn't sure what happened to the displaced Temple ghosts. Did they disperse to other mansions and find new places to haunt? Or invest in retirement condos in the world's most haunted cities, Savannah being one of them?

Yet, it feels like old times to speak of ghosts. She always knew that funerals attracted them, and now it seems that weddings do, too.

"That hurricane is an interesting coincidence," Rose says.

"I always knew your mother was a force of nature," Violet says, remembering how Miss Temple left critiques in the kitchen in the mornings. Critiques of meals, and initially, critiques of her housekeeping abilities, until Violet figured out exactly what she wanted. To work there, Violet had to grow a thicker skin and not take anything personally, though Miss Temple's critiques were always personal. Telling Violet that she wasn't smart enough to comprehend her needs, or that Violet's cooking skills lacked finesse.

With a white monogrammed handkerchief pulled from the pocket of his purple suit, Spud wipes a smattering of perspiration from his brow. He is right to worry. How will Queenie take this news? She can get stormy herself if she thinks the fates are messing with her.

Katie returns to the kitchen to eat a banana, her latest snack. "What are you guys talking about?"

Violet, Rose, and Spud exchange a look. An entire book is needed to tell this story instead of a sentence or two. It appears Violet has been elected to offer a summation.

"Iris and Spud were an item many years ago," she begins, "and while we initially thought that your Grandmother Temple's ghost was finally resting in peace, now there's a genuine concern that she may be crashing Queenie's wedding."

"At least metaphorically," Rose says.

Angela laughs, as though entertained by hearing about ghosts crashing a wedding.

"That's what you get for moving to the South, sweetheart," Katie says with a playful southern accent, all the while holding her belly.

Everyone joins in the laughter before things turn serious again.

"Do we know when the storm is due?" Violet asks.

"The hurricane is a long shot," Rose says. "It may never materialize."

"That's right," Spud says. "Hurricanes never hit Savannah. The big storms head north or south of us, to Charleston or Florida."

Violet is relieved that she hasn't heard a peep out of her left shoulder, her early warning system for bad things.

"There's something else you should know about," Rose says to Violet. "We have yet another unexpected visitor coming."

"Ghost or real person?" Violet asks.

"I'm assuming real," Rose says.

"Good," Violet says. "I prefer real. Who?"

"It seems Edward has a daughter that he didn't tell anybody about."

"You've got to be kidding."

"I kind of wish I were," Rose says. "She's been giving Regina a hard time, so Regina sent her here."

"Here?" Violet can't believe how much has happened while she fought with Queenie's zipper.

"She's driving here from Atlanta this very minute. Evidently, she wants to meet us."

The day is getting more complicated by the minute. While the others scatter to do different tasks, Violet glances at the kitchen clock and speeds up her process. She adds water and sugar to the three large glass pitchers with cut lemons on the bottom, to make lemonade the way Old Sally always makes it.

Violet pauses. Where is Old Sally? By this time of day, she is usually in the sunroom at her window seat, but with the wedding, she is probably taking a short nap. She already dressed hours ago, so now all that's left is showing up.

After finishing the lemonade and arranging the flowers, Violet sprinkles water around the house to keep evil spirits away like Old Sally taught her. A precaution. As far as she knows this ritual doesn't work with hurricanes. But she will welcome any help she can get. Gullah folk magic has proven to be more complicated than she initially imagined. Roots. Spells. Medicines. Rituals. Stories. Spirits. Subtle yet powerful. As with anything, it takes a belief that it will work for it to be effective. And Violet believes.

Many traditions fade away with modern times. However, thanks to Old Sally, the Gullah traditions aren't dying away, they are changing form. To survive, Gullah folk magic is becoming more secretive and protected.

In coming years Violet plans to pass these traditions along to Tia and Leisha, who already spend a lot of time with their great-grandmother now that they all live here on the beach. But first, Violet reheats the gumbo, a meal with an okra base and a host of other vegetables, spices, and meats. The Frog-more stew is on simmer in Rose's kitchen. Violet combined the sausage, shrimp, corn, and potatoes this morning. It will be brought out and served steaming hot at the reception. Both recipes were passed down to her from Old Sally and those who came before her.

"I guess I need to break the news to Queenie," Spud says to Violet. "I wouldn't want her to find out about Iris without me."

Violet wishes him luck. "And tell her that my shoulder isn't concerned," Violet adds.

He says he will.

"Oh, is my bow tie straight?" he asks, before walking away. "It won't be long until I become Mister Queenie Temple." Spud gives a short, nervous laugh.

Violet steps in front of him and tenderly tightens the bow tie of the kindest man she has ever known.

"Where did you find this one?" Violet asks.

"Queenie had it made for me in Charleston," Spud says.

The bow tie is yellow and dotted with purple saxophones. A couple of years ago, Spud would have never worn custom-made ties, and Violet would have never lived in a big, fancy home on the beach, even if it was an expansion of her grand-mother's much smaller house.

Before the reading of Miss Temple's will, Spud was a butcher at Piggly Wiggly, and Violet was Miss Temple's house-keeper and cook. Everything they now possess is thanks to Miss Iris Temple of the Savannah Temples. Naming a hurri-cane after her seems appropriate. She was an extra-large personality. While Violet hasn't missed dealing with a mansion full of Temple ghosts every day—along with the eccentricities of a *living* Miss Temple—what she did in leaving Violet the estate in her will changed her life, and she is forever grateful.

Although the mansion burned to the ground shortly after, the insurance money helped them build this current house, as well as open Violet's long-dreamed-for tea shop in downtown Savannah.

As for Miss Temple, may she finally rest in peace, as well as quietly blow out to sea.

CHAPTER FIVE

Old Sally

While everyone prepares for Queenie's wedding, Old Sally walks down to the breaking tide. Weddings are essential rituals, a moment of light in a family. She pulls her summer shawl tight around her shoulders. Born in the year 1900, Old Sally has stayed on this earth much longer than she thought she would. The only way she can make sense of it is to believe that her Gullah ancestors still have plans for her.

A whirlwind dances up the beach, tossing loose circles of sand, and Old Sally admires the outfit Rose found for her to wear. The cotton dress is the color of sand with red and purple flowers stitched around the collar and hem. If Old Sally had her way, this would be her funeral dress, too. The cemetery at the far end of the island is where her ancestors are buried. All her life Old Sally has known her body would end up there, too, when her spirit rejoins her ancestors. This thought comforts her. No fear involved. Like a story, every life on earth has a beginning, a middle, and an end. Sometimes a life story lasts only hours. Sometimes days, years, or decades. A few last over a century, like Old Sally's, with no rhyme or reason for who goes first or last. It is not about the lucky or the unlucky. The good or the evil. Old Sally knows better than to think she can figure out this mystery. It is not a crime novel, after all. Life and death are in an eternal dance just like that whirlwind. Wind and sand. Sand and wind. A dance across time.

We might as well try to enjoy the dance and the story that goes with it.

Someone calls her from the dunes. It is Jack, Violet's husband, who reminds her of a man from her past she loved with her whole heart. A man nicknamed Fiddle. Someone she has been thinking about more and more, now that the time draws near for her passing.

"Violet asked me to check on you," Jack says as he joins her.

"That sounds like our Violet," she says with a smile.

Jack is a good match for her granddaughter. He is thoughtful and kind and an excellent father to their two daughters. He teaches at the community college and some-times invites his students to visit with her. With the group of young people gathered around her, she will tell them how things used to be for black people.

Old Sally likes having her great-granddaughters around more now that they are all living here in this great big house. After the Temple mansion was destroyed, Violet presented the idea of adding on to her small home here on the beach, where they could all live together. Old Sally was hesitant at first. Her mind was trapped in a little box of how things had to be. But the Lord's ways are mysterious. Now she has a house full of family again. Family that is related by blood, and the added family that a person chooses. Soul family, she calls them.

People found in a moment of grace, while that whirlwind keeps dancing up the beach.

As for family related by blood, there are Queenie and Violet, Violet's teenage daughters, Tia and Leisha, and Jack. Her soul family is Rose, her husband Max, their daughter, Katie, and Katie's special friend, Angela. And after today, Spud will live here, too.

Old Sally even has soul pets. Keeping all their names straight helps her mind stay active. Lucy and Ethel are Rose and Max's border collies. Katie's little white dog is named Harpo. Angela's two cats are Zelda and Gertrude. And Tia and Leisha's pet turtle is named Jake.

Families live so far away from each other these days. Old people go to nursing homes instead of living with their families. Some are perfectly fine. But too many people die lonely. With this arrangement, they all live together yet have their separate spaces. Old Sally might die alone, but loneliness is impossible. Especially with her belief that her ancestors are waiting for her.

As they look out over the sea, Old Sally takes Jack's arm. He is tall and handsome, a lovely black man.

Last fall, to get their minds off the 9/11 tragedy, Old Sally taught Jack and Max how to fish the Gullah way, with weighted casting nets. Now they catch fish, crab, and shrimp from the creeks on the island. Sometimes Old Sally watches them standing knee-deep in water throwing nets and realizes that Dolphin Island is becoming a part of them, too.

Old Sally enjoys having men around again. Her husband, Samuel, died in the Second World War, so she has been a widow for over fifty years. Their wedding was on the south end of the island at the small church, now in ruins.

"Do you want to stay here a while longer?" Jack says. "I need to get back. Guests will be arriving any minute."

"I think I'll walk a little more and gather my thoughts," Old Sally says.

Before leaving, Jack kisses her hand as if they have just finished a dance. She offers him a slight bow.

Old Sally settles into the silence again, memories rising from her bones. Memories of playing on this beach as a girl, living in a house built for her mother by her uncles and grand-father, before Sally was born. Her mother had three children. Two sons and then Sally, the youngest.

Her mother would never recognize this house now. It is beyond grand. Before, it had only two bedrooms, but that seemed like a castle when Sally was a girl. Now it has seven, as well as a cottage in the back. It surprises her sometimes how big her life has become in the last year. Right when most old people's lives are getting smaller.

In June of 1920, it was Old Sally who was preparing to wed. Of course, back then she was called Sally; there was nothing "old" about her. Her mother and her Aunt Polly decorated the small church on the island. Palm fronds lined the aisle, with white hydrangeas tied on the end of each pew. Aunt Sissie Mainer, her mother's older sister, made Sally a beach-shell wedding bouquet with a bleached white starfish lying in the center of purple flowers. She still has the starfish in her collec-tion of unique things.

Her wedding dress was stitched by hand by her grand-mother who lived with them—her other grandmother died before Sally was born—who also made sugar cookies shaped like sand dollars, and a wedding cake with two white starfish sitting on the top of sea-blue icing sprinkled with brown sugar to look like sand.

Old Sally still remembers the look of the scars on her grandmother's arms as she made these things. Injuries from a grease fire in the Temple kitchen while she worked there, back in the slave-owning days. She was finally freed in 1865, right after the war ended.

When Old Sally closes her eyes, she feels her mother's gentle touch. Even though her mother always came home exhausted, she would fix Sally's hair before bed to ready it for school the next day. All these years later she still misses her mother. To lose a loving mother is like a heartache that never goes away. However, it was her grandmother she was closest to growing up. Some would call her unlucky to be a servant all her life, but she was lucky to have such loving people around her.

Old Sally looks out over the ocean. Waves were a constant lullaby growing up. A continuous source of comfort. Even now she can recognize the sound of high tide, low tide, and everything in between. Right now, the tide is going out, the beach expanding in time for the wedding.

For seven years—after she married Samuel and before he died in the war—Sally didn't live on the island. They lived in Savannah in a small apartment because Samuel wanted to break free of the old ways. Sally didn't see the point of breaking free of something so central to her, but Samuel was her husband, so she did it anyway.

After his death, Sally moved back in with her mother, young children in tow. Ivy came much later, after Old Sally's other children were already grown and out of the house. She was a change-of-life baby fathered by Iris Temple's father. Making Iris and Ivy half sisters. No consent to it. Old Sally wanted to keep her job. But those days no longer hurt her. She wasn't the one who did anything wrong.

Years later "Ivy" became Queenie, a name given to her by Rose and Violet when they were girls and called themselves the Sea Gypsies. An image rises in front of Old Sally of Rose and Violet running on the beach as girls, the sequined scarves she made for them flowing behind them. In her mind, they will forever be Sea Gypsies.

Old Sally takes a deep breath and walks back to the house. Memory works in strange ways. She can't remember yesterday that well, but she can recall details from eighty years ago. Some memories are painful. Others surprise her with their tenderness. All are a gift.

On the front porch, Violet greets her with a cup of steaming ginger tea—Old Sally's favorite. She places it on the small wooden table beside Old Sally's rocking chair. They each take a rocker, though Violet looks about as harried as Old Sally has ever seen her.

"You okay?" Old Sally says, a shared greeting in their family.

"Just need to catch a breath," Violet says. "Guests are arriving."

"How's Queenie?" Old Sally asks.

"Nervous," Violet says. "She's touching up her makeup."

"And the groom?"

"Nervous, too."

"Marriage be nerve-wracking when you've never done it before," Old Sally says. *Can you hear me?* Old Sally adds, thinking this instead of speaking.

Violet smiles. "I heard you."

"Good," Old Sally says, feeling pleased. "Good," she says again, more to herself than Violet.

Sometimes an opening occurs between two souls where thoughts can get through. It can happen with mothers and daughters, grandmothers and granddaughters, or two people who have been joined together in a common fate. Like Old Sally helping Iris Temple transition to the next world, although that didn't entirely work. Old Sally and Violet are hearing each other's thoughts more often these days. That's because Old Sally's time to leave this world is getting close.

"When you get quiet, what are you thinking about?" Violet asks her.

"I be visiting the past since there's not much future left," she tells Violet. "Lots to explore there."

Old Sally is surprised that Violet is taking the time to be with her with so much going on around them. Cars pulling in the driveway. People walking to the wedding tent on the beach. Max and Jack taking turns telling people where to park or running to get something they need. Yet, it is all getting done, and somehow Violet has accepted that. Anyone who knows Queenie knows that her wedding will not start right on time. It would be out of character.

"You know, if this wedding is too much for you, Queenie will understand," Violet says.

Violet's protection of her means a lot to Old Sally.

"I'm not about to miss this wedding," Old Sally says. "I was honored that Queenie wanted me to take part in the ceremony."

From inside the house, Queenie lets out a frantic call to Violet.

"I'd better go see what's up," Violet says.

Old Sally agrees that may be best.

Violet leaves her on the porch, and Old Sally raises the tea to her lips. Her hand has a slight shake to it these days, like she is getting ready to wave goodbye.

She looks forward to laying her burdens down, as the old

spiritual goes. But first, Old Sally must bless Queenie's wedding.

CHAPTER SIX

Queenie

Queenie fans herself with an issue of *O* magazine sporting Oprah's smiling face on the cover. Oprah has Stedman but has never officially married, and for years Queenie was convinced that she was destined to follow in her footsteps. Now she wishes she could call her up and ask her if she knows something Queenie doesn't know. Maybe marriage isn't something enlightened women choose to do in the twenty-first century.

A gentle knock on the door breaks her steady stream of second thoughts.

"You okay, sweet pea?" Spud's voice is muffled through the closed door.

Queenie has forgiven Spud for being in love with Iris for all those years, although she still has trouble understanding it.

"You aren't supposed to see me before the wedding," Queenie calls. "It's bad luck."

"We got all our bad luck out of the way years ago," Spud says.

That little devil sure knows what to say and how to say it, Queenie thinks. "Well, if our marriage only lasts a week, it will be your fault," she says, opening the door.

The look on Spud Grainger's face makes Queenie quit second-guessing herself. Tears spring to his eyes, and hers, too, and she dares them to mess up her mascara.

"You are the most beautiful creature on God's green earth," he says.

Queenie's glee gives her a quick shiver. She is too old to feel like a teenager in love, but there you go. If she has learned anything in the last year, it is not only to seize the day but seize any moments of happiness she can grab.

"Where in the world did you find a purple suit?" Queenie feels the fabric of his lapel to see if it is velvet and then looks on the back to make sure there isn't a picture of Elvis.

"I have my sources," Spud says. "I know your favorite color is purple, and I wanted to make you happy."

Queenie pulls him inside the bedroom and gives him a kiss that steams up his glasses. It still surprises her how her heartbeat quickens every time she sees him. Finding true love with a skinny white vegetarian butcher was not something she saw coming. Ever.

"Why do you smell like lemons?" she asks. "You been cleaning with Lemon Pledge or something?"

"Rose had me cutting lemons to keep me distracted." Spud smiles, sniffing the backs of his hands.

"I guess a wedding wouldn't be a wedding without Mama's lemonade," she says.

He agrees.

"You think we should go ahead and start the honeymoon now?" she asks.

He matches her grin and gives her a loving pat on her ample backside. "I still can't believe I get to do that," he says.

Spud stretches an arm toward the zipper on the back of her wedding gown, and Queenie stops him.

"Come to think of it, honey, I guess we'd better wait. I may never get back in this dress once I take it off."

With a sigh, Spud agrees and takes a handkerchief from his pocket to rub the steam from his glasses.

"How's it going out there?" Queenie asks.

Spud looks away, a sure sign that he isn't telling her something.

"Out with it." Queenie places her hands on her hips. She is not to be underestimated. Something about wearing a wedding gown makes her feel like a superhero. Powerful and gracious at the same time. She may have to wear this more often. Maybe in a slightly bigger size. But then she imagines dragging her train everywhere—through the Piggly Wiggly and the Gladys Knight and the Tints beauty parlor—and thinks better of it.

Queenie regains her focus and waits for Spud to answer.

"It's kind of funny when you think about it," he says, still not looking her in the eye.

Queenie pulls him toward her by the same lapel she admired earlier. They are almost the same height, but she has a good fifty pounds on him.

"Spud Grainger, don't even think about lying to me."

"Two things." His eyes soften as he looks at her. "First, it seems that Edward Temple has a daughter who is coming to visit today."

Queenie laughs. "You are such a joker," she tells him. "This is not April first, and I am nobody's fool."

When he doesn't join in the laughter, she tightens her lips. Queenie has despised Edward Temple with a passion ever since he cornered a teenage Violet in the garden shed at the Temple mansion.

"Since when does Edward have a daughter?" Queenie asks.

"Evidently, it's a recent discovery," Spud says.

"What's the second thing?" she asks, though she isn't so sure she wants to know.

"A hurricane is forming in the Atlantic."

"And why should I care?"

"It's probably nothing," Spud says, "and I hesitate to even mention it, but—"

"But what?"

Spud hesitates.

"All I've wanted for the last six weeks is for this wedding to come off without a hitch. Is that too much to ask?"

"Is that a rhetorical question?" Spud responds.

Queenie lets out a sound that is a cross between a scream and an *oomph*. She drags her train to the window and sees blue skies.

"Seriously, is this a joke?" Queenie asks again. "There's not a cloud in the sky."

"There is a funny part to it," Spud says.

"Funny, ha-ha, or funny strange?" Queenie asks, narrowing her eyes at him.

"Funny strange."

Queenie puts her hands on her hips again, but it isn't the same as before. She doesn't feel powerful or graceful at all. She feels plus-size, awkward, and hot-flashy.

"Tell me before I bust a zipper or something," Queenie says to him, her voice low.

Spud pauses as if being careful of his word choice. "You

know how the National Weather Service names storms when they have a certain wind speed and reach hurricane status?"

"Yes, I know that," Queenie says. "Where in the world are you going with this?"

"Well, the letter they've worked their way up to is *I*." He looks at her as though waiting for a lightbulb to go off over her head.

"*I?*"

"Yes, *I*." Spud winks.

"What in heaven's name are you trying to tell me?" Queenie taps her size nine shoe.

Spud's face turns a light shade of red and begins to glisten from the beads of perspiration forming.

"Well . . ." Spud stutters, "they've named the hurricane Iris."

Queenie laughs like she has just heard the funniest joke of all time, but then realizes that she is the only one laughing.

"That witch will not ruin my wedding," Queenie says, thinking the b-word would suit Iris better. When it comes to spoiling a special event, Queenie will not put anything past Iris Temple—dead or alive.

Queenie feels like one of those cartoon characters whose face turns fire-engine red right before the steam shoots out of their ears. Spud tells her not to panic, but it seems that that ocean liner has already sailed. Holding up her dress so she doesn't trip, Queenie pushes past him into the hallway and down the steps that lead to the kitchen.

When they see her coming, Rose and Violet exchange a look that says the hurricane coming starts with a *Q*, not an *I*, and her name is Queenie.

"Try to stay calm," Rose says, meeting Queenie at the entrance to the kitchen. "You look beautiful, by the way," she adds.

"Try to stay calm?" Queenie's voice rises, skipping right over the compliment. She drops the skirt of her gown and enjoys a brief rush of cold air up her legs.

"Don't worry," Rose says. "Edward's daughter isn't due for a couple of hours. It will be the middle of the reception by then."

"Since when does Edward have a daughter?" Queenie asks.

"It was news to us, too," Rose says. "Evidently that was another one of those Temple family secrets."

"God help us," Queenie says. "When in heaven will those secrets finally stop haunting us?"

"Good question," Violet says.

"Do you think she's a fake and just trying to get Edward's money?" Queenie asks.

"She supposedly has a birth certificate that proves his paternity," Rose answers.

"Well, why is she coming here?" Queenie asks.

"I'm not exactly sure," Rose says. "I think Regina wanted to get rid of her. But I could be wrong."

"Well, I'll get rid of her," Queenie says with another tap of her shoe.

Spud places a calming hand on her shoulder. When she looks at him, she is reminded of Barney, that purple dinosaur that all the kids love. Except this Barney is skinny.

"And that's not even the biggest news," Queenie says. "What about this storm?"

"Hurricane Iris is nowhere near here," Violet says, trying to untangle the train of Queenie's wedding dress.

Queenie huffs when she hears the name of the hurricane again.

"Is my wedding a cosmic joke?" Queenie asks Rose. Tears threaten to come next. *Ugly tears,* as Oprah calls them.

Spud, Rose, and Violet look at Queenie as though she is a nuclear reactor threatening a meltdown.

"It's going to be a wonderful wedding," Violet says. "The sun is shining, and we've got plenty of food—"

"Oh my Lord, what time is it?" Queenie shrieks before swooping up the stairs for her last-minute preparations, cussing Iris on every step.

CHAPTER SEVEN

Rose

Rose thinks of Edward's daughter somewhere on the interstate from Atlanta, curious what this potential niece might be like. Rose was naïve to believe that the mansion burning down had brought an end to all the Temple secrets. Another layer is bubbling to the surface. Maybe her Temple ancestors will never rest in peace until that Book of Secrets is destroyed. Or should she say *books*?

Celebrations shouldn't be stressful, she decides.

But she can't quit thinking about those Temple ledgers. Does Regina have a copy of the secrets that Edward released to the Savannah newspaper in the weeks leading up to the fire? Maybe she knows exactly why Edward's daughter is coming. Maybe Edward kept the juiciest secrets for a future release. Blackmail goes a long way in business negotiations or in generating cash. Rose isn't sure why she should even care. However, if the books exist, they can potentially do harm, and the Temple family is not free.

Finally dressed, she checks out the tent and seating arrangements on the beach. Queenie will be pleased. She takes a moment to look out over the ocean, comparing it to her former view of the Rocky Mountains. Adjusting to East Coast living again has taken some time.

Rose hasn't been able to paint since she got here, and this concerns her more than she wants to admit. Last week, Rose dreamed her mother hid all her paints and paintbrushes. She couldn't sleep the rest of the night after that and has slept fitfully ever since.

Twenty-five years ago, Rose knew she had to leave Savannah or she would spend her life in her mother's shadow and never recover her self-esteem. Even now, her presence still looms, if only in memory. How ironic that the hurricane out in the Atlantic carries her mother's name. Is the storm reminding Rose that her mother is always watching, always lurking on the edges of her life? Rose takes a deep breath of ocean air to clear the past away. *But will it ever go away completely?*

Painting is the only time Rose feels like she is doing something she is meant to do. Two galleries in Sante Fe, New Mexico, carry her Western landscapes. But she doesn't live in the West anymore, and moving back to the East Coast required more energy than she anticipated. If that wasn't enough, the Temple mansion burned down, which was where they had planned to live. Followed by Plan B, the renovation and move into this house. Followed by 9/11. She hears herself making excuses and stops.

A blank canvas is sometimes a good thing, she tells herself. *I can go in a totally different direction if I want.*

However, new directions take time and patience, and she hopes she is up for the task.

When Rose returns to the house, Old Sally is sitting in the

living room by the front window with Katie. Just seeing Old Sally makes Rose feel more settled. Katie rises when she sees Rose and excuses herself to go to the bathroom again.

"Can I get you anything?" Rose asks Old Sally.

"If you could return my teacup to the kitchen, that would be helpful," she says.

It is only lately that Old Sally has been asking for help with little things, like taking a teacup or helping her stand if she's been sitting. The cup rattles gently on the saucer, her hand not as steady as it once was.

Tea leaves deposit a message in the bottom of the cup. Do they spell out danger? Is the stranger coming to town going to change their lives forever? Rose has read enough novels to imagine the worst. If the stranger were anyone other than her brother's offspring, Rose might look forward to meeting a new family member. But Edward was a carbon copy of their mother. Manipulative. Controlling. Always wanting to have the most power in a room. All attributes guaranteed to make Rose cautious about meeting his daughter.

When Rose returns, Old Sally pats her hand and thanks her. They are waiting for Queenie to come downstairs to start the procession as the guests continue to arrive and walk down to the beach.

"Earlier today, I remembered how you and Violet played on this beach as girls," Old Sally says. "You called yourselves the Sea Gypsies. Remember?" Old Sally laughs a short laugh. "You two were the beginning of a promise to me. You gave me hope that someday color wouldn't matter in this world."

"Queenie was always around, too," Rose says. "Now I know why."

"Yes, you do," Old Sally says, patting her hand again.

Rose can't imagine how hard it must have been for Queenie, at nineteen, to have a child that she kept secret. A child that was sired by Rose's father. A fact that still shocks her when she thinks about it.

Do children ever know who their parents really are? Rose wonders.

Family secrets in the South are like kudzu; they grow like crazy and are nearly impossible to get rid of. For years she thought her father was an honest and kind man. Never would she have imagined that he might take advantage of Queenie in that way, or in any way.

Dear, sweet Queenie, Rose thinks.

Unfortunately, he wasn't the first white man to take advantage of the people who worked for him. Nor can Rose imagine Old Sally's life—living in the South as a black woman for over a hundred years. A servant most of her life. A servant to Rose's family.

A familiar guilt rises and flushes her face. While her mother wore entitlement every day of her life like a set of pearls, privilege has never sat well with Rose. Old Sally has more integrity in her pinkie finger than Rose's mother had in her entire body. Rose looks at her hand, where her fingertip is missing. A small sacrifice to the past, thanks to Edward and a Temple sword.

"You know how much I love you, don't you?" Rose kneels next to Old Sally's chair so they can be eye to eye.

Old Sally covers Rose's pale hand with her dark one. "You be my English Rose. My beautiful girl."

Tears come to Rose's eyes. A moment of peace amidst all the wedding preparations.

Old Sally turns her gaze to the objects on the table, her ritual for as long as Rose has known her. Mementos that stand in for people Old Sally sends healing to and protection from the harshness of the world every single day.

"I have a favor to ask," Old Sally says.

"Anything," Rose says, and she means it.

"There be only a few people left that I watch after these days. Most of them are right here in this house. Would you take over when I'm gone?"

Rose pauses with new tears. It is another day of moisture in the low country. At breakfast, Violet said that she was more emotional than usual today, and Queenie admitted the same. The three of them agreed to not question it and flow with it.

"I would be honored to carry on for you," Rose says to Old Sally.

Old Sally thanks her and takes a deep breath, as if this is one more thing she can let go of before she goes.

Although Rose and Old Sally have never spoken of the key, she is sure Old Sally noticed it there. Rose placed it on the table the day she met Regina, Edward's secret wife. Regina gave Rose an unopened envelope that contained correspondence between her brother and her mother. If Regina had known what was inside, she might never have given it to Rose. Along with the key, there was a letter that told of a second, older safe-deposit box that contained another Book of Secrets. Rose's first instinct was to throw the key away and let that old book rot in the vault until all those secrets could die away, along with her mother and Edward.

Old Sally picks up the key and hands it to Rose. "It be time to lay all the ghosts to rest."

"Lay the ghosts to rest?" Rose repeats, wondering if Old Sally heard her thoughts.

"You're the next in line in the Temple family," Old Sally tells her. "The responsibility falls to you."

Rose has trouble meeting Old Sally's eyes. It's not like a person can choose their lineage. Rose is tired of being a

Temple and lugging around all the history that comes with it. Old Sally talks about her ancestors in such a positive way, but Rose wishes hers would leave her alone. She grew up with their lavish portraits staring at her in every room of the mansion. Meanwhile, Old Sally's family seems less encumbered, despite being fated to live in the shadows of wealthy white people.

Rose offers a reluctant nod and places the key in the pocket of her dress. She has no idea what Old Sally means by the Temple history being Rose's responsibility. She has watched Old Sally pass on the Gullah ways and their rich history to Violet—at times, almost enviously. But the Temple traditions are about amassing power and more money than you could possibly spend in a lifetime. Is that a heritage that needs to be passed on?

Despite the warm breeze moving through the house, Rose shivers.

CHAPTER EIGHT

Violet

The wedding nearly under way, Violet takes a last look at the reception table. She adjusts a serving spoon here and there before deciding it is as good as she can make it. Meanwhile, Tia and Leisha escort guests to the white folding chairs under the rented white tent. The girls wear matching dresses, and their hair is in matching beaded braids that Old Sally fixed for them yesterday, like she fixed Violet's hair when Violet was their age. They were each allowed to invite one friend to the wedding, and wear makeup, which they are usually not allowed to wear. They appear more grown-up than usual. They are beautiful young women.

"Is Queenie ready?" Rose asks Violet in the kitchen.

"She's in her room sitting in front of three oscillating fans to keep from sweating," Violet says. They exchange a smile.

"Should we take her a glass of wine or something?" Rose asks.

"She's fine, just a little nervous."

"It's amazing how much time and energy goes into a twenty-minute ceremony," Rose says.

Violet agrees and pulls a baking sheet of peach turnovers that she had almost forgotten out of the oven.

Rose asks what she can do to help.

"Maybe put these on a serving plate once they're cool?"

Rose nods.

Violet and Rose have agreed that they will be so relieved when Queenie's wedding is over. It has been the topic of conversation between them for weeks—that and the birth of Katie's baby.

Fortunately, the day is sunny, with no hurricanes in sight. The weather people have been wrong plenty of times. Countless storms have been predicted to hit the Georgia/South Carolina coast that never did, and this one is merely a projection, too—so far.

Jack calls Violet from the front door. She doesn't like the tone of his voice. Not upset, but concerned.

Violet meets him on the porch, where he lowers his voice to a whisper. "Have you seen Spud?"

"No," she whispers back. "Where is he?"

"I'm not sure," he says.

"When did you last see him?" Violet lowers her voice another notch.

"I was getting the parking area set up, and he left in his car. Mumbled that he had forgotten something and took off in a flash."

Reflexively, Violet rubs her shoulder, though it doesn't seem to be speaking to her right now.

"He was awfully nervous when I saw him in the kitchen this morning," Jack says. "He isn't the type to leave Queenie at the altar, is he?"

"No," Violet says. "He values his life more than that."

Jack chuckles.

Violet and Spud have been friends for years. It isn't like him to abandon someone, especially at the altar.

"Spud loves Queenie," Violet says. "He would never hurt her like that."

"I didn't think so, either."

"Well, maybe he forgot the rings or something," Violet says.

Jack pulls two silver bands from his suit pocket. "He gave them to me this morning, so he wouldn't lose them."

They exchange concerned looks.

"Is his family here yet?" Violet asks.

"Both his sister and brother are sitting in the first row, groom's side," Jack says. "But Spud left before they even got here."

Violet glances at her watch, thinking how out of character this is. It's time for the ceremony to begin. If Spud doesn't get back soon, the aftermath of Queenie being stood up at the altar may be more devastating than anything they can imagine.

"I'd better tell Rose, just in case," Violet says.

"She's at the tent already, greeting guests," Jack says.

Violet takes off her apron and hangs it over the back of a rocking chair. She finds Rose greeting people at the entrance of the tent. Rose has done a beautiful job creating a simple, elegant beach-themed wedding. White tent, white chairs, white flowers tied to the end of every row. Large potted plants of peace lilies in full bloom on each side of the altar. All very elegant.

Rose talks to a woman wearing a canary-yellow hat who must be Spud's sister. She looks like Spud but with more hair and minus the bow tie. When Rose is free again, Violet steps in

and steers them to a section behind the chairs, where they can
have more privacy.

"Could you tell that was Spud's sister?" Rose asks with a
wink.

"Spud's missing," Violet whispers.

"What?" Rose says, full-voiced.

People turn to look. Rose smiles and waves to convey that
all is well.

"Where is he?" Rose asks, her tone matching Violet's
whisper.

"Jack saw him leave in his car. He said he forgot something."

"What in heaven's name did he forget?"

Violet shrugs, but not without concern.

"This is not good," Rose says, looking at her watch again.

"It may be nothing," Violet says, looking at her watch, too.
They have been checking the time all morning, rushing to get
everything handled. Now they may not even have a groom.

"Does Queenie know?" Rose asks.

"It's way too quiet in the house for Queenie to know,"
Violet says. "There would be screaming and wailing."

"You want to tell her?" Rose asks.

Violet's eyes widen.

"I didn't think so," Rose says.

"Let's give him ten minutes to show up," Violet says. "We
have to trust that he'll be back. We have to." She pauses,
wondering what the best strategy might be in this situation. "I
guess I'll go up and try to prepare Queenie for it, just in case,"
she says.

"Good luck with that," Rose says.

A minute later, Violet approaches Queenie's bedroom and
realizes she has no idea how to tell her mother that her fiancé
is missing. When she knocks on the door, Queenie yells for her

to come in over the hum of the electric fans. Violet steadies herself and garners her courage before stepping inside.

When Violet enters, Queenie is holding two magazines, one in each hand. She uses them to fan her face, while Oprah's image flutters on the covers, a chaotic photo montage.

"Vi, I've got flop sweat. It's a hundred degrees in here, and I can't stop sweating!"

To Violet, the room is chilly with all the oscillating going on, and the unsynchronized movement makes her feel dizzy. Where did Queenie find all these fans anyway? Maybe Spud is in line at Walmart this very minute buying Queenie a few more, chatting it up with the cashier about the pros and cons of orthopedic socks.

"Please tell Spud I need him," Queenie says. "And tell him to bring clean beach towels. I need to mop up some of this perspiration."

Should she tell Queenie that Spud has vacated the premises? Or that he was called away for a family emergency, even though his only remaining family is sitting in the front row of the wedding tent? She has never been good at lying. But she also has things left to do before she dies.

"What in heaven's name is wrong with you?" Queenie asks. "Don't you see I'm melting here? I'm like the Wicked Witch of the West. Get Spud!"

"I need to tell you something," Violet says finally, her voice reaching for the calmness Queenie lacks.

Queenie stops fanning herself and tosses the magazines on the bed. She approaches Violet in a whoosh of white that feels slightly intimidating. The fans oscillate toward her to observe what will happen next.

"What do you need to tell me?" Queenie asks.

It is the soft volume of Queenie's voice that alarms Violet the most. It can only get louder from here.

"Well—" Violet pauses and holds her right shoulder, even though she has no pain despite the possibility of another Chernobyl. "We can't find Spud." Anticipating an explosion, she cowers. But instead, Queenie rolls her eyes.

"You scared me there for a minute. I thought something horrible had happened. Spud is around here somewhere."

"He left in his car," Violet says.

Queenie hesitates. "Why would he leave in his car?"

"He told Jack he forgot something."

"Well, maybe he did."

"He's not back yet," Violet says.

Queenie looks at the clock and then crosses the room to look out the window. Squinting, she scans the crowd as if looking for a purple beacon of hope.

"He'll be here," Queenie says, but her certainty seems to have taken a hit. "Help me put myself together again, Vi. By the time I get downstairs, I bet Spud will be here. At least he'd better be," she concludes.

While the electric fans toss intermittent waves of coolness in their direction, Violet helps Queenie dry her face and freshen her makeup. Then she straightens Queenie's yellow scarf and red hat. A dash of color, indeed.

They leave Queenie's bedroom for the bride to take her place and begin her procession, no groom in sight.

CHAPTER NINE

Queenie

Queenie walks down the stairs and finds Old Sally standing at the front door, waiting to walk her daughter down the aisle. A small bouquet of white roses is tied around Old Sally's slender left wrist.

At the door, Rose hands Queenie the wedding bouquet Violet made for her—white roses mixed in with seashells. Though Spud is nowhere in sight, the three of them act like nothing is wrong.

"That man had better show up at the altar in the next two minutes," Queenie says to Violet, who gives Queenie's stubborn wedding train a final straightening.

Clearly, if Spud doesn't show up, Queenie's heart will be broken. *Perhaps along with his neck,* Queenie thinks.

"He'll be here," Violet says, a dash of hopefulness in her voice.

In the distance, the white tent is filled with seventy-five family members and friends. All of them waiting and shifting in their seats. The young priest looks in Queenie's direction as though wondering what he should do without a groom standing beside him. For sixty years Queenie has imagined being a bride and walking down the aisle. If Spud leaves her stranded at the altar, at least she will have this moment in the spotlight. Or in this case, the sun.

Queenie motions for the priest to start. He pauses, giving her a look that says, *Are you sure?* She repeats her *let's get this show on the road* hand motion. The young priest gives a brief shrug before asking everyone to stand. Family and guests turn in her direction, and Violet kisses Queenie on the cheek. Queenie takes a deep breath and holds Old Sally's arm. Then the two of them walk down the porch steps to where a sheath of white paper leads the way down the walkway through the dunes to the beach.

Queenie decided that there would be no music at the wedding. The sound of the waves would serenade her down the aisle. But that was a mistake. She wants to hear "Here Comes the Bride" or the "Alleluia" chorus. Something to mark such a momentous occasion. In an instant, the wedding she dreamed of is ruined, with no music and no groom.

Old Sally squeezes Queenie's arm as if sensing her growing upset. They begin their slow procession. "It be all right, child," she says. "Enjoy this. It's your day."

Queenie wonders if she is about to be stood up at the altar by the one person in the world she thought incapable of bailing on her. An undertow of grief threatens to pull her beneath the waves.

Suddenly she hears the notes of a familiar melody.

A splash of purple rises from the dunes as Spud emerges, playing his saxophone. It is a jazz rendition of "Here Comes the Bride." The beauty of his playing brings joyful tears to

Queenie's eyes. She has cried more today than she has in ages.

Queenie wipes her tears with the yellow scarf tied around her neck, beaming a smile toward the dunes. Spud nods his saxophone in her direction. The melody soars.

As she approaches the tent, all the guests smile at Queenie as if she is the most beautiful bride in the world. Most have tears in their eyes, too. Queenie has never heard Spud play better. After Iris broke off their relationship, he didn't play saxophone for decades and disbanded his jazz quartet. It was only after Iris died that he started playing again.

Iris.

Queenie looks at the sky, expecting angry clouds to greet her, but the day remains clear. A perfect day for a wedding. The hurricane named after her nemesis has stayed away. Her groom has returned. There is music. Queenie's day will not be ruined.

Queenie and Old Sally join the sandaled priest down front, who looks like he might pull out a guitar and sing "Kumbaya" at any moment. Thankfully, Queenie prefers jazz. Spud ends his solo. A rush of purple approaches, and he hands his saxophone to his brother in the front row, who looks like a plump version of Spud with a blond toupée. The young priest who buried Iris invites Old Sally to join him at the front.

Spud and Queenie stand side by side, and Queenie steals a look at her intended. Not only does he play a wicked saxophone, but she loves him with her whole heart.

More tears fill Queenie's eyes, making her grateful for waterproof mascara. Tears that signal a new chapter in her life. A life that a few years ago she could have never imagined would include this much happiness. Or this much purple.

CHAPTER TEN

Old Sally

An image emerges from the past. It is what Old Sally does these days. Remember things. She patches together memories to create a picture of her life. At ten years of age, Queenie wore one of Old Sally's white slips on her head like a wedding veil and walked with great pomp and circumstance down the hallway to the kitchen. Like many little girls, she dreamed of this day. Fifty years later it is finally happening.

Celebrations are as necessary as the air she breathes. Katie stands near the front of the gathering practically busting with another celebration to come.

Death can be a celebration, too, Old Sally thinks. A celebration of a life lived fully.

Old Sally stands at the front facing Queenie, Spud, and the gathering of guests. Goosebumps climb her arms. A signal that a spirit is near. She senses her grandmother in attendance. A woman who passed to the other side many years ago. A strong woman in a long line of strong women stretching into the present day.

A chuckle rises from somewhere deep inside her. Old Sally should have known her grandmother would attend. For years she taught Old Sally the Gullah secrets as Old Sally is now teaching Violet.

To begin the ceremony, Old Sally welcomes everyone and then asks them to stand. Violet joins her at the front and begins to sing an old Gullah spiritual. The song is about how the Gullah people rode the water to this place and how the water will take them home. It is the tempo of a slow walk along the beach. A walk through all the ages that their people have lived here.

Guests sway to Violet's singing, including the young priest from the all-white Catholic church in Savannah. For a time, it resembles a revival meeting instead of a wedding. Old Sally remembers her first love and imagines him playing his fiddle in the dunes, as Spud played his saxophone. For several moments her vision blurs with tears.

In between the verses, Violet leads them on the refrains.

This is how it should be, Old Sally tells herself. *It's Violet's time to lead.*

Old Sally looks beyond the guests to her grandmother watching from the edge of the dunes, nodding and clapping with the passing of the mantle. Old Sally has done her part to not let the traditions die out. So many of their young people have moved away from the island—distracted and enticed by modern times. However, some will return, and some will stay.

Old Sally is reminded of the gathering outside the Temple mansion as the fire raged on. Violet's voice uplifted them in the darkest times. It can bring people closer together in the best of times, too.

In her imagination, Old Sally is transported to another time. A time far away when her ancestors first arrived on this island and named it after the dolphins frequently seen along the coast. She imagines other weddings taking place on this beach, weddings in the past and in the future. When Violet stops singing the guests are silent. Only the waves are heard. Waves from thirty feet away. Waves that sing the ebb and flow of life.

"You must remember the live oaks that grace this coastline," Old Sally begins, her voice clear. "Their roots join under the earth. Now Queenie and Spud be joined, too. The roots of their families now merge. Each of us merges with all Creation. The Creator blesses Queenie and Spud's union because of the genuine love here. This is all you can hope for in this life. To be blessed by love."

Old Sally looks at her grandmother, and for a moment sees a faint reflection of herself standing next to her.

The ceremony continues, and Old Sally steps aside for the priest to say the traditional vows to make Queenie and Spud's marriage official in the eyes of the law.

Queenie and Spud say, "I do," and kiss.

Gullah has mixed with Christianity over the years, adding another layer to the story of Old Sally's people. Most of those who stayed on the island now go to the island church that worships both Jesus and the tides. These are people who believe in the earth's seasons and in the resurrection. Water is central to both faiths.

Finally, the priest takes a step back and leaves Old Sally in front to say the final words.

"Ritual be what unites us all," she begins. "Ritual anchors us to this place and time. With love in place, there be no room for hatred. Love will save us."

Queenie and Spud stand holding hands with their heads bowed, as do all their family and friends, including Old Sally's grandmother in the dunes.

"May we be a lighthouse for each other through every storm," she says, realizing this is not something she had planned to say. Then she looks at Queenie and Spud and adds: "May you spread your joy to all who meet you. May you stay safe from harm and honor your ancestors. May you love each other for the rest of your days."

Violet says, "Amen," and the guests respond with the same. With Violet leading, they call and respond several times, tossing "Amen" across the tent among all those gathered. Laughter and clapping end the ceremony.

CHAPTER ELEVEN

Rose

Never has Rose seen a more colorful bride and groom. Queenie with her white wedding dress, red hat, yellow scarf, and purple pumps. Spud with his purple suit, white shirt, and purple-and-green bow tie. Nor has she ever seen a happier couple.

The wedding reception is at the house and in full swing. Violet is busy refilling different serving dishes.

"Let me do that," Rose says. "You don't work for the Temples anymore."

Rose seldom thinks of herself as a Temple, though she kept the name after she married, as her mother did. Maybe she is more of a Temple than she thinks.

"Don't be silly," Violet says. "I'm good at this."

Violet seems more confident since she started her tea shop a few months ago. Is this what happens when someone finds their true calling? If so, Rose needs to start painting again. Every day that she doesn't, she disappoints herself. But now that Queenie's wedding is over, she plans to get out her easel and paints and set up in the small light-filled studio at the back of their cottage.

The last time Rose mingled was after her mother's funeral, when Savannah's upper crust was paying their last respects and reshuffling the old Savannah power structure.

Rose raises a glass of tonic water with lime, minus the vodka, for an imaginary toast.

Rest in peace, Mother.

Across the room, Old Sally is showing signs of weariness. The priest is unusually talkative, so Rose crosses the room to rescue her. If Old Sally is one of the hundred-year-old live oak trees on the island, the young priest is a sapling.

"Excuse me, Father, can I borrow Old Sally for a moment?" Rose asks.

He offers a brief Kumbaya smile and then pivots to the next listener.

Old Sally holds onto Rose's arm like she is clinging to a life raft. "He kept asking me how all of us could possibly live in this house together without being at each other's throats. You would think a priest would believe in harmony."

Rose agrees. They walk down the hallway toward Old Sally's room, the noise fading as they get farther away from the party. Her bedroom is simple. A bed. A chair. One dresser. Perfectly neat. A knot of "five finger" grass hangs on the bedpost, meant for restful sleep. A large window faces the ocean, with a windowsill filled with seashells Old Sally collects on her walks. One corner holds a piece of driftwood that was the base of an old tree. While Queenie's room is full of color, Old Sally's is the color of the beach. Almost no separation exists between her bedroom and the sand and dunes.

Rose helps Old Sally take off her sandals and lift her legs

onto the bed. She lies back onto her pillow and lets out a long sigh.

"I was saving all my energy for the wedding," Old Sally says. "Now I be like a balloon that's lost all its air."

"You rest for a while, and you'll feel much better," Rose says. She gently massages Old Sally's hands as Old Sally did for her when she was getting her ready for bed as a girl. She traces Old Sally's lifeline and the veins on the backs of her hands. Then Rose moves to the end of the bed and massages Old Sally's feet, something she has taken up doing since she has lived here. Old Sally thanks her, her eyes closed. The tops of her feet are the color of leather, the bottoms the color of sand. Cool, wrinkled, and sandpapery dry. Feet that have been walking the earth for over a hundred years. Millions of steps. Walking. Running. Dancing. And at one time, skipping and jumping.

No wonder she's tired, Rose thinks, grateful that she can give back to this woman who gave her so much.

With every second that passes, Rose is more aware that a stranger is coming to the island. A stranger who claims to be Edward's daughter, her brother being the one person in her family she wishes she could forget ever existed.

"Edward's child be almost here," Old Sally says, not opening her eyes.

This is the second time today that Rose has thought Old Sally was reading her thoughts. Is Rose that transparent?

"How did you know that Edward's daughter was coming today?"

"I forget," Old Sally says.

"Should I be concerned about her?" Rose asks.

"Too soon to know for sure."

Rose covers Old Sally with a light blanket from the end of the bed and watches her fall asleep.

When she returns to the living room, Max is greeting a stranger at the door. Upon seeing Heather for the first time, Rose emits a slight gasp. Heather looks like a younger version of Rose's mother. The same upturned nose. The same hair color, though Heather's is long. The same ramrod-straight posture and overture of entitlement. She is dressed like the Junior League version of a Jehovah's Witness. Heather's blue eyes narrow when Rose approaches the door. No DNA evidence is needed. The resemblance is immediate. Heather is not only her brother's child but her mother's grandchild.

They introduce themselves. Heather's gaze burrows into Rose, before looking around as if to assess the value of the house.

"I didn't mean to interrupt anything," Heather says, though she doesn't seem to mind. "I guess that's what I get for not calling first. I got your address from Regina."

"Yes, Regina called me."

"She did?" Heather's look of surprise appears rehearsed, or maybe Rose imagines it.

"I don't know Regina very well," Rose begins. "I met her once for a short time last year, and we've talked briefly on the phone. She called me this morning to say you were on your way."

Heather nods like someone who has practiced a speech for hours and now must skip several note cards ahead to find a new place to start. A crack in the façade?

"I didn't know you were having a party," Heather says, which feels genuine.

"It's actually a wedding," Rose answers. She starts to say that it is Queenie and Spud's wedding, but she isn't sure she wants to share that much with someone she has only known for half a minute. Someone who also bears an uncanny resemblance to her mother.

Is this a joke? Rose wonders. *Why didn't Regina warn her?* Then she remembers that Regina probably never met her mother.

Rose also questions the timing of Heather's arrival. They are in the middle of a celebration, with a storm barreling toward them, and a long-lost relative has washed up on the beach via Atlanta.

"My father was your brother," Heather says, as if this is a news flash.

"I can see the resemblance," Rose says, thinking it is not only her brother she resembles.

"You can?" Heather's small eyes widen, and Rose notices for the first time her smile. A smile, she imagines, that required several years of orthodontia to achieve. At least the smile is a departure from her mother, who rarely partook in something so frivolous unless she wanted to impress someone.

"You have Edward's bone structure, hairline, even his hair color—at least when he was younger." Rose feels generous saying this much.

Heather's cheeks redden. "Regina didn't seem too convinced."

Regina probably wouldn't admit it, even with DNA proof of paternity, Rose thinks.

She wonders what Heather hopes to gain from their meeting, and then asks herself when she became so cynical. It isn't like her to think the worst of people.

Max gives Rose a look that asks, *Can I go now?* She nods, and he rejoins the party.

For an awkward moment, Rose and Heather stand at the front door, neither speaking. If first impressions are to be trusted, Rose's first inclination is to lock up the silverware. Her second, to return to Wyoming, where she lived for twenty-five years to get away from her mother.

"How can I help you, Heather?" Rose's politeness sounds insincere, even to her. She wants this young woman out of her house.

"I'd like to ask you some questions," she says.

Rose challenges herself to give the young woman a chance. She directs Heather to the rocking chairs on the south end of the porch, where they can have some privacy. Two guests from the wedding are on the other end, but far enough away that they won't be able to hear.

"My mother died six months ago," Heather says. "I didn't know who my father was until I found my birth certificate in her papers."

"I'm so sorry for your loss," Rose says, wondering why Heather's mother didn't share this information with Heather sooner. Did Edward threaten the woman? Pay her off?

Rose reminds herself to listen, instead of appointing herself judge and jury. She notices how perfectly Heather is dressed. Her sleeveless dress reveals an attractive figure. Tanned legs. Nice sandals. Toenails painted a dusty rose color that matches her purse, as well as her lipstick. Rose half expects her to be wearing pearls.

"Your father and I were never close," Rose says, which is the truth.

"You weren't?" Heather looks almost irritated, like she has come all this way for nothing.

"No, I'm sorry to say we weren't."

Rose's absence of warmth isn't like her. Is this self-protection? They pause again, their awkwardness cresting like the nearby waves.

Until now, Rose has never been an aunt. This will give Katie a cousin, too. A hereditary windfall in some ways. But something isn't sitting quite right. Rose blames it on wedding fatigue and tells herself to be nicer.

"What was my father like as a boy?" Heather appears to renew her excitement, and smiles as if imagining something that involves frolicking.

Rose pauses. How does she tell Heather that her father was a first-class bully? A near-perfect copy of their mother until he betrayed her at the end by releasing the Temple secrets.

"He was older than me," Rose says instead. "He had a totally different set of friends than I did. We rarely played together." Her pinkie finger vibrates where Edward cut it off with one of the Temple Confederate swords when she was five. Is that the kind of story Heather wants? Or does she want to hear how he would shove Rose against walls as he passed or try to trip her on the staircase or trap her in her bedroom?

"Do you know about the fire that took his life?" Rose asks.

"Yes. My mother had a copy of the newspaper article in her things."

Heather straightens her hair, blown by the ocean breeze. Rose can't remember a single time her mother came to the beach, even with it being this close to Savannah. Meanwhile, Heather shows no remorse for Edward's death. No apparent longing for what might have been. Or perhaps she is good at hiding it. Rose was good at hiding her emotion at her mother's deathbed, too. It was the first time she had been back to Savannah since she married Max.

Is Heather here to merely meet her long-lost aunt? Or is she here with a purpose in mind that she isn't talking about? If she is, Rose is intent on finding out what it is.

CHAPTER TWELVE

Violet

The reception is a hit. The crab cakes and shrimp cocktail are well received, and Violet's cocktail sauce—as always —has guests asking for the recipe. When she was in Miss Temple's employ, receptions were frequent. Mounds of seafood, finger foods, and fresh fruits were standard. Depending on Miss Temple's mood, sometimes even a chocolate fountain was prepared, along with strawberries for dipping. At Violet's new tea house, she bakes. Muffins and pastries. Banana and pumpkin bread. Pies and cakes. She must admit she has enjoyed putting together something that doesn't involve quite as much sugar and white flour.

With all the serving bowls and platters full again, Violet turns on the small television in her bedroom for the weather. Tia and Leisha and their friends stand in front of the mirror in her bathroom, putting on additional eye makeup. Tia will be sixteen soon, and Leisha will graduate from high school next week. In a little over two months, Leisha will be leaving for the

College of Charleston, a school they never could have afforded a couple of years ago. Edward tried to prove in court that his mother had been out of her mind when she changed the will in Violet's favor, but it was not overturned. Somehow Edward was the loser in the will. Something that surprised Violet considering how loyal he was to Miss Temple. At least she always thought he was loyal, until she found out that Edward was the person who was releasing all those secrets. Evidently, not everything and everyone is as they seem.

On the news, a weather map shows a tight twist of clouds in the Caribbean. The hurricane has made landfall in St. Croix as a Category 3 storm. Violet still can't believe the coincidence of a hurricane named *Iris* forming on the day of Queenie's wedding. It sounds like something Miss Temple might have arranged just for spite. Do spirits have that much power? If any might, it would be Miss Iris Temple.

"What are you watching?" Tia flutters her eyelashes, thick with mascara, in Violet's direction.

"Just the weather," Violet says, seeing no need to excite them any more than they already are. Like Spud noted, Savannah has a history of predicted hurricanes that hit some-where else. This storm is still far away. She imagines it will fizzle out after making landfall, which they often do.

Honestly, what worries Violet more than a hurricane is the notion of Tia and Leisha leaving home. She's not sure how to deal with an empty nest. Although even without them, their communal nest will be far from empty.

When Violet returns to the kitchen, the party is full of life. Happy to be on the fringes, she loads the dishwasher and then washes a few things by hand. If anyone else knows about the storm, they don't seem that concerned.

Meanwhile, Queenie and Spud dance to Lionel Richie in

the living room. Queenie waves for Violet to join them, but Violet smiles and waves her suggestion away. Even with all the preparations, there is still plenty to do.

Rose enters the kitchen followed by a young woman. Violet stops washing dishes and her eyes widen. She shivers like the warm day has suddenly turned cold. Heather could be Miss Temple's ghost, if she had died when she was twenty instead of eighty.

Rose lifts an eyebrow as if to say, *You see it, too?*

Her gesture reminds Violet of when she and Queenie used signals during the long meals with Miss Temple at the Temple mansion. Meals where silence was required of them.

"Heather found out recently that Edward was her father," Rose says. "She's come here to meet us."

Heather is taller than Violet and looks slightly down on her. A position that feels all too familiar. She decides not to bring up the fact that she is Heather's half aunt. That would require too much explanation on a day when she is so tired. Besides, she can barely keep all the family connections straight as it is.

"You have a beautiful home," Heather says to Violet.

She wonders if Heather thinks that she and Rose are a couple. Their living situation has perplexed many people, especially those who could never imagine living with a collection of souls who are in some ways related by blood, and in other ways not related at all.

"I'd better check the food," Violet says, telling Heather that it was nice to meet her, though she isn't so sure it was.

Compared to Tia and Leisha, who aren't that much younger, Heather seems sophisticated, worldly. Violet isn't entirely convinced it isn't all just an act. She has known families where genetic traits appear to skip a generation, but this is almost creepy. Violet recalls dusting early photographs in solid gold frames in Miss Temple's bedroom that could be of Heather instead of Miss Temple.

Violet stands at the sink overlooking the wooden walkway that connects the big house to Rose and Max's cottage. The sky is a deep blue with no clouds in sight, but according to the weather reports that could change as the storm progresses.

Katie walks into the kitchen with Angela not far behind. Katie's Lamaze classes usually meet here on Saturday afternoons. Right about now they usually have a living room full of pregnant women and their husbands or partners, pushing and blowing until Violet thinks she might give birth herself from all the encouragement. Because of the wedding, they won't be meeting today, which is probably a good thing. That crowd would have devoured all the food by now.

Angela steps up to dry the dishes Violet recently washed. "Have you heard about the storm?" she asks.

"I doubt there's anything to worry about," Violet says. "We never get hurricanes around here."

She bases her confidence on how her left shoulder would be aching by now if there was a danger. Although, her shoulder has never predicted weather-related incidents before. Probably because there haven't been any.

"We never get hurricanes where I'm from, either," Angela says.

Katie dips a cucumber slice into the avocado dip that Violet will soon return to the reception table. "I guess it's safe to say we're all novices in the hurricane department," she says, offering to help, too.

When all the dishes are dry and put away, Katie and Angela join the party in the living room. Tia and Leisha are now dancing with their friends, eyes brilliant with shadow, mascara, and thick eyeliner, and circles of wine-colored rouge on their dark cheeks.

The music stops and the bride and groom collapse, smiling, onto the sofa. The wedding, as far as Violet can tell, is a complete success. Thanks to Old Sally, the ceremony was lovely and meaningful. Afterward, she heard several people say that they felt part of something extraordinary. They were also complimentary about Violet's singing. Most importantly, Queenie was pleased.

It has only been two years since Violet found out that she is Queenie's daughter. Given how close they always were, it seems obvious now. But sometimes the obvious isn't noticeable at all. Sometimes the truth is hidden right in front of you. She wonders what other secrets have been kept from her, and what secrets are in this room right now. Besides possibly Heather.

Meanwhile, Old Sally is nowhere in sight, and Rose and Heather have moved to the back patio. What could they possibly be talking about that has Rose looking so somber? Somber like she was as a girl whenever she was around Miss Temple, who corrected her almost nonstop. Violet would have asked Heather to leave by now simply because of the creepiness factor, but Rose has always had trouble telling people no. Especially people who look like Rose's mother.

Violet should have known that the Temples weren't the type to rest in peace. Even though Edward's ghost isn't hanging around the rafters, now his daughter has shown up.

Let's hope it's not to make trouble, Violet thinks.

Violet is too tired to deal with trouble. Too tired to deal with anything other than letting her thoughts wander.

If Edward hadn't accidentally started the fire that burned down the mansion, they would be living in that grand old house in Savannah. Yet, despite the tragedy, everything seems to have worked out for the best. Violet is honored to be learning the Gullah secrets and her family's history. Honored to be entrusted with what Old Sally knows. Their Gullah ancestors have been here for almost two centuries. They brought with them a rich ancestry from Africa and built a culture here. A culture based on ancient medicines, rituals, and folk magic. Preserving that history is essential. What they don't know, however, is where their Gullah story will go from here.

CHAPTER THIRTEEN

Queenie

With all the guests finally gone from the reception, Queenie and Spud sit on the couch, their arms entwined. Queenie wants to bottle this happiness and drink from it the rest of her life.

"Hello, Mrs. Grainger," Spud says, his voice soft and affectionate.

"Hello, Mister Grainger," she responds, marveling at how skinny his arm is compared to hers.

What she doesn't tell Spud is that she wants to keep her old name, but she doesn't want to hurt his feelings. It is the twenty-first century, after all. If Oprah ever marries Stedman, Queenie doubts she'll change her name, either. It occurs to her that maybe she could ask Spud to change his name to Spudman, but then thinks better of it.

Marrying Spud has taught her something about change. Mainly that you never know what will be good for you until you try. Before falling in love with Spud, Queenie rolled her eyes at interracial couples. She is sorry about that now.

People can change their minds, thank goodness, otherwise the world wouldn't evolve at all, she thinks, her lightheartedness taking a turn. *Heaven knows we need the world to change.*

Last fall, on September 11, the world changed the instant the first plane hit the towers. Now all these white people think that dark-skinned foreigners are the enemy.

Well, aren't we all foreigners? she asks herself. *Didn't every single one of us come from somewhere else?*

"What are you thinking about, lemon drop? You suddenly went away."

"Those towers," she says with a sigh.

Spud looks puzzled and perhaps surprised she would be thinking of 9/11 on their wedding day, but then he lowers his eyes. After those towers came down, he stayed quiet for days. Queenie likes that he is sensitive. Musicians are often like that, at least the best ones are. But for the life of her, she can't figure out how he was ever a butcher. He will capture a mouse and relocate it instead of killing it.

People are a mystery, Queenie thinks.

Spud squeezes her hand and smiles at her. "Let's not ruin our wedding day worrying about the state of the world," he says.

Queenie agrees, though he's done plenty of worrying as far as she can tell. She shifts her thoughts and looks at him lovingly.

To her unending surprise, Spud Grainger is every bit as sexy to her as her longtime heartthrob, Denzel Washington. Turns out it doesn't matter what a person looks like as long as your two hearts match up.

Queenie gives Spud a full-out kiss right there on the couch.

Her shoes drop to the floor and her toes tingle. When Spud played "Here Comes the Bride" on his saxophone she thought she might keel over in the dunes from the surge of love that came through her like a lightning bolt.

A young woman comes in the back door with Rose. A stranger. But someone who looks somehow familiar.

"Who's that?" Queenie asks Spud, motioning toward the kitchen.

"That's Rose's brother's daughter I told you about. Heather."

Queenie's eyes narrow in instant distrust. Mean people should not be allowed to reproduce. Especially someone like Edward Temple.

Queenie pulls her glasses from her cleavage and puts them on. When Heather comes into focus, Queenie covers her mouth and lets out a scream. Mostly it is covered up by the music playing, but a few people turn.

"What is it?" Spud straightens his bow tie with a flash of alarm.

"Edward's daughter is the spitting image of Iris before she got old!" Queenie says.

Spud squints in the direction of the kitchen. If he notices the resemblance, he doesn't let on, which—come to think of it —is a brilliant move. He gives Queenie's love handles a squeeze as if to remind her that they are here to celebrate. But Queenie is not ready to let this go. Violet joins them in the living room and Queenie motions toward the kitchen.

Violet nods, confirming Queenie is not imagining things.

The lights flicker, and Queenie jumps. "You don't think that's Iris, do you?"

Spud laughs and shakes his head like this is the last thing he wants, too.

Even though the spirits of the Temple mansion were

silenced in the fire, she wouldn't put it past Iris to figure out a way to haunt her on her wedding day. In fact, it seems the entire Temple clan is conspiring against her. What with Edward's daughter showing up out of the blue, and the news this morning that a hurricane named Iris is hovering somewhere out in the Atlantic. Odd coincidences, at best. Every now and again, Queenie finds herself missing her half sister, which is even more bizarre.

"I've been thinking about the past today," Spud says.

Queenie is so distracted, she forgot Spud was even there. She turns to give him her full attention. Is he going to tell her that his love for Iris goes beyond the grave?

"What is it?" she asks, telling herself not to panic.

"I need to tell you something." Spud looks more solemn than Queenie likes.

"Uh, oh." Queenie holds her breath.

"No, no. It's nothing bad."

She exhales. "You want me to have your love child?" Queenie asks. They laugh, and she thinks about Katie, ready to burst with new life. When Queenie was pregnant with Violet, she did her best to hide it. Mister Oscar told Queenie that if she ever told anyone that Violet was his child, he would have to fire Old Sally and make life difficult for Queenie and Violet. Mister Oscar was weak compared to Iris and could be kind, but he was still surprisingly good at delivering a threat.

"You sure it's nothing bad?" she asks.

"Positive."

"Promise?"

"Promise. Now can I tell you what I wanted to say?"

Queenie pauses while Spud clears his throat.

"I've been thinking about Iris today—"

Queenie puts a hand over her heart to keep it from breaking.

"Let me finish, please," Spud says, his look stern, yet loving.

The lump in her throat tightens with the fear that an annulment is looming.

"When I was with Iris, I was so young I didn't even know what love was," Spud begins again. "It was infatuation if anything, but what you and I have, Queenie, is love. Real grown-up love."

Her eyes mist and she kisses Spud. A passionate kiss meant to curl his bow tie, not caring if anyone sees it.

All those years she was single, she has missed kissing the most, and wants to make up for all that time lost. In an hour, she and Spud are scheduled to leave for their week-long honeymoon in Hilton Head.

A hot flash fans the flames of Queenie's love, followed by a sudden chill that cools her sweat. She breathes in sharply. The last time a chill climbed her spine was before the Temple mansion was destroyed and all those ghosts got displaced. Now she seems to see Iris everywhere she looks. Has her half sister found a new way to haunt her?

CHAPTER FOURTEEN

Old Sally

Waking from her nap, Old Sally remembers why she felt so tired before. A heaviness set in after the wedding. She senses that dark forces are coming together. For the last three nights, she has slept fitfully. Her tea leaves this morning spelled disruption, too.

People wonder how she can read the future from a few leaves left in the bottom of a cup. But the otherworld talks to her whenever she lets it, using anything that is around as a messenger. Sometimes a tree leans in the direction she is to go. Sometimes the mood of the ocean tells the story. Sometimes a whisper hides in the breeze, telling her everything she needs to know.

Old Sally returns to the empty living room. What is left of the party has moved outside. From the front window, she sees Jack and Violet walk arm in arm down the beach, with Tia and Leisha and their friends behind them. Violet stops on the beach and looks back at the house.

Do you need me? she asks, sending her thoughts in Old Sally's direction.

No, Old Sally responds. *But thank you.*

Are you sure? Violet asks.

I'm sure, Old Sally answers.

Old Sally and Violet have begun to converse this way only recently. It is how she knows her time is growing short, and that the opening between this world and the next is growing wider. Old Sally sees this as a blessing. Her spirit is ready to be released.

Rose sits on the front porch with a young white woman. Old Sally narrows her eyes before widening them again. She shouldn't have been napping. A fox has entered the hen house while she wasn't looking.

She goes outside and greets Rose and the stranger on the porch. Some people are like storms and create chaos wherever they go. A trickster, the Gullah people would call her. Someone who turns things upside down and often deceives. Caution is required. Old Sally asks her ancestors for Rose's protection.

"Did you have a nice nap?" Rose asks.

Old Sally nods, not taking her eyes away from Heather.

Rose introduces them.

"I know who you are," Old Sally says. "I be praying for you for a long time."

"You've what?" Heather turns to Rose as if to confirm that the old woman is demented.

"Old Sally is the matriarch of this house," Rose says. "None of us would be here without her."

"Nice to meet you," Heather says, not offering her hand.

In her imagination, Old Sally sees Iris Temple as a little girl hiding under her bed waiting to see how long it would take for her mother or father to find her. Her parents never noticed she was gone. Nobody even came looking except for Old Sally. That little girl became someone who insisted on attention of every kind. This young woman feels the same. Confirmation lies in how much she looks like Iris. The ancestors are offering another attempt for the Temple family to heal and choose something different.

"Can I talk to you?" Old Sally says to Rose. "In private."

Rose follows her into the house and closes the door.

"Something about her makes me tired," Rose says.

"You must be very careful," Old Sally says. "She drains your energy to use for herself. She doesn't do it on purpose, but the Temple wound be so deep you must be careful not to get pulled in."

"The Temple wound?" Rose asks.

"Edward abandoned this girl. Never acknowledged her existence. So, as a Temple, she be looking for you to do that. You're the only one left."

"Can you believe how much she looks like Mother?" Rose asks.

"Traits often skip a generation to remind us there still be stuff to deal with."

"I feel horrible that I don't like her," Rose whispers.

"It be history weighing on you," Old Sally says.

Iris Temple was unrelenting in how she criticized Rose. All to mold her into what she considered to be a true Temple. Edward was treated this way, too. Standards impossible to live up to. Rules that weakened instead of strengthened the Temple family. It surprises Old Sally the burdens parents put on their children when their only job is to love and protect them. And notice them.

"Should I tell her to leave?" Rose asks.

"These old energies never move on unless you take time to

acknowledge and understand them," Old Sally says. "You can either do it now or wait until it shows up again."

Rose gives an exasperated sigh. "I thought I'd dealt with this already."

Old Sally removes a small burlap sack the size of a deck of cards from the pocket of her dress. The bag contains a root that looks like a gnarled knuckle, a rough pearl the size of a marble, and a piece of indigo-blue fabric.

"Take this," Old Sally begins. "My grandmother gave this charm to me when I was a girl, and I've carried it every day of my life since. It will protect you from anything harmful."

Rose tries to refuse it, but Old Sally won't let her. "You must take it," Old Sally says, closing Rose's hand around it. "If I need it back, I'll ask for it."

Rose finally agrees, and Old Sally hugs her, telling her everything will be all right. Something still to be seen.

"Do you know where Katie is?" Old Sally asks. "We were supposed to meet after the reception."

"She may be napping," Rose says. "She does that a lot these days."

I do, too, Old Sally thinks.

Births and deaths take place at the same threshold. Old Sally's grandmother said that one is God's inhale and the other is God's exhale. Old Sally likes thinking of it this way. Each of us a part of the breath of our Creator.

Old Sally and Katie spend time together every day to get ready for the birth. If Rose is her *soul* daughter, then Katie is her *soul* granddaughter. Everyone is connected. Blood family and spirit family. Now she needs to make sure that everyone she loves stays safe for whatever is to come.

CHAPTER FIFTEEN

Rose

All afternoon, Rose's unexpected niece has hovered around her like a mosquito looking for a place to bite. With Old Sally off to find Katie and the small charm in her pocket, Rose now feels emboldened enough to tell Heather that their family reunion will have to wait until another time.

Earlier, Rose gave Heather a quick history of the Temple family—it would make Rose's mother proud to know how much Rose has remembered. However, Heather showed only a vague interest in what Rose told her. Had she already researched the Temple family? That would be easy to do these days with the world wide web.

Rose returns to the front porch to find Max and Heather sitting together. Max makes friends easily these days, having traded in his cowboy boots for flip-flops. Sometimes he says more in a day than he said in an entire week at the ranch. Rose doesn't know what brought on this transformation, but it has taken some getting used to.

"We were wondering what happened to you," Max says to Rose, patting an empty rocking chair beside him.

"Old Sally needed my help," Rose says, aware that it was actually Old Sally who helped Rose.

"Heather was asking how we could afford such a beautiful house," Max says. "I told her it was a matter of combining inheritances and—" He stops. The look on Rose's face tells him that he has already said too much.

How is it that the quiet cowboy I've been married to all these years now overshares?

For all Rose knows, Heather is here to collect whatever Temple money she feels entitled to.

"Max invited me to stay the night," Heather says to Rose. Her eyes sparkle like a child receiving precisely what she wanted for Christmas.

When Heather isn't looking, Rose tosses a wary glance at Max. The last thing she wants to do tonight is to have Heather reminding her of her mother and everything wrong with the Temple family.

"I'm sure you have family or pets to return to," Rose says to Heather.

"No, it's only me. No family. No pets."

"But you don't have any of your things with you," Rose says.

Heather smiles as though moving her knight into position to take Rose's queen.

"I packed up some things in the car before I left."

Rose's suspicion may be a direct result of being a Temple. Whenever people in Savannah find out who her family is, they often become intimidated, enamored, or sometimes greedy. Meanwhile, the tip of her little finger throbs and weighs in on her hesitation.

Max excuses himself to go to the kitchen. He knows he's in trouble and food will fortify him to face the fallout.

Heather excuses herself to get her things out of the car. Her profile reveals how much she looks like Rose's mother.

Rose shivers and removes the charm from her pocket.

"You were supposed to protect me," she says aloud with no one to hear.

With the wedding finally over, Rose had planned to put on her pajamas and curl up with a good book. A nice stress-free evening. Now it seems the mystery novel will have to wait, replaced by the mystery of why Heather is here and what old energy, as Old Sally would say, needs to be resolved.

She glances at the sky. It's been hours since she's heard a weather report. Is her mother's storm still out there somewhere? A double dose of trouble, counting Heather's unexpected visit?

Violet walks through the dunes to go to the house, leaving the rest of her family on the beach.

"What's going on?" Violet asks Rose.

"It turns out Heather will be spending the night," Rose says.

"You're kidding."

"I wish I were."

"How did—"

"Max invited her."

Violet mirrors how Rose feels. A stranger in the house means they won't get to fully relax.

"Dinner is fend-for-yourself," Violet says. "I'm too tired to come up with anything else."

Rose agrees. "Have you heard anything about the storm?" Rose refuses to call it Hurricane Iris. The irony is too perfect. Rose's entire childhood was spent avoiding her mother's larger-than-life nature. She thinks again of Heather, whom she hasn't yet figured out how to avoid.

"The hurricane is still in the Caribbean," Violet says, looking unconcerned.

But Rose wonders if her mother is staging a little karmic revenge.

"What did you find out about Heather?" Violet asks.

Rose glances to the left, where Heather's car is parked, to make sure she isn't coming. "I'm not sure why she's here," Rose says. "It appears she wants to know things about her father, but there's something else going on, too. Old Sally thinks she's here to resolve something from the past."

They exchange a look that reminds Rose of how long they've been friends.

"Why do I feel like Mother is messing with us again?" Rose asks.

"It's weird, but I've been feeling the same," Violet says.

"Do you think it's possible for history to bubble up?"

"I do." Violet looks out to sea.

As girls, Rose and Violet were good at putting puzzles together, and it feels like they are putting a puzzle together now. A giant one that includes strangers coming to visit, history bubbling up, and Gullah spells.

"Something about the whole situation feels troubling," Violet says.

Rose's shoulders tense. "Do you ever feel like you're the only one left in your generation to deal with things?"

"I do," Violet says. "I never dreamed I'd be the keeper of the Gullah secrets."

"Just like I'm the keeper of the Temple secrets," Rose says. "Except I don't even know where the Temple secrets are anymore."

"Maybe it's time to go find out what that key opens. And soon," Violet says.

Queenie and Spud emerge from the far deck and the mood shifts. Spud's bow tie is askew, and it appears he has a copper-colored rash on his face from Queenie's lipstick.

"I wondered where you two were." To Rose, mature love seems so much more hopeful than young love.

"I think I'm going to like being married," Spud says to them, causing Rose and Violet to laugh.

The newlyweds go inside. Seconds later, Heather rolls a large suitcase up the front walk, as if she might stay for a month instead of one night. Storm clouds gather in Rose's thoughts. Whatever happens next, she hopes the charm works.

CHAPTER SIXTEEN

Violet

Tiny brass bells jingle to announce another customer coming through the door. First-timers are easy to identify. Violet often catches a moment of delight in their eyes, as if surprised to find her small tea shop tucked away off a side street behind a tiny courtyard full of tea roses. The large front window has fancy purple-and-gold lettering that reads: VIOLET'S TEA SHOP.

Earlier this morning, Violet carried a heavy sandwich board out to the corner of the main street and set it up. A giant arrow below the name points down the alleyway—with the same purple-and-gold lettering—so that people won't miss it. Like most of the structures in downtown Savannah, the building is historic, meaning ivy covers the brick, the water pipes talk to you on occasion, and everything smells like the most ancient of mildew when it rains. But this seems a small price to pay for a sense of history.

When it comes to storms, however, downtown Savannah

isn't an ideal location. Even a heavy thunderstorm can flood the street and courtyard. It is hard for Violet to imagine what might happen during a hurricane.

"Don't borrow trouble," Violet tells herself, which is something Old Sally reminds her often.

The next customer through the door makes Violet hesitate, a ghost from the past brushing by her. It is Heather. The Heather who spent the night at the house last night, much to Rose's dismay. Violet was so exhausted after the wedding she went to bed early and was out of the house this morning before anyone was up and about.

Heather glances at the African violets in the large front window. A jungle of purple blooms in clay pots are stacked on bricks at different heights. Bricks that at one time made up the exterior of the Temple mansion and that Violet gathered and carried in the trunk of her car for this purpose. Her only reminder that the estate belonged to her, if only for a short time. Seeing Heather makes Violet wonder if Miss Temple would approve.

Whether at a wedding reception, like yesterday, or a downtown tea shop, Edward's daughter seems somehow out of place. Violet wonders why she isn't at work somewhere or going to college classes. It is eerie how much she looks like Miss Temple.

Violet wonders if Heather will gravitate toward the small tables for two around the edges of the shop, where she'll have more privacy. Or if she will choose the openness of the main tea room, where bigger tables are set up so that people can gather and talk. Heather picks a seat on the fringes and puts her umbrella on a chair.

"Nice to see you again," Violet says when Heather approaches the counter.

"You, too," she says, though neither of them seems to mean it.

Why does Violet feel like she should be wearing her outdated maid's uniform? The one Miss Temple insisted she wear.

"Did you sleep well last night?" Violet asks, pushing the past from her mind.

"I did," Heather says. "Rose told me about your tea shop this morning, so I thought I'd visit."

Is that a dull pain pinging Violet's shoulder again or does she imagine it? She doubts Heather came here only to have a cup of tea. Her entire demeanor is of someone who wants something much more substantial than tea.

"What can I get for you?" Violet asks.

She often tries to guess what people will order. Are they the English breakfast type? Earl Grey? Herbal tea? She has difficulty pinning Heather down.

Heather eyes the pumpkin bread in the glass case.

Too many calories, Violet can almost hear her say.

"Coffee, black," Heather says.

"Of course," Violet says, remembering this is how Miss Temple drank her coffee, too. If she drank tea, she insisted that Violet use two tea bags to keep it from being weak.

If Queenie were here, she would quip something funny in response to Heather's request for black coffee. Something like, *Yes, I am black. Been this way since I was very young.*

But Violet has never had Queenie's sense of humor. If anything, Violet is much too serious. Jack tells her sometimes that she should lighten up. Although Violet has been slow to embrace all the changes of the last couple of years, she has also welcomed them. Violet and Queenie have weathered the storm of Queenie's secret maternity quite well, though she doesn't think she will ever be able to call her anything other than Queenie. As a girl growing up without a mother, Violet would have given anything to have had someone to call *Mama*, but it feels too late for that now. Maybe that will change over time. A lot of other things have.

Violet asked Tia and Leisha to look after Old Sally this morning while Rose went to the bank. Not that Old Sally needs looking after, but at the end of April, they celebrated her one hundred and second birthday. Something about the largeness of that number prompted them to always have someone around if she needs anything. Besides, Violet likes the influence Old Sally has on her girls. After spending time with her, they seem more grounded and thoughtful.

Heather digs into her sizeable purse, as if on a search for buried treasure instead of two dollars and some change.

"It's on the house," Violet says.

Heather stops digging and thanks her. For a moment, Violet wonders if she uses this ploy often.

Violet was good at reading the moods of the ghosts who haunted the Temple mansion and is learning to read the energy of living people, too. But this young woman is not so easy to understand. If Violet had to guess she would say Heather is, underneath all the pretense, desperate for something. A sense of belonging, perhaps. Or a way to fill her emptiness.

"A fresh pot of coffee will be ready in a minute. You can have a seat, I'll bring it to you," Violet says.

Without thanking her, Heather returns to the corner near the window. A table that people often pick their first time in. Violet arranged the tables to accommodate every type of personality. The shy, the outgoing, the college student, the elderly couple, singles, and groups.

As soon as it's ready, Violet brings over the coffee. She refuses to use paper cups except for to-go orders. A person should have a nice cup of tea or coffee in a container that won't begin to disintegrate as soon as hot water hits it. Violet also brings Heather a small slice of pumpkin bread. A slice small enough to not evoke much guilt.

"Oh, I didn't order that," Heather says.

"I know," Violet says. "It's on the house, too."

Heather looks at her as though wondering why Violet is so nice. She doesn't appear to trust easily. Or perhaps at all. Another attribute of Violet's former employer.

"Rose told me that owning this tea shop is like a lifelong dream or something?"

"It is." Violet doesn't mention that before she fulfilled her dream, she was a servant to the Temples, and therefore to Heather's biological father and look-alike grandmother. Violet was someone who wore a uniform to work, lived in a small apartment, and drove an old car. But that has changed.

Violet excuses herself, telling Heather to let her know if she needs anything else.

Most of the morning crowd are older and retired. People who become invisible in the culture after a certain age. Yet, Violet sees them all. At times, Violet thinks she should hang out a shingle. But she isn't so much a psychologist as she is a reader of tea leaves. From Old Sally, Violet has learned to see the invisible clues of who people are. Tea leaves left behind in their cups reveal short journeys. Long journeys. A new romance. A sudden illness. Their lives revealed under their noses and at the bottom of their cups.

The Gullah ways in her family have passed through the maternal line. It isn't always so. There are male root doctors, too. Yet, Violet is becoming well versed in protection spells, healing elixirs, and where to find the different plants and roots needed for both. Not to be forgotten are the teas. Ginger root tea can cure all sorts of female problems. Dogwood root tea mixed with cherry root and oak bark cures muscular swelling. Cockroach tea helps cure coughs. And earthworm tea works on rashes if combined into a salve with lard. However, Violet imagines that most of these teas will never be sold in her tea shop, no matter how beneficial they are.

Violet's favorite customer, Marylou, enters. Her local customers usually come at the same time every day and order the same thing. Orders she begins fixing as soon as they walk through the door. They count on her to remember the teas and pastries they enjoy.

Marylou is twelve years younger than Old Sally and walks with a silver cane. A colorful scarf is wrapped around her neck, her solid white hair in a pixie cut. She used to be a dancer and was quite famous at one time. Every morning, Marylou orders Earl Grey tea with a cheese Danish warmed in the microwave. Violet makes her tea, thinking again how lucky she is to be working at her very own tea shop instead of in Miss Temple's kitchen.

It is still early, just after nine o'clock, but it already seems a lighter crowd than usual. On a typical Sunday, the tea shop is busy. Queenie usually comes in to help with the lunch crowd, but not today. She is away on her honeymoon.

It is probably Queenie's presence that explains why they can barely catch a breath from 11:30 until 2:00 every day. Queenie draws people like bees to flowers with her laughter and folksy manner.

Violet smiles, remembering when they left for Hilton Head last night, Spud's car covered with the JUST MARRIED announcements that Tia and Leisha drew on the sides and back window.

After Violet delivers Marylou's tea and pastry, she stops by Heather's table. The pumpkin bread remains untouched.

"Everything okay here?"

Heather says that everything is fine, but there is something ominous in the way she looks at Violet. Something in her eyes holds a secret.

CHAPTER SEVENTEEN

Queenie

Queenie and Spud walk along the waterway near the lighthouse on Hilton Head Island. A tower built for display, not necessarily function, but that has a lovely panoramic view if you take the time to trek to the top. A feat Queenie only did once, when she started coming here with Spud.

Occasionally Queenie sees tourists looking at them. She imagines a plus-size black woman and an undersized white man wearing a bow tie aren't a typical couple seen here. But diversity is what makes life interesting. At least that's what Queenie tells herself whenever she's being stared at. She would have thought judgment of this nature would be a thing of the past in 2002. Queenie must bite her lip sometimes to keep from saying what she is thinking, which is that people should keep their stares and smirks to themselves.

"What were those men talking about in the restaurant?"

Queenie asks her new husband, squeezing his arm to make sure he is real.

"Evidently Hurricane Iris is building up speed and has turned toward the southeastern United States."

"That's us," Queenie says, her eyes widening.

"Well, us, and a whole lot of other places," Spud says.

"Hurricane Iris." Queenie scoffs. "Isn't that just our luck, to be pursued by a storm named after you-know-who?"

"*Pursued* may be too big a word," Spud says. "She may still peter out." But his eyes reveal how seriously he is taking this.

Spud puts an arm around her, telling her not to worry. "No matter what happens, I'll take care of you," he says.

Queenie giggles before she can stop herself. Since when is she someone who titters like a schoolgirl? She hates to admit that she likes the idea of being taken care of, but she can't help thinking it comes at a cost. Doesn't everything have a price, whether it's independence or codependence? For a moment, she sounds like Oprah, and this pleases her. Spud Grainger has become one of Queenie's Favorite Things. A gift wrapped in a bow tie just for her.

More and more people are talking about the storm. When Queenie is paying for a colorful new scarf at one of the harbor shops, Spud tells her he thinks they should talk.

"I don't want to upset you," he begins, "but I think we should head back to the island. The others may need us if this hurricane takes the course they think it might," he continues. "We may need to prepare the house for the high tides and high winds."

Should have known Iris would ruin my honeymoon, Queenie thinks, but what she tells Spud is altogether different.

She says they can leave, sounding more submissive than she feels. But the truth is she doesn't want her mama to go through a storm without her, no matter how many other people are around.

"We can continue our honeymoon after the storm passes," Spud says.

She agrees, hiding her disappointment. "I've waited this long. I can wait a little longer," Queenie says, which is actually true.

He opens the car door for her in the parking lot near the harbor. They will return to his condominium and pack up to go back to Dolphin Island less than twenty-four hours after they arrived. Queenie admires the elegant red-and-white lighthouse again. It couldn't be more different from the one on their island that has been abandoned for years. A structure that may have been helpful at one time, now bolted closed and dark.

A gust of wind shakes the car door as she is getting inside, and Queenie can almost hear her dead half sister laugh. The same half sister who insisted at every opportunity that Queenie wasn't a true Temple but a watered-down version, and who treated Queenie with scorn for thirty-five years.

It's not funny, Iris, Queenie tells the wind, wondering if she will ever escape the woman who haunts her memories at every opportunity. Iris was larger than life while alive and is perhaps even bigger in death in the form of a hurricane.

CHAPTER EIGHTEEN

Old Sally

You best be waking up now, little girl, her grandmother says. *Things need to be done to get ready for what's coming.*

Like what, Granny? Sally asks, half-asleep.

You got to build the courage fires to keep everybody safe.

Courage fires? Sally asks. She loves her grandmother more than anyone, but this doesn't make sense.

The water going to get high, over your head. You remember how to swim, don't you, little girl?

Yes, Granny, Sally says.

Don't forget now. Sally's grandmother looks at her with so much love, tears spring to her eyes.

I won't, Sally says.

Promise me, girl.

I promise.

. . .

OLD SALLY STARTLES AWAKE, putting her hand on her chest to calm her racing heart.

"Granny?" she says aloud, wishing the spirit to return. Old Sally's grandmother died ages ago, yet in the dream she was as alive as anything and passing down her wisdom as she was prone to do. Things like the past, present, and future travel together, like three sisters who refuse to be separated. She also told Sally that everything alive grows on top of something that was before. A live oak can grow right on top of another fallen tree and be nourished by it.

But what does any of that have to do with courage fires? she asks herself.

Gullah people have an intimate relationship with nature and spirits. Spirits are benevolent ancestors who are not forgotten. Unlike the Temple ghosts who shocked and scared people, her ancestors try to help. They pass on wisdom to those who will listen.

It isn't always that way. Spirits have different personalities. Some want to do good, and some don't. Whenever her grandmother shows up, Sally knows she wants to help.

Old Sally thinks again of the dream. She's never heard of such a thing as courage fires. And why would her grandmother ask if she remembers how to swim? A tingle travels the length of her spine. Her old bones know something she doesn't.

Old Sally doesn't need a weather forecaster in Savannah to tell her that a storm is coming. She has been studying these things since she was a little girl. She can smell a storm on the wind and feel it in her body. If that isn't enough, the birds act differently. They start preparing long before anybody else. But that doesn't mean it will be a hurricane. They do the same thing before a significant rain.

Old Sally gets out of bed and shuffles toward the kitchen,

surprised by how late it is. She usually gets up by sunrise, and here it is almost noon. The house is oddly quiet. Tia enters the hallway, Violet's youngest.

Such a pretty girl, she thinks, *a lot like Violet was when she was this age.*

"Mom is at the tea shop. Can I make your breakfast?"

"That be awful nice," Old Sally says, thinking again of the dream. "You girls know how to swim, don't you?"

"Sure," Tia says. "Daddy taught us when we were young. Why?"

"No reason," she says, although there are plenty of reasons.

In the kitchen, Tia makes Old Sally a bowl of her usual oatmeal, adding a little butter and brown sugar on top. Old Sally could fix it herself, but it seems necessary to let people help her these days. Not only for her benefit, but for theirs, too. After Old Sally is gone, they will know they were helpful to her, and that will comfort them in their loss.

Leisha comes in and gives Old Sally a hug. Violet's two girls are as different as the sun and the moon. One is shy, the other is outgoing. Tia is tall and athletic like her father, Jack. Leisha is more petite like Violet and into making good grades at school. But both are strong in integrity like their parents. Soon they will go off on their own. They are at the beginning of becoming who they are, while Old Sally is at the end.

"Where's your daddy?" Old Sally asks Leisha.

"He and Max are returning the rental chairs," Tia says.

All those wedding preparations now be reversed, Old Sally thinks. Life is a constant building up and breaking down. Ebb and flow. Rise and fall.

Tia and Leisha stand in the kitchen like Old Sally used to stand and wait on the Temple family, meeting their every need.

Old Sally eats her oatmeal, thinking how strange it is to be catered to.

"When I was your age, I was living on this island with my mother and grandmother just like you are," Old Sally says.

Tia sits next to Old Sally as if knowing a story is coming. Leisha pours herself and Old Sally each a small glass of orange juice before sitting, too. Old Sally thanks her.

"Back then, cars hadn't been invented yet, and no one on the island had a telephone," she begins. "My grandmother worked for the Temple family and made seven cents an hour. It felt like a step up to be paid at all. Before that, my family had been Temple slaves."

The girls' attention doesn't waver. Old Sally thinks again of the dream. Courage fires. They will need to call on all their strength soon. The last foretelling dream Old Sally had was before Edward started the fire at the Temple mansion. Old Sally dreamed that Queenie was in danger. Now, this new dream is pointing to something, too.

"Anybody home?" Queenie calls from the front door as Spud carries in the bags. They join them in the kitchen.

"What happened to the honeymoon?" Tia asks.

"We thought we should be here to help out with that hurricane coming," Spud says.

"A hurricane is coming?" Leisha asks, her wide eyes begging it to be so.

"Well, not officially," Spud says.

"You okay, Mama?" Queenie asks Old Sally. "You look like you've seen a ghost."

"A dream has me riled up," Old Sally says, relieved that Queenie and Spud are here. If something big is going to happen, she wants to have all her family around her.

"Where are Max and Jack?" Spud asks. "I thought they'd be boarding up windows by now."

"They're returning the rental chairs in Max's pickup," Leisha answers.

"I thought you said it isn't officially a storm," Queenie says.

"It isn't," Spud says. "There is absolutely no reason to think we may get a hurricane."

According to Queenie, Spud is a person who likes to be helpful. Sometimes too helpful, as far as Queenie is concerned. Last September Queenie had to talk him out of going to ground zero in New York City to help with the recovery effort. Perhaps he would have been more in the way than helpful, but it was an impulse Old Sally admired.

"Mind if I change clothes in your bedroom?" Spud asks Queenie.

"You can change clothes in my bedroom anytime, handsome," Queenie says, and adds a wink.

"Gross," Tia says, which makes everyone laugh.

"Just wait," Queenie says. "Someday, you'll find yourself a handsome hunk of man like this one, and you'll say things you never dreamed of saying, too."

"Doubtful," Leisha says, kidding her sister.

Despite the playful banter among the people she finds dear, Old Sally's concerns deepen. An ill wind is blowing in. She is sure of it. Or near certain. But what do courage fires have to do with anything? She hates a riddle she can't figure out.

While the others talk, Old Sally is deep in thought. Both Queenie and Spud can swim, she's seen them out in the ocean. Rose can, too. In fact, Old Sally taught her one summer when she was five or six. She taught Violet, as well, and she has seen Jack swim with the girls. But Max? She will ask him the next time they have a moment alone. Although she isn't sure why she is so concerned about swimming.

High water. That's what Old Sally's grandmother said in the dream. But maybe that will only happen if Old Sally doesn't heed her warning.

What are you trying to tell me? she says to her grandmother.

Her grandmother doesn't answer, but Old Sally imagines she will find out soon enough.

CHAPTER NINETEEN

Rose

Rose drives over the Talmadge Memorial Bridge into Savannah, the key from Old Sally's table sitting on the passenger seat. A key Regina gave her from the overlooked package Iris sent her son, Edward. At the time it seemed odd that Regina would give it to Rose. Perhaps she hadn't intended to, or maybe she just wanted to get rid of it. Rose had not planned to go to town today, but with Heather showing up and after the strange dream Rose had last night, it felt important.

Living with Old Sally has her paying attention to her dreams. Old Sally is convinced it is how their ancestors communicate. Rose isn't so sure she wants to hear from her ancestors, but at the same time, if it prevents her from doing something unwise, she is all for it.

In her dream, Edward was searching for the second Temple Book of Secrets and wanted to find it before Rose. She has a feeling something inside that second book will change everything.

As if things haven't changed enough, Rose thinks.

Maybe Heather is after the second Book of Secrets, too. She seems to be after something. Rose still can't believe there are two ledgers. Until her return to Savannah, she had forgotten all about the Temple's lifelong obsession with collecting secrets. Secrets that helped leverage the family's power in Savannah. This is not a game Rose has ever played, but she wants to make sure the books don't create further damage. She still has no idea where the first Book of Secrets ended up after Edward shocked Savannah with it around the time her mother died. He released a secret a day in the Savannah newspaper for weeks. An act of revenge to get back at their racist mother. At least that's what Regina said the day she and Rose met for the first time.

When the weather report comes on the radio, Rose turns it up. The storm has taken a turn over the Atlantic and is now heading toward the southeastern coast. After living in Wyoming all those years, severe weather has become routine. Blizzards happened every winter, with tornados in the spring and summer. But she has never experienced a hurricane before. Not even in her first twenty years of life living here in Savannah.

At the bank entrance, Red Mason waits for Rose. His hair has never been red; the nickname is short for Redmond. Red's hair has turned gray, and he wears a pair of gray slacks with a light blue shirt and loafers without socks.

"I didn't know you were back in town," he says to Rose, flashing the same smile he gave her from the varsity basketball court as she sat in the stands back when they went to school together.

"My husband and I moved back to Savannah after Mother died," she says, unsure why she feels the need to tell him she is married, except that the high school crush he had on her was intense.

"I heard you married a cowboy," he says.

"I did, indeed." Her face momentarily warms. She never knows these days if she is embarrassed or having a hormonal surge. She changes the subject. "Do you think that hurricane will amount to anything?"

"Iris?" He smiles again, as if the irony isn't lost on him, either. "Much ado about nothing," he says, from the high school play they were both in.

Rose pauses, wishing she had thought to bring Max along. "Thanks again for meeting me."

"No problem," he says, glancing at his loafers as though they could use a polish.

Rose's mother would like that the Temple name can still get a banker to come into work on a Sunday. It is unusual for Rose to take advantage of that fact. But something about it feels urgent.

"You mentioned finding a key to a safe-deposit box of your mother's?" Red asks.

Rose hands him the old key, and his eyes widen.

"That's from the original bank, the oldest section," he says. "I didn't think there were any of those left anymore."

Red's expression changes to one Rose can't quite interpret. Does he not want her poking around? She chides herself for imagining things, the chiding something her mother did quite often.

After unlocking the front door, Red leads the way up the stairs and then down a hallway. His loafers squeak on the marble floors, sounding almost comical. They enter a section of the building Rose never knew existed. The sign on the door reads ARCHIVES.

"What you're looking for will be back here," he says, opening the door.

They walk into a musty room filled with old wood filing cabinets. Even with windows lining one wall, the place is dark. Red flips on a light switch and fluorescents hum and flicker until they bathe the room with unnatural light.

The farther back they go, the older the furniture gets.

"It's like we're walking through history," Rose says, more to herself than to him.

"Yeah, I guess we are."

At the end of the room is a large walk-in safe that takes up an entire wall. Red takes a small index card from his shirt pocket and turns the silver dial to the correct numbers like in every old movie she's ever watched with a bank vault scene. She looks around to make sure they aren't in the middle of a film set.

"You have the number with you?" Rose asks.

Red pauses, like he didn't think she'd notice.

"I had it just in case." He beams his charm at her again, but this time it isn't the least bit charming.

"You acted surprised when I showed you the key," Rose says, thinking something doesn't add up.

Red swings the door open and ignores her comment. A whiff of old papers and history rush toward them, suddenly disturbed. Rose steps into the vault and feels instantly claustrophobic. She steadies herself against the cold metal of the safe, taking deep breaths of the musty air, the smell something akin to old attics.

Red asks her for the key that Rose had forgotten she was holding. He goes over to an iron box that looks like it could be pre–Civil War. A safe within a safe, the size of a small coffee table. He opens it with the key.

"A couple of years ago, I let Edward in here," he says, as if feeling a need to confess.

"Edward was here?" Her throat tightens. "What was he looking for?" she asks.

"No idea," Red says. "But he was acting strange that day."

"What do you mean by strange?" Rose asks.

"Like secretive, but full of himself at the same time," he says. "Come to think of it, he was almost gleeful, and shortly afterward those secrets started showing up in the paper."

Rose imagines Edward's delight was from knowing he was finally getting back at their mother. But Rose admits she didn't see this need for revenge coming. She always thought Edward adored their mother.

"Edward came in again a week before the fire," Red begins again. "He stood right where you're standing now. That was horrible about the fire," Red adds, sounding genuine.

Rose's little finger tingles, remembering its sacrifice in the war with her brother. When he died, her grief was more about what could have been instead of what was.

"Do you know what Edward was looking for?" Rose asks.

"The same thing you are, I imagine." He lifts an eyebrow.

"But I don't know what I'm looking for," Rose says.

"You don't?" Red's voice registers mild surprise.

Rose wonders what Red knows that she doesn't. Do bankers have access to every vault and safe-deposit box and what's inside? Or maybe her mother was right about Rose imagining things.

"This is where I disappear," Red announces. "You can stay up here as long as you like. I'll be in my office on the first floor." He hands her back the key that she had already forgotten about.

Red exits the long room, his squeaky footsteps growing

softer in the distance as Rose's sneaking suspicions grow. She reminds herself she is not a reliable witness as far as sneakiness is concerned. In the past, Rose imagined complicated plots and ulterior motives where nothing was confirmed.

Alone now, Rose pulls a wooden office chair into the vault and sits in front of the open safe-deposit box, at eye level. Timid, she reaches inside the box, almost expecting to fall headfirst into the past.

Inside the box is a metal drawer at the top, deep enough to hold an old fountain pen and a bottle of petrified ink. A blotter like the one that sat on her father's desk when Rose was a girl sits next to it. Below is a stack of papers and different ledgers. She is surprised cobwebs aren't strung between the pages. Except that Edward was here before her.

One after another, Rose carefully lifts out the papers crisp with age. Ledgers. Deeds of different properties dated before the Civil War, along with stacks of receipts for various goods: furniture, weapons, the chandelier that used to hang in the Temple mansion. Then an entire folder holding receipts for large deposits to different people—the faded ink a light gray—for services unknown. Payoffs?

Rose regrets she hadn't stopped at Violet's shop to order a large coffee to go. She needs caffeine if she's going to sift through the Temple past. An abundant and dark past, if she imagines correctly.

Minutes later she comes across an old ledger that looks familiar. Wasn't this in her father's office when she was a girl? The Book of Secrets was leather like this one. Could the second book be the same? And how did Edward even know there was a safe here full of Temple papers? Did their mother tell him about it? Or perhaps their father? Rose can't remember a time when so many unanswered questions rushed at her.

When she opens the ledger, she realizes it is actually the Book of Secrets that Edward used when he leaked the confidences to the Savannah newspaper before their mother died. This information was never shared with Rose, but maybe as the male heir, her brother had access. It seems the quest for secrets and leverage was generational and never-ending until now.

Rose is relieved that Regina doesn't have the book. At least in this old safe, it can't do any more harm to reputations. Power is a fascinating thing, and if you combine power with secrets, it can be both dangerous and advantageous for whoever has access to the secrets.

Rose puts the ledger back where it was for safekeeping. She will give some thought to what she wants to do with it now. A bonfire at the beach is still a possibility.

Rose goes through more papers, digging through the Temple past. Mostly records of everything acquired and ample evidence of status. It is hot in the safe, the air conditioning unable to reach inside. She tires quickly, not even knowing what she is looking for. Then she stops, deciding on a different tactic. She pauses and closes her eyes, asking her ancestors what they want her to find. This is something Old Sally or Violet might do.

Rose waits, feeling silly at first and then recommitting to the question. When she opens her eyes, she is drawn to something about halfway down in the right corner of the large safe-deposit box. It is another thick ledger, similar to the Book of Secrets, except the pages are more yellowed, and the cover is faded. She opens it to find that the pages are indeed more brittle, the ink even more faded. The dates are from the early

1800s. Pages have fallen out and been stuck back in. If this is the precursor to the Book of Secrets Rose saw as a girl, she feels she should be wearing gloves. It is like a museum piece. It seems to be a diary containing dates and meetings. Some of the things are written in her great-great-grandfather Temple's hard-to-read scrawl. Page after page gives a list of names and dates of transgressions. It's not the second Book of Secrets. It is the original one. Confirming that the secrets Edward leaked to the press were much newer.

After thumbing through several more pages, Rose comes across a list of names, knowing immediately what it is. A shudder passes through her that feels as old as the names. Does she want to see the evil deeds of her ancestors? She thinks of Old Sally and Queenie and Violet—people who are dearer to her than any family member other than Katie and Max—who are the descendants of the people listed in this ledger. Page after page.

Most of the names are written in the same hand, but with varying dates and shades of ink. A first name only. Age. Children. Where they were assigned to work. Near the middle of the third page, Rose recognizes the name Sadie, Old Sally's grandmother, whom Rose has heard stories about her entire life. A child is listed. A boy named Adam. Sent to the Temple plantation near Charleston at ten years of age.

Rose pauses and closes her eyes. "Forgive us," she whispers.

Even if the people are no longer living, an apology is inadequate. She closes the book to erase the truth written in the ledger. A boy was taken away from his mother at age ten? Old Sally's grandmother must have been heartbroken. And what must it have been like for the boy?

Rose covers her mouth, feeling queasy, and leaves the vault to find a restroom. Her footsteps echo on the marble floors.

How does someone several generations later make up for the sins of her family's past? she wonders.

In the restroom, Rose splashes cold water on her face and dries it with paper towels. The bank is as quiet as the Temple crypt in Bonaventure Cemetery. She could probably spend weeks in the bank vault exploring the past. But for now, she needs to figure out what Edward was searching for. She guesses that it is somehow linked to Heather being here.

After returning to the vault, she takes another deep breath of history and allows herself ten more minutes to look through the ledger to see what she can find. It isn't fair to keep Red here much longer.

Rose wonders what else her ancestors want her to see.

Near the middle of the book, she finds more secrets. She recognizes the name Rivers. Bo Rivers was her mother's attorney. But this is a Harrison Rivers who was living in 1834 and had an unlawful child named CeCe, who was sent to Vicksburg to live with a maiden aunt. She imagines how scandalous it would have been and thinks of Edward's daughter. A present-day scandal hardly worth noting.

Another name comes to her attention: Mason. She imagines this is one of Red's ancestors. She leans forward to read the faded ink. Several dates follow the name along with a series of numbers, all to do with embezzling from the bank. This bank. The oldest bank in Savannah.

"You about done?" Red says, suddenly behind her.

Rose jumps. "You scared me!"

His apology sounds sincere, but she wonders why she didn't hear him walk up. Perhaps he knows what secrets concerning his family may be in there. Or perhaps it is simply a coincidence.

"I promised my wife I'd spend time with her and the kids today," Red says.

"Of course," Rose says, momentarily flustered. "Sorry, Red. I lost track of time. Can I take this?" She holds up the faded ledger with the yellowed pages stuck in here and there.

"Everything in there is yours," he says, his eyes on the papers, not her. "You can take anything you want."

She closes the fragile ledger and then carefully puts it in her purse, grateful that she is carrying one of her bigger bags today.

"Find anything interesting?" Something about the way he asks makes her question his intention.

"Just a bunch of old papers."

Rose realizes how inconsistent this is to her calling him on a Sunday morning with a special request to get into the bank.

"Your family is one of the reasons this bank has survived," he says, as if no apology is needed.

For years Rose didn't question how her mother could get anything she wanted from just about anybody. She wouldn't have thought twice about keeping a banker from his family for an entire Sunday for weeks or months on end. Her mother's needs trumped anyone else's.

They walk down the marble stairs, Red holding her arm. Manners are essential in Savannah. Important all over the South. Southern men have impeccable manners, even while embezzling, siring illicit children, or laundering money.

Instead of going home, Rose drives to Violet's Tea Shop. After she parks, she pulls the faded ledger from her purse. Rose has no idea why she is bringing it home. Or why she is sitting here in the car wanting to hold it. But something about this record of the past feels significant, and she is determined to find out why.

CHAPTER TWENTY

Violet

When the bells jingle to announce the next customer, Violet looks up to see Rose enter the tea shop.

"What are you doing here?" she says when Rose reaches the counter.

"I need coffee," says Rose, who seldom looks this weary in the afternoon.

Violet reaches for the pot, but Rose insists on fixing it herself and is even more adamant than usual. Rose has helped Violet out enough to know where everything is and comes behind the counter for a coffee cup.

"How did it go at the bank?" Violet asks.

"You don't want to know." Rose doctors her coffee with cream and two sugars, cleaning the counter after she finishes.

"You seem upset," Violet says. She was surprised that morning to hear Rose's plan to visit the bank on a Sunday and when a storm was coming, but she trusts her friend had a good reason.

"I'll fill you in later when we have some privacy," Rose says.

Violet agrees and then nods in Heather's direction. Rose looks and then quickly turns away. They stand behind a display of pastries and cookies, keeping their voices low.

"What is she doing here?" Rose whispers. "And who is that guy with her?"

"He came in a few minutes ago. I guess he's a friend." Violet looks out into the tearoom at the two people, who are deep in conversation.

"Isn't he one of those Goth people?" Rose asks.

"Complete with trench coat," Violet says.

"Doesn't he know it's ninety degrees outside?"

"I don't think he cares," Violet says. "They're a very odd-looking couple, aren't they?"

Rose agrees. "But in a weird way, they look kind of related."

"I think that, too," Violet says. "It's like they wear the same mascara and eyeliner."

Rose laughs. "I'm serious."

Violet apologizes. "Maybe they're in on something together," she says.

"You sound like me," Rose says. "I hate thinking the worst of people."

"You're not thinking the worst, you're cautious," Violet says. "It's okay to be cautious." Violet narrows her eyes while looking in their direction, a model of cautiousness.

The bells on the door jingle again, and Violet leaves Rose still blowing on her coffee. While Violet fixes an order, Rose watches the corner table near the window.

"I think I'll confront them," Rose says after Violet finishes the order. A sentence Violet doesn't think she has ever heard Rose say.

Before Violet has time to stop her, Rose is already

approaching the table. From a distance, Violet tries to decipher what they are saying. Regarding their body language, it is the young man with the black lipstick who appears to be the most ill at ease. Rose seems to be holding her own. Every now and again her childhood friend surprises her. She didn't expect Rose to be this bold.

The door jingles again and Tia and Leisha enter, pulling Violet's attention away from Rose. Jack is behind them. When Violet worked for Miss Temple, her family never stopped by. Not once. But now, since Violet owns the tea shop, they visit often.

"Mom, the storm is coming straight for us!" Tia's excitement is tangible.

Jack gives Violet a quick kiss.

"Is it true?" she asks, her shoulder offering a twinge for the first time in months.

Jack nods. "We're under a hurricane watch."

From Violet's understanding, a hurricane watch means that the storm is still only a possibility. It is a hurricane warning they fear, saying the wind is imminent.

Leisha eyes the pastry counter. This adventure might require a lemon poppy seed muffin.

"When is the storm supposed to be here?" Violet refuses to call it Iris. It is too strange.

"Sometime in the early morning," Jack says.

Mondays are her slowest days, so at least the storm may not affect her business too much.

"Have you been busy?" Jack asks.

"Not really," she says. "I guess the possible hurricane is keeping people away. Even the threat of a tropical storm has people standing in line at the Piggly Wiggly, their carts full of canned food, bread, and milk."

"You're right, it's a zoo. We picked up bottled water just in case," Jack says. "Max has plywood in the truck to board up your windows. He's right outside."

Violet glances at the large window, the most beautiful and fragile part of the shop. The door jingles again and Max comes in, waving to her and Jack.

"Isn't it a little early to board up windows?" Violet asks. "It's only a hurricane watch. Still a long shot."

"Better safe than sorry," Jack says. "Max is dropping off the plywood. We'll be back right before closing, and if it looks like it's not going to happen, we won't do anything."

"I still think you're overreacting," Violet says.

Everyone gathers at the counter—the girls and Max and Jack—and then Rose returns, looking flushed. "What did they say?" Violet asks.

Rose greets the others before pulling Violet into the back room, keeping her voice lowered like they did when they shared secrets as girls.

"Evidently he's a friend that goes to Savannah Art and Design," Rose says. "Heather said they grew up together."

"Okay, so nothing to worry about, right?" Violet asks.

"Something still feels fishy to me," Rose says.

"What are you two doing back here?" Jack asks.

"Just talking," Violet says. She will fill him in later about the Heather saga.

"We need to catch the latest weather report," Jack says.

"Did I miss something?" Rose asks.

"Looks like we may get that hurricane after all," Violet says.

"Worse-case scenario, downtown Savannah could get six to eight feet of water," Jack says. "Dolphin Island even more."

A sharp pain shoots through Violet's shoulder, putting to

rest the concern she had about losing her sensitivity. Her thoughts immediately turn to preparations for the storm.

CHAPTER TWENTY-ONE

Queenie

Queenie stacks several wedding gifts in the top of her closet to deal with later, along with the thank-you notes.

"You've got nerve messing with my honeymoon," Queenie says to her deceased half sister. She looks up at the closet light to see if it flickers with Iris's answer.

When still alive, Iris Temple was known for her revenge tactics, and for all Queenie knows she has ordered this hurricane from the grave. According to Spud, they are under a hurricane watch. It is still far away, a Category 3 storm and growing. Knowing Iris, she will settle for nothing less than top tier, a Category 5.

When Queenie lived in the Temple mansion there were daily hauntings by various dead Temples, Iris being the last of the Temple spirit legacy. Cold air rushed down hallways or rattled dishes and glasses when no one was in the kitchen. Plants tipped over for no reason. Ancient perfumes and scents lingered in bedrooms. As far as she knows, however, all the Temple spirits were destroyed along with the mansion, along with Edward, who died in the fire.

Of course, Queenie knows that a hurricane named Iris and the woman who made her life miserable for over three decades are not the same. Or are they? Unexplained mysteries happen all the time. Like the fact that she loathed Iris, yet still misses her. Queenie is a perfect example of what occurs when you combine Gullah folk magic and an old Savannah family. All her life she has struggled to find her place in the world—she, herself, is a mystery. Since Iris died and Queenie is no longer her personal assistant, she hasn't known what to do with herself. Until recently, her entire life revolved around Iris's needs, not her own.

Spud told her they must take this storm seriously, and Queenie is doing just that. She checks on Old Sally, who is busy making a smelly concoction on the stove. It is not unusual to smell strange substances brewing. Things that don't, in Queenie's opinion, belong in a cooking pot. Gnarled roots, parts of frogs and chicken bones, human hair and sometimes fingernails. Along with the ever-present graveyard dirt kept in an old metal canister at the top of the kitchen cabinet over the sink. A canister Queenie remembers from when she was a girl, the FLOUR label already faded with age.

Long ago Queenie stopped asking what these ingredients were for. Lately, Violet has been brewing things with Old Sally, writing complicated recipes down in her notebook while standing alongside the stove, though not today.

Queenie has never been interested in spells. It never made sense to her how the bark of one tree and the mud from a certain Georgia swamp could heal or prevent something bad from happening. It also never made sense to her that putting a favorite cereal bowl at someone's gravesite will keep the spirit happy forever. Do people eat Cocoa Puffs in the Afterlife? She hopes not. She hopes there are better options. Like croissants from a heavenly bakery, covered with real butter and home-made raspberry jam. Her mouth waters.

"What are you cooking up?" Queenie asks Old Sally, not really wanting to know, but she is suddenly hungry.

"A protection spell." Old Sally seems more thoughtful than usual. She gets this way when something is going on *between worlds*, as she calls it. Evidently, there are two worlds instead of one. The visible one that Queenie is standing in here in the kitchen and the invisible one her ancestors live in, and where everyone who dies crosses over to.

Queenie has never understood the Gullah ways. The only time in her life she took an interest in folk magic was when she asked her mama to make her a love potion for a boy she had a crush on in the fourth grade. Her request did not go over well. Gullah magic was not to be used to manipulate matters of the heart, she was told, so Queenie never asked her to do it again.

She knows that if she had somehow managed to marry before now, it would not have been the *right* man for her. Her eyes tear up, and it's not from what is cooking on the stove. She cannot believe how much she loves Spud Grainger.

Well, not his bow ties, she tells herself. *I could spend the rest of my life without those.* But he doesn't wear them much anymore since he has retired.

Queenie never dreamed someone would treat her so well. Bringing her socks to put on in bed if her feet are cold. Putting a Hershey's Kiss on her pillow every night, even though she has recently brushed her teeth. Giving her a neck rub if she has the least bit of a pain. Iris was an idiot to end her affair with Spud Grainger all those many years ago.

With Old Sally stirring smelly stuff on the stove, Queenie wonders if her mama has ever loved someone as much as she loves Spud. Queenie's father was Edward Temple, and Old Sally's only husband had already died before Queenie was born. Old Sally had Queenie when she was in her early forties, having long before planned to not have any more children. But life, it seems, rarely goes as planned.

"Mama, who was the love of your life?" Queenie asks. She doesn't usually speak of intimate things with her mama like some daughters do, but she is genuinely curious. She takes a seat to wait for the answer.

"A man named Everett Moses," Old Sally says, without hesitation. "But everybody called him Fiddle. He was said to be the best fiddle player east of the Mississippi."

"Everett Moses?" Queenie pauses. She has never heard that name before. "Why haven't you ever told me about him?"

"It was a long, long time ago." Old Sally gives the pot another stir.

"Well, how did you meet him? What was he like?"

Old Sally stops stirring and looks up, surprised by Queenie's interest. But then she returns to it, this time like she is stirring her memories.

"Everett was from Charleston," Old Sally begins. "We met at a revival my family took me to over at Edisto."

"I've never heard this story," Queenie says.

"I never told anybody before." Old Sally chuckles when she sees Queenie's face. "Nice to know I can still surprise you," she says.

"I'll stir. You talk." Queenie takes the spoon and motions for her mama to sit in one of the chairs. "I need to hear what happened between you and Fiddle."

The smell coming from the pot makes Queenie want to gag.

But it is the price she is willing to pay to hear her mama's story. This concoction smells strong enough to ward off anything. Iris the hurricane *and* Iris the ghost.

"Fiddle be eighteen, with me two years younger," Old Sally begins. "He was playing at a three-night revival. A gorgeous man if ever you saw one. Black as a moonless night, with beautiful eyes and straight white teeth. He could smile at you and weaken your knees."

Queenie stops stirring. Her mama looks suddenly younger. Her eyes sparkling with the memory.

"The first night, he watched me," Old Sally continues. "On the second night, we talked before and after the service. By the third night, Fiddle and I snuck away from the tent and talked the night away under a live oak with a full moon watching over us. My family thought I was spending the night with a girlfriend," she continues, "but I was spending the night with Fiddle under the stars. Then the next week he drove over from Charleston and tried to talk me into eloping with him. But I didn't want to hurt my mama by moving so far away."

"Charleston was too far away?" Queenie asks, thinking it is a two-hour drive if that.

"It seemed far away back then," she says.

Old Sally looks out the window, as though looking into her past. The sparkle in her eyes begins to fade.

"That night, I snuck out and met him at the lighthouse. Most wonderful night of my life." Old Sally lowers her head, as well as her voice. "On the way back to Charleston the next morning, he died in a car accident. A bus hit his car straight on."

Queenie gasps mid-stir. "Oh, Mama, I'm so sorry." She walks over and hugs her, being careful not to embrace her too tightly. She seems so fragile these days. "I can't imagine losing

Spud so soon after we found each other. I'm not sure I would ever get over it."

"I'm not sure I ever did."

Old Sally pauses for what feels like a long time.

"A baby girl came out of that night at the lighthouse," she begins again, her voice even softer. "A baby girl who died at six days old. Broke my heart into tiny pieces."

Queenie's eyes fill with tears. She can't imagine losing Violet, either, even if she didn't officially claim her for over four decades.

"Is that why you walk to that lighthouse all the time?"

Old Sally nods. "Life be full of heartache, daughter," she continues, emotion choking the words. "That's why when love comes you got to celebrate it as big and loud as you can."

Queenie gets them both tissues.

"I wish you had told me sooner," Queenie says.

"Sometimes we lock hurtful things away, just so we can carry on," Old Sally says.

Queenie thinks of the secret she kept for so many years. Maybe she locked that away so she could carry on, too.

"What was the little girl's name who died at six days old?" Queenie asks.

"Annabelle," Old Sally says. "She looked like Fiddle, too. Dark and sweet as sunlight."

"Annabelle," Queenie repeats. She realizes now that she's had two half sisters: one black and one white.

"He came to me in a dream the other night," Old Sally says.

"Fiddle did?"

Old Sally nods. "At first I only heard him play. But then I saw him, and he had so much love in his eyes I woke up crying."

"You missed him so much," Queenie says.

"No. I be crying because I get to see Fiddle soon."

Queenie puts a hand to her heart. For years now, her mama has been ready to go. But it doesn't mean a daughter wants it to happen. Violet will be the one to help Old Sally transition to the next world since Queenie knows so little about the Gullah tradition. But she does see the importance of death rituals on the Gullah side of her family.

"I need to lay down for a minute," Old Sally says.

Queenie asks her if she's okay, knowing that nothing can make losing a child okay, no matter how long ago it was.

"I be fine," she says, though she doesn't look fine. Queenie turns off the stove and follows her into the bedroom. She helps her take off her sandals and lie on the bed.

"It's been a big weekend," Old Sally says. "More excitement than I've had in a long time. I just need a quick nap, and I'll be fine."

Queenie closes Old Sally's door and returns to the living room. She goes over to the collection of objects near her mama's chair and finds a small black-and-white photograph, worn with age, of a dark man playing a fiddle. Next to it sits a small square of pink fabric with an *A* embroidered on it. Almost threadbare, it is as if someone held this piece of cloth every day for over eighty years. How many times has Queenie passed this table and never taken in how each object is a story in her mama's life? Not a shallow connection. Not a collection of ghosts. But an assortment of living memories of the people she continues to love.

CHAPTER TWENTY-TWO

Old Sally

S *ally, honey, wake up.*
Her grandmother Sadie bustles around the room, a stooped-over Gullah woman.

What is it, Granny? What are you doing? Sally asks.

It be time to light the courage fires, girl. The driftwood be already piled high on the beach. Your grandpa piled it up this morning.

But I don't have anything to light it with, Sally says.

Yes, you do. You be the only one who has the light. If you don't light it now, everyone will be lost.

As a girl, her grandmother expected Sally to know things that she had no way of knowing.

What time the tide be, girl? she would ask. *If you don't know, we all be sunk.*

Sally's mother was tired before her time. Her grandmother was a different story. She had the energy of three people and expected Sally did, too.

Old Sally floats in and out of the dream like she is time

traveling. One minute she is young Sally searching for matches, the next she is Old Sally watching everything unfold.

Her grandmother looks under the bed and all around the room, repeating that she must find the light, or everyone will be lost. She repeats it until Sally covers her ears and can't hear it anymore. She wants to go back to sleep. The island school doesn't start for another three hours. The sun isn't even up yet.

Then her grandmother grabs her by the shoulders and lifts her from the bed.

This be serious, girl. Go to the lighthouse. The water's coming. Get up those stairs!

Old Sally wakes with a start, gasping for air as if coming up from a giant wave. Fully awake, she sits up, her heartbeat echoing in her ears.

CHAPTER TWENTY-THREE

Rose

Rose decides to stay and help Violet at the tea shop, her time at the bank still on her mind and in her nose. The smell of musty old ledgers has seeped into her clothes. Her purse hangs on a hook in the back room of the tea shop. When she has a chance, she wants to look through it. If this is the original Book of Secrets, she can't imagine anything it contains is pertinent today. But the question remains of why Edward would have gone to the bank to try to find it. And why is Heather in Savannah hanging out in the wings like that crazy storm?

"You seem distracted," Violet says to Rose between customers.

"I'm still thinking about that trip to the bank," Rose says. "I barely scratched the surface. There were receipts, deeds, and accounts from the last two hundred years. Most of it useless, I imagine."

"Might as well check it out just in case," Violet says.

"Might as well," Rose repeats.

"I wonder what my Gullah ancestors would have kept in a bank vault," Violet says. "Recipes, maybe. Spells or different folk magic remedies. Maybe a few special roots." She smiles.

Rose doesn't tell Violet about the lists of dozens of her Gullah ancestors who were slaves owned by Rose's family. If the situation were reversed, she imagines Violet would feel a similar shame. But the situation isn't reversed. A long line of Temples owned people. Lots of people, it seems like. People forced to run not only the mansion but a Charleston plantation as well.

To keep an eye on the storm, Rose suggested last night that Violet bring in a small television from home to sit on top of a filing cabinet in the back. Violet, Jack, Rose, and Max gather in front of the local weather report. It reminds Rose of when they watched the towers go down on 9/11. Like the dust of the buildings that fell that day, a profound sense of helplessness fell over Rose. But this isn't a terrorist attack. It's a hurricane. A hurricane spinning wildly out in the Atlantic Ocean, due to turn further inland any minute, where it will collide with a low-pressure system and determine their fate.

Minutes later Rose's fear is confirmed when the weatherman reports that the hurricane watch has just been upgraded to a hurricane warning. Their fate sealed, they exchange looks revealing their surprise. The hurricane is heading this way.

The news report now includes information on how to prepare for the storm. Stocking up on bottled water is recommended, as well as canned goods and batteries. Jack tells them about driving up to Charleston to help some cousins clean up after Hurricane Hugo hit in 1989.

"I've never witnessed anything so destructive," he says, shaking his head.

The word "evacuation" flashes across the television screen. Rose feels a knot in her stomach. She doesn't want to evacuate her new home. Her life has seen enough upheaval lately. Half of the people she talks to are skeptical the storm will even hit. People keep saying how many storm paths predicted for Savannah don't materialize.

Meanwhile, possible evacuation routes are shown on the screen.

"I think you should close early," Jack says to Violet.

"I do, too," Rose says.

Heather walks into the back of the shop and startles Rose, who is standing closest to the door.

"I didn't hear you walk up," Rose says.

"I'm wondering if I should go back to Atlanta," she says to Rose.

"That's up to you," Rose says. Her distrust of Heather nags at her again. When Regina first talked about Heather on the telephone, she practically called her a con artist, and she implied birth certificates could be forged.

"Do you mind if I come back after this storm has blown over?" Heather asks her. She looks back at her friend standing at the door.

Rose says she doesn't mind, which isn't the truth. The truth is she wishes Heather had never shown up in the first place. She would prefer to not deal with this hurricane, either. Or the mystery of whatever is in that old bank vault. Rose wants a peaceful life. One without drama. But at this moment, that seems an impossible request.

CHAPTER TWENTY-FOUR

Violet

Whole Violet makes out Sunday's bank deposit, Max and Jack nail plywood over the large tea shop front windows to protect them from breaking during heavy winds. They also get everything off the floor, since the street Violet's shop is on floods during a hard rain. Before they leave they stack sandbags in front of the door to keep high water from coming in.

When Violet locks the door from the outside for the day, she offers a silent prayer that her tea shop is here when she returns. She wishes now she had brought some of Old Sally's graveyard dirt from home to spread around the shop to protect it. Violet is not someone who enjoys starting over. Who does? But she will if she must.

On the drive home, Jack and the girls are in their other car somewhere in front of her. Weatherwise, it has been a perfect day in Savannah, though hot, and the thought of a hurricane bearing down on them is hard to imagine. The sunset in her rearview mirror is a masterpiece of yellow and orange. Despite the hurricane warning, forecasters say there are still other paths the storm could take. Hitting their island is only one of them. She finds comfort in the possibility that the hurricane may veer north at the last minute and amount to nothing.

Home again, Violet sees that the house is lit up as if they are hosting another wedding party. A peculiar odor greets her on the front porch. A root mixture has been rubbed along the door and window frames of the house. Old Sally's doing, no doubt, for further protection against the storm.

Violet finds everyone in the kitchen except for Old Sally. An animated discussion is going on about the storm. Jack puts an arm around Violet when she steps close. Tia and Leisha have made iced tea for everyone, placing lemon slices on the rims of the glasses like Violet did for Miss Temple's fancy dinners. She hasn't missed serving the silver-headed patriarchs and their wives who keep old Savannah alive. Although they are welcome to visit her tea shop at any time, not one of them has passed through its doors. She offers a wry smile.

Angela fixes Katie a snack. Green grapes and green olives have been her latest craving. When Violet was pregnant with Tia, she ate her weight in apple slices dipped in Peter Pan peanut butter. She looks forward to having a baby around. Good practice for when Tia and Leisha have babies, if they choose to. But before any new life is welcomed, they need to get through this hurricane.

Queenie and Spud enter the kitchen. "We're going back to Hilton Head as soon as this storm passes," Queenie says to Violet, after noting her surprise at seeing them back.

Spud gives Violet a wave, sporting one of the many Hawaiian shirts he has collected since he retired, his idea of leisure wear.

For years Violet thought of herself as an orphan, her mother deceased and a father who had no name. But now she has Queenie and a stepfather in Spud. Violet smiles at this thought despite her tiredness and sits on a stool at the kitchen island. She will check on Old Sally after she rests for a moment.

Weather reports now play on the hour. Violet sighs. She is already tired of this storm, and it hasn't even happened yet. Katie turns up the volume on the television on the kitchen counter, and they watch yet another update. The forecaster has taken off his suit coat and rolled up his sleeves. The storm is skirting past Cuba with 150 mile-per-hour winds, still heading in their direction.

The inevitability of the hurricane reminds Violet of childbirth—that moment during her labor with Leisha when she realized there was no turning back. Nature rules over everything and everyone. Like a newborn, the storm will arrive whether they are ready for it or not.

Violet is curious why her shoulder isn't hurting anymore. She had one sharp but brief pain at the tea shop, and now nothing. At times she has prayed that this sensitivity would go away, but she didn't realize how much she relies on it.

"I need to check on Old Sally," Violet tells Jack.

"Good idea," he says, not taking his eyes from the weather report.

When Violet gets to Old Sally's room, she finds it empty. She checks the bathroom before finding the side door slightly ajar. She goes outside and calls Old Sally's name and then follows the deck around to the front of the house. It is almost dusk, and Old Sally is standing on the beach looking out over the ocean. Violet walks through the dunes to join her, the crests of the waves tipped in the last moments of sunlight.

Violet often finds Old Sally like this these days. Deep in thought. Visiting a silence that takes her full attention.

"Are you okay?" Violet asks her.

Old Sally nods as she studies the waves.

"An ill wind be blowing in," Old Sally tells her.

"I thought so," Violet answers. "How should we prepare for it?"

Old Sally doesn't answer and keeps staring at the waves. "Do you know what courage fires are?" she asks after a long pause.

"No. What are courage fires?"

"I'm not so sure myself," Old Sally says. "But they sound important."

It is not often that Violet sees Old Sally at a loss or confused. But something has her off balance.

Together, they look out over the waves as if the sea holds the answers they seek. The tide is coming in.

"Are you worried about the storm?" Violet asks.

"This one be different somehow."

Old Sally's words make Violet uneasy. She shudders and wraps her arms around herself.

"I may need you later," Old Sally says.

"Of course," Violet answers. "Just tell me what you need."

"My grandmother came to me in a dream yesterday. She told me to build courage fires, but I don't know what that means."

"Well, whatever they are, we'll figure it out." Weary, Violet glances back at the ocean, wishing the waves could carry her tiredness out to sea so she could be more available to Old Sally.

"Thanks for your faith in me," Old Sally says, touching Violet's arm.

It strikes Violet as an odd thing to say. She has never lost faith in Old Sally. She has counted on her to be there every moment of her life, and Violet has never been disappointed. It never occurred to her that faith might be involved.

"Has everyone made it home?" Old Sally asks.

Violet says they have. "I need to go in. You coming?"

"Soon," Old Sally says.

Violet turns and heads back to the house. Two crows pick at a dead crab on the beach. They stagger away when Violet walks by. Life and death hold hands here on the island, where land and ocean meet. To see crows this late in the day is odd. Depending on who you talk to, they can either be a sign of good luck or death coming.

The crows take flight, their wings flapping loudly as they pass on both sides of Violet. Close enough that she can feel the wind from their wings on her face. She walks through the dunes, remembering a story Old Sally told her about a Dr. Crow who lived on one of the barrier islands near here. He was a root doctor like Old Sally. Rumor was that he could take the form of a crow whenever he set a notion to. But these are not human crows as far as she knows. She hopes they are bringing a sign that good luck is coming. Sounds like they could use it with this storm.

An ambitious gust of wind causes the dune grasses to twirl —a whisper, perhaps, of the shouting to come.

CHAPTER TWENTY-FIVE

Queenie

Several of Queenie's housemates gather in the kitchen to view the latest weather report. The weather map on the television shows a giant swirl of tight clouds heading toward the southeastern coast of the United States.

"Heaven help us," Queen says, a frequent phrase of late.

"Looks like that hurricane is building steam," Spud says. He puts an arm around Queenie, resting it on her hip. "Don't worry, we'll be fine, Sugar," he adds.

Queenie gives him a sideways glance. "Mister Grainger, since when do you call me *Sugar*?"

His smile is followed by a quick kiss. "Husbands and wives are supposed to have pet names for each other, aren't they?"

Queenie resists slapping him. This storm has her agitated. Not only has it cut her honeymoon short, but now Iris is sucking up all the wedding excitement. A bride is meant to bask in the glory of her wedding day for weeks. But that once-in-a-lifetime memory is now replaced by weather maps and preparation lists.

"Max and I call each other 'honey,'" Rose says. "We haven't called each other by our real names in years."

"We do 'honey,' too." Katie smiles at Angela.

"What would you like to be called?" Queenie asks Spud. Not *Sugar*, she hopes.

For a moment, he looks perplexed, but then another smile crosses his face. "How about, *You sexy devil, you?*"

She gives Spud a playful nudge in the ribs. "You wish, old man."

Everyone laughs, except for Tia and Leisha, who roll their eyes. Queenie imagines this is more than they want to know about their grandmother and new step-grandfather.

For decades, Queenie's love life was only a periodic fantasy that involved movie actors. But now, in her sixties, all has changed. The first time she and Spud made love she was literally weak in the knees. She had heard the phrase before but never experienced it. Now she doesn't feel weak but emboldened. At times, she even feels forty years younger. However, this storm is aging her fast.

"Lord have mercy," Queenie says after the weather report ends. "Are those weather people deliberately trying to scare us? Every time we watch, the news gets worse."

Amidst the chatter, Queenie reminds herself to ask Rose what happened to Heather, as well as what happened at the bank today. It seems a lot more is going on besides this storm, and Queenie hasn't had a spare minute to catch up.

"We need to get busy," Max says to everyone gathered in the kitchen. "You know what they say: prepare for the worst and hope for the best."

Queenie moans. This is not what she had in mind for enter-
tainment this evening. Max and Jack hand them rolls of
masking tape and instruct them to put a large *X* on each
window that doesn't have storm shutters. Canned goods and
other foods are to be gathered. Water jugs filled and labeled.
Batteries and flashlights collected. Matches and candles put in
dry, waterproof containers.

Queenie gets tired just hearing them talk about all that
needs to be done. She hasn't recovered from the last big event,
and now they are getting ready for another one.

Nor has my honeymoon adequately commenced, she thinks.

With that thought, Queenie gives Spud a wink that appears
to confuse him. Who, after all, gets amorous during hurricane
preparations? It seems her sexual prime has coincided with her
AARP membership and senior discounts.

But it's good to surprise yourself, she decides, *especially as
you age.*

The kinds of surprises she doesn't like are unexpected
weather events. But truth be told, this hurricane could ruin a
lot more than Queenie's honeymoon. Just a little while ago
Jack showed her some photographs of the aftermath of Hurricane Hugo. Oprah even did a show there at the time, but Iris
refused to let Queenie attend. Hugo left houses on Sullivan's
Island and Isle of Palms in shambles or swept them off their
foundations. Some of the homes were washed a block or two
away. It didn't help that the drawbridge to the islands was
blown off its hinges, too, and people couldn't get home for
weeks. A bridge very similar to the one on Dolphin Island.

Hurricanes, like Iris Temple in her day, are never to be
underestimated, in Queenie's opinion. Iris was a blowhard for
sure, and she was also destructive, especially if you got on her
wrong side.

Not that Iris had a right side, she thinks.

Queenie had thought those evil days were over. But it seems her stormy stepsister is making an encore appearance with the clear intent to destroy Queenie's happiness.

CHAPTER TWENTY-SIX

Old Sally

For all the years Old Sally has looked out over this same sea, she has never seen it with this many deep purple hues. Something is churning up from its farthest depths. A similar churning is happening in her gut. Her grandmother was the one whose intuition was the most refined in her family. She predicted the loss of her boy, Adam, who was sent away to the Charleston plantation, and ultimately put a curse on the Temple family for sending him away. She predicted the First World War and the Second. In fact, she predicted her own death right down to the hour.

Old Sally isn't as good at predicting world events, but her gut tells her when something dangerous is close to home. The ill-tempered wind she sensed earlier is growing in anger and heading in their direction. Old Sally's dreams were different last night, too, churned up by the sea. Every night it seems that something new washes up on the beach of the dream world that she is to look at.

This isn't the first time this has happened. The night the Temple mansion burned to the ground a dream warned her. The morning Fiddle died in a car crash her dreams foretold that, too, as well as the death of their child together, and Maya's death—from a tragic car crash, too, more than forty years ago. Now her latest dreams have her grandmother telling her to prepare for something dangerous. Something that requires courage.

Old Sally pulls her shawl tighter and thinks again of Violet. The Gullah ways have been perfected over several centuries stretching back to Western Africa. It would be impossible for anyone to learn everything in only a few months, and harder still for modern people to embrace the old ways. What more does she need to pass on to her? Every human thinks they will have more time, but the truth is, nobody has any guarantees of living any longer than the next second.

Only recently did Old Sally and Violet begin to experiment with tonics Violet might sell in her tea shop. Root teas. Teas that keep sickness at bay, as well as dark forces. But Old Sally wonders if Savannah is ready for such cures.

She walks in the direction Violet went moments before and falters. For the last twenty-four hours, dizziness has visited her. At first, she thought it was the excitement of Queenie's wedding. Now she realizes it may be the storm.

Once inside the house, she stands in the entryway to steady herself. Then Queenie comes to greet her in the hallway like a sudden gust of wind, if the wind were happy to see someone.

Because of her advanced age, Old Sally is often the center of attention, as if everyone is anticipating her keeling over in front of them. The older she gets, the more her final day crosses her mind. But it doesn't frighten her like it seems to scare them. To Old Sally, it is her reward for living. Her last breath here will be followed by her first breath there—the land of her ancestors.

However, it seems that since she is still breathing, her work in this world is not yet finished. Thank the heavens she is good at waiting. Otherwise, it would be harder than it is. Longevity has burdens, too, as well as lessons—as does everything in life. In the meantime, Old Sally directs an unspoken message to Violet to further test their ability to communicate with their thoughts.

Violet emerges from the kitchen.

Was that you? she asks, without speaking.

Old Sally gives a single nod, and she and Violet exchange a smile. Their connection is getting stronger.

Is there something more we should be doing about this storm right now? Violet asks.

Even our best conjuring spells can't keep this storm away, Old Sally tells her. Although she did create something earlier to try.

The truth is this hurricane is as inevitable as Old Sally's passing. The wind and sea are riled. Once nature sets things in motion, there is nothing humans can do.

Old Sally joins Violet in the kitchen, feeling a sense of urgency.

"With this storm, things be speeding up," Old Sally says aloud. "There are a few things left for me to tell you and now seems the time. Can we talk later?"

Violet agrees. As far as Old Sally knows, Violet's notebook contains the first written record of the Gullah beliefs and potions, as well as the stories going back to when her people first arrived on this island.

Until she began teaching Violet, the stories Old Sally heard when she was young were part of an oral tradition. But Violet's book of Gullah secrets gives her hope that their traditions will live on in written form, too. Tia and Leisha also give her hope. They have Gullah blood in them, and an interest in the old ways.

Old Sally yawns. She naps a lot these days to conserve her energy for what is coming. She tells Violet she needs to lie down, and on the way to her bedroom, she glances at the front door. Someone is about to arrive. The doorbell rings and Rose answers it. Old Sally lingers long enough in the living room to hear that it is Edward's daughter again. She is certain Heather is part of the ill wind blowing in.

Tiredness threatens to overcome her as she continues to her bedroom. She must sleep and gather her strength.

CHAPTER TWENTY-SEVEN

Rose

Seeing Heather at the door reminds Rose of that saying about how bad pennies always turn up. After they last spoke at the tea shop, she imagined she wouldn't hear from Heather again. At least not anytime soon.

"Did you forget something?" Rose asks.

"Let me explain." Heather pushes past her, reminding her of how her mother always insisted on being center stage.

Rose would never walk into someone's home uninvited. Southern manners were bred into her as habitually as brushing her teeth. She rubs her temples with the beginning of a headache.

"This isn't a good time," Rose says. "We're getting ready for a storm here."

Heather doesn't move and readjusts her purse on her arm.

Rose wants her out of the house and steps onto the front porch. Thankfully Heather follows. A bitter smell around the door reminds Rose of the roots Old Sally cooks on the stove for her different spells. Rose crosses her arms, body language for *Go away*. Words Heather doesn't appear to understand.

"First of all, I appreciate you talking to me," Heather begins. "Second of all, I don't think you realize how important it was for me to find you. I never had a family growing up except for my mom and now that she's gone—"

Rose's arms loosen their grip. For the first time that day, Heather appears to have broken character.

"How did my brother meet your mother?" Rose asks, taking advantage of the opportunity.

"She worked for him in Atlanta."

It doesn't surprise Rose that Edward would take advantage of someone under him.

"Did you tell Regina that?" Rose asks.

"I was afraid to," Heather says, which sounds honest enough. "I wasn't sure if they were already together by then."

"That was probably smart," Rose says.

"Well, it didn't work, anyway."

"Why?" Rose asks.

Rose is surprised by her own directness. Directness is not a southern thing.

Heather pauses. Is she revisiting her strategy? Or maybe choosing her words carefully?

"I read the article in the newspaper when the Temple Garden was dedicated," Heather says. "It said you had returned to Savannah after being away for a long time. You sounded like an outsider," she continues. "Someone who might understand my situation."

"Regina didn't understand your situation?"

Heather rolls her eyes. "She threw me out of her apartment."

"Threw you out?" Rose doesn't reveal her wariness. This is more drama than she wants to deal with today or any day.

"She didn't actually touch me," Heather says, "but she strongly suggested that I leave, or she would call the police."

Heather sounds convincing. Not that Rose knows Regina that well, either. But why should she believe anything either woman says? Heather is Edward's daughter. A brother she never trusted. And Regina married her untrustworthy brother. It also makes no sense that Regina would threaten to call the police. From what Rose remembers, Regina has some muscle to her. If anyone were in physical danger, it would be Heather. And why did Regina give Heather her address without even asking her?

"I'm confused," Rose says, uncrossing her arms.

"She thinks I want my father's money," Heather admits.

If Heather is covering up her motives, she sure is sloppy about it. At least in this current version of herself. Besides, isn't Edward's money now Regina's money?

There must be more to this, Rose thinks, feeling even more cautious.

"I didn't know who my father was until six months ago," Heather continues. "When I was a kid and asked my mother, she said he was an anonymous sperm donor who was college educated and athletic."

"Well, he was those things, too," Rose says.

"He was?" Heather smiles and then twists a silver bracelet on her wrist. Is she imagining father-daughter dances and doubles tennis matches?

"I'm athletic, too," she adds. "I haven't gone to college yet, but I plan to."

Rose can't discern if Heather is innocent or cunning or both.

"Edward was a lot like our mother," Rose offers, wondering if Heather has any idea how much she looks like her.

"What was your mother like?" Heather's attention doesn't waver.

A simple search at the library would reveal a wealth of information about Rose's mother *and* her mother's wealth. Newspaper clippings from the society section don't tell the real story of who a person is, but they do offer clues. Given Heather's way of presenting herself, Rose would have thought she had studied Iris Temple for years.

"Look," Rose says. "I can't do this with you right now." She sounds like her mother, a fact that makes her recoil.

While Rose withers, Heather stands taller. It seems the Temple ghosts are back after all, in the form of inherited behaviors. For as long as Rose can remember, her quest was to be nothing like the infamous Iris Temple. Or Edward, either, for that matter. Her mother's prized son. Yet, as much as Rose has tried to get away from them both, it seems they have been personified in Heather.

After going to the bank this morning, she now knows the Temple ruthlessness goes back many, many generations. Documented proof is in the faded ledger in her purse.

Rose softens her voice. "We'll have to do this another time, Heather. A hurricane is coming, and we need to prepare."

A hurricane with the same name as my mother, she thinks.

A flash of anger crosses Heather's face that comes and goes so quickly Rose wonders if she imagined it.

"I need to go back inside," Rose says. She takes a step toward the door and stops, aware that Heather is about to follow her again. "You mentioned coming back after this storm has blown over," Rose says. "Let's do that. We can meet at Violet's Tea Shop and have a talk about your father and grandmother and any other Temple you want to know about."

Instead of retreating, Heather steps forward, blocking her way. It reminds Rose of when Edward cornered her as a girl. Or when her mother lectured her on how she should act. Both made her feel trapped.

Rose extends her arm and takes a step forward, refusing to play the game. "Give me a call after the storm, and we can set up a date." A generous offer on her part. She could be like Regina and threaten to call the police.

Heather takes a step back, and Rose goes inside. She considers locking the door but doesn't want Heather to hear the latch. Meanwhile, she can feel her presence on the other side. When Heather finally walks away, Rose takes a breath and finds herself hoping that her long-lost niece never returns. Something about this whole mess doesn't add up.

To Rose, the world became more complicated after 9/11. The entire country now lives with a heightened sense of danger. Reminders of how safe or unsafe they are on any given day come in yellow, orange, and red alerts. Here on Dolphin Island, they are probably safe from terrorist attacks. But Rose's trust in humans has lessened.

Violet enters the living room wearing casual shorts and a sleeveless top, as though ready to get to work on storm preparations. "You look upset," she says to Rose.

"Heather was here."

"I thought she went back to Atlanta."

"That's what she said at the tea shop, but then she ended up back here again."

Violet rubs her left shoulder.

"Are you getting a hint of something dangerous?" Rose asks.

"No, I'm not getting anything. That's what's odd. Do you suppose intuition can go on the blink? I got a hit at the tea shop, and then nothing again."

Rose cannot relate to Violet's sensitivity, though she did sometimes see the spirits in the Temple mansion when she was growing up.

"Can you believe all those ghosts we put up with over at the other house?" Rose asks. "It seems the memories still haunt me. I think of them quite often."

"I can't say I've missed that crew," Violet says.

"Me, either," Rose says, thinking again of the ledger in her purse. In a way, that book is full of ghosts, too.

Marrying Max and moving to Wyoming was a way to escape everything the Temple family represented. Rose wanted a new life, and Max gave her that. Now Rose has given him a *new* life back.

"You look a thousand miles away," Violet says.

"Two thousand, actually. Can I tell you something unrelated?" Rose asks.

Violet says she can.

"I feel a little shaky with this storm coming."

"Do you?" Violet says, touching her arm. "I do, too."

"You do?"

Violet nods. "It's important to remember that it may not amount to anything, though."

"I hope you're right," Rose says.

Queenie joins them near the door. Without thought or plan, the three of them lock arms like they did when they were Sea Gypsies. A celebration of lightheartedness.

"Are we having a secret meeting?" Queenie smiles.

Queenie was an honorary member of the Sea Gypsies, the secret club created by Rose and Violet when they were young.

Rose wonders if Katie's child will grow up to be a Sea Gypsy, too. The thought pleases her, even if he is a boy.

"Sea Gypsies aren't afraid of storms," Violet says, as though speaking it will make it so.

"They are absolutely not afraid of storms," Rose says, her tone perfectly serious.

"Tell that storm to stay the hell away," Queenie says, snapping her fingers.

"Stay the hell away!" Rose repeats with a smile, her voice raised.

Violet snaps her fingers, too, and says the same, matching Rose's volume.

They laugh, the three of them snapping their fingers at the ocean to keep the danger away. As girls, they would have liked nothing better than a hurricane coming ashore to give their lives some adventure during the long, dull days of summer. Rose sometimes wonders what happened to that little girl in her. It's like she was never seen again after she left home. Hidden away in the scrapbook pages of her memories.

While Rose could never get close to her mother, Queenie and Old Sally were the people she depended on to love her no matter what. They have never let her down in that regard. Rose feels better thinking these old friends will be with her during the storm. And a small part of her now thinks of it as an adventure.

Max comes in the back door, and they unlock arms as if their playfulness is as secret as the Sea Gypsy handshake. He hands them each a roll of masking tape.

"What's this for?" Rose asks, although she knows perfectly well.

"Taping the windows that don't have storm shutters," he says.

They weathered plenty of storms on their ranch in Wyoming, and none required masking tape.

"I thought we did that already," Rose says.

"There are still a few left upstairs," he tells them. "Iris's ETA is about nine hours from now," he continues. "She'll come ashore somewhere, we don't know where. But we might as well be prepared."

Queenie and Violet leave, and Rose leans into Max's broad shoulder. "Tell me what your gut says. Do you think we're in danger?"

After thirty years of marriage, Rose trusts Max's hunches.

"Honestly?" he asks her.

"Yes, honestly."

Max pauses, his brow furrowed. "Truth is, nobody has any idea what this storm is going to do, but my guess is we're in for a humdinger."

"Then let's get ready for it." Rose thinks of Heather again. She has no idea what Heather is going to do, either. But there's no time to worry about that now. With masking tape in hand, Rose sets off to prepare for their unexpected summer adventure.

CHAPTER TWENTY-EIGHT

Violet

Violet makes sandwiches enough for everyone in case the
power goes out. She puts them in a cooler and then
packs chips and fruit to go with them. Whatever happens, they
will have food.

With a few more minutes of light left, Violet decides to go
on a short walk down the beach. She breathes in the salt air,
letting it take her tiredness away. After all those years of
dreaming about having a different life, it seems she is finally
living her dream. Not only of owning her tea shop but having
a purpose to her days. A life in which she is learning about her
Gullah ancestors from Old Sally and creating a written
record.

Though she is half-white, like Queenie, she can relate more
to the Gullah side of her family. A side more mysterious than
she ever realized. Increasingly, Violet can hear Old Sally's
thoughts when the intention is set. A gift she is counting on to
continue after Old Sally returns to the ancestors, as her grand-

mother calls it. And a gift she hopes will make what feels unbearable more bearable.

Darkness falls quickly now. Violet stops before getting to the lighthouse, uncertain of why she even headed in this direction. She usually walks down the beach instead of up. Violet makes an X in the sand before turning around and going back. A ritual that is written in her notebook of Gullah secrets. She isn't sure why the X is essential, except that many of their rituals are related to avoiding lousy luck or attracting good fortune.

Violet glances at the lighthouse before turning around. For years, it faded into the background of her life, as though hidden behind an invisibility cloak, like in the *Harry Potter* books her daughters have read. Then one day she started seeing it again. Violet has done this with people, too. For many years she took her Aunt Queenie for granted until she found out that Queenie was her birth mother. Then memories of her always being there for Violet rushed forward.

The water birds on the beach move frantically along the shore, using the last seconds of daylight to eat their fill. All the while, several pelican formations head north, zigzagging up the coast like an airplane pulling a banner behind to advertise tours of the island. Other than these clues, it would be impossible to imagine a storm on the way. What was it like for her Gullah ancestors who didn't have Doppler radar and advanced warning systems?

Violet remembers the mermaid story Old Sally told her yesterday and hopes that if someone has captured a mermaid they soon return her to the sea.

Home again, Violet is grateful the foundation of the house was raised eight feet during the renovations. A suggestion made by their contractor. With this hurricane, this could be a crucial eight feet. Even a thunderstorm can be dangerous when you live on a barrier island and are exposed to the elements.

Leaving her sandy sneakers on the top step, Violet shakes out the small, colorful rag rug outside the front door and wonders if Old Sally is up from her nap. Every evening Violet sweeps sand from the wooden floors, something she remembers Old Sally doing when Violet was a girl. Tradition gives her comfort these days. The knowledge that some things carry on, despite death and natural disasters.

The only voices in the kitchen come from the television someone left on in the corner. A different weather reporter talks about a best-case-scenario, which has Iris skirting the coast with winds of 80–100 miles per hour. A storm surge of 4–6 feet. That would have waves breaking against their front steps before returning to the sea.

This is the best case scenario? she asks herself.

Violet goes to check on Old Sally. She knocks gently and then opens her door. Eyes closed, Old Sally lies on the bed. Violet watches for her gentle breathing, the movement of her chest up and down—signs of life. When someone is Old Sally's age, the end is expected. Like the hurricane, it cannot be ignored and falls somewhere on the prediction spectrum between a Watch and a Warning.

"I be awake," Old Sally says, her eyes still closed.

"Did you have another dream?" Violet asks.

Old Sally pats the bed beside her, and Violet comes to sit. When Old Sally opens her eyes, there is a weariness there that Violet hasn't seen before.

"These days, the ancestors come every time I close my eyes," she says.

"Does it scare you?" Violet asks.

"Oh my, no," Old Sally says with a chuckle. "I welcome them."

Violet wonders if she will be like Old Sally when her time comes. Not fearing death but looking forward to it as a family reunion. Old age is a privilege, not a birthright, Violet heard somewhere. Not everyone gets to grow old.

"My grandmother came again in the latest dream," Old Sally begins. "She was braiding my hair on the old front porch, and I sat cross-legged a step below her with my favorite rag doll in my lap. It was a brown doll she made me that wore an outfit that was made from the same fabric of her favorite dress," Old Sally continues. "That doll had black buttons for eyes and black yarn stitched on for her hair." Old Sally pauses as though seeing the doll anew. "In the dream, I could feel Granny's breath at my back. Her soft touch working to tame my hair into a braid after rubbing the oil into it that makes it relax."

Violet's scalp tingles.

"You feel her presence, too?" Old Sally asks.

"I do," Violet says, "at least I think I do."

"That be your great-great-grandmother," she says.

Violet soaks in the feeling of another presence in the room. The vibration is like a fan on its lowest setting, except it makes no breeze. The tingling spreads from her scalp into her torso and then down into her arms and legs.

"Why do you think you have so many memories from back then?" Violet asks.

"Because it be close to my time."

Violet lowers her head.

"No, sweet girl," Old Sally says, with a gentleness Violet has come to expect. "Don't be sad for me. I have been here long enough. I am ready for the Great Beyond. More than ready. I overdue."

Violet never thinks of people being overdue, as in late to depart this life. A jar in the kitchen is full of change for when it takes Tia and Leisha longer to finish a library book than the due date allows. Ten cents a day for an overdue book. She wonders what the cost is for an overdue person.

"I'm worried more about me than you," Violet says. "I hate thinking of you not being here anymore."

"But I will be here." Old Sally smooths out the wrinkles on Violet's forehead with her warm, soft touch." *And we can still talk to each other.*

Violet hears the last statement in her thoughts, transmitted on a secret Gullah airwave. A few months ago, she would have never thought it was possible to talk to her grandmother this way. Violet still questions sometimes if she imagines it.

When Violet looks up, Old Sally is watching her.

"What's troubling you?" she asks.

"I hate it when you talk about going," Violet says. "I know you're ready to go and all that, but I've learned so much from you, and I don't know what I'll do without you here to teach me."

"I felt the same way about my grandmother," Old Sally says. "It was much harder on me when she died than anyone else in my family. But after a bunch of years, I finally figured out that this is exactly how nature works," she continues. "We're like flowers that bloom for a while and then fade away to make room for the next blooms."

Violet thinks of the blooms on her African violets at the tea shop. They love the window they sit in front of and bloom for months on end. She likes to think of people flourishing that way if they find the right spot to thrive.

Except for the mother she thought she had lost when she was a little girl, Violet hasn't lost anyone close to her. Jack's mother died a few years ago, but Violet and her mother-in-law didn't have a close connection like she does with Old Sally. Old Sally raised her. Violet lived with her for the first twenty years of her life until she married Jack. Besides Queenie, Old Sally is the most constant presence in her life.

But Violet doesn't want to bloom at Old Sally's expense. "I'm not sure what to say." Words feel inadequate to express the weightiness of the moment.

Old Sally touches her hand. "You don't have to say anything."

"Will you tell me what you need me to do? I mean when the time comes?"

Old Sally says she will. *Though I imagine even if I couldn't, you would know.*

Violet pauses, hearing her thoughts and wondering if this is true.

Moments later, Old Sally sits up. "What's the weather doing?" she asks.

"I guess you could call it the calm before the storm," Violet says. "It's absolutely beautiful out there. A clear and glorious night."

"That will all change soon," Old Sally says.

Violet's left shoulder twitches for the first time in hours, as if waking from a long nap. It has given her mixed signals or no signals all day. Either way, Violet must prepare for what is coming.

CHAPTER TWENTY-NINE

Queenie

Queenie's bedroom is in total disarray from the ceremony the day before. Her wedding gown is thrown over a chair near the far window, along with her red hat, yellow scarf, and purple pumps. Several fans sit in silence. Queenie has been known to thrive on excitement, but this weekend has been too much even for her.

A hurricane is churning out in the Atlantic and according to the weather forecasters has just turned inland. Spud's place up the beach was to have summer renters living there starting this week since he would be living with Queenie after their wedding. But an hour ago, they called to cancel their stay because of the hurricane.

Last week, Queenie cleared half of her walk-in closet for Spud and gave him two drawers in her large dresser. One for his socks and underwear and another for his bow ties. Spud has a bow tie for almost every day of the year and in every color. Queenie has yet to see the fascination, but Spud doesn't understand her loyalty to Oprah, either. She supposes living with each other's weirdness is what marriage is all about.

"Honeypot?" Spud steps out of the bathroom, naked, every gray hair on his head sticking straight up.

"Who are you calling *Honeypot?*" If he weren't so cute Queenie might throw something at him. "Why are you so obsessed with finding me a nickname?"

"I don't know," he says. "Maybe I should just call you Queenie."

"Now there's a novel idea," she quips. "It is my name after all." But in truth, she is not the least bit irritated. She likes how hard he tries to please her. So far in this marriage, she has no complaints. Well, except for the fact that a hurricane named after his ex is threatening to spoil everything.

A knock on the door has Spud ducking back into the bathroom.

Violet enters.

"I need to talk to you," she says.

"You mind if I stay here in my chair?" Queenie asks. "This weekend has tuckered me out."

Violet says she doesn't mind at all and sits on the end of her bed.

"What is it?" Queenie asks. "You look worried."

"It's Old Sally," Violet says. "She's talking about things she doesn't usually talk about."

"Like what?" Queenie sits straighter.

"Like dying."

Queenie bolts from the chair. "Does she think she's dying now? I just saw her a couple of hours ago, and she seemed as good as ever."

"She's fine," Violet insists, "but she's having a lot of dreams about when she was a girl, and her grandmother keeps visiting her in her dreams, too. She seems to think it's a sign."

Queenie calls to Spud in the bathroom. "Can you get out here, please?"

When Spud comes out his hair is combed, and he has a bathrobe tied tightly around his skinny waist. It smells like he got a little overzealous with the aftershave.

Is all that primping in the bathroom for my benefit? She smiles at the thought.

Spud's legs are white and thin and remind her of a chicken's legs, which then reminds Queenie of Kentucky Fried Chicken, and Iris, and the stupid storm heading in their direction.

"What is it, sweet cakes?" Spud says. "You look upset."

"Oh, good heavens," Queenie answers with a reluctant smile. "I am nobody's sweet cake."

Spud greets Violet like they are old friends, which they are. Queenie sometimes forgets how close they were before Spud and Queenie started dating.

"Violet says Mama is talking about dying."

Queenie tells Spud about how hard it will be when her mama passes. She has been her only parent, after all, for her entire life. Her father for sure never claimed her. He only barely claimed Iris, who was his legitimate daughter.

When Spud hears all this, he gives her such a loving and compassionate look that tears spring to her eyes.

"What should we do?" Queenie asks him, dabbing her eyes with a tissue.

He pauses for what feels like a solid minute. "I don't think you'll like what I have to say."

"Tell me." Queenie trusts him to tell her the truth, even if she won't like it.

"I think we should let her go," Spud says.

"Let her go?" Queenie glances at Violet, who to her surprise doesn't appear as shocked as Queenie is. This is the last thing she expected to come out of the mouth of Spud Grainger, who has a hard time letting go of anything. He still has bow ties he wears from back in the sixties.

"What else can we do?" Spud asks.

Queenie puts her hands on her hips. It is all she can do not to scream or cry. She is a big woman after all, with big thoughts and big feelings. Spud knows how much Queenie hates feeling helpless. It is her least favorite feeling in her feeling collection. And with this storm coming she was already heading in that direction. She is tired. And when she gets tired, she is not good at handling anything.

She had hoped to hide all her oversized emotions from Spud for at least the first year of their marriage, but here it is on the second day.

"I just thought you should know," Violet says to them.

"You did the right thing by telling me," Queenie says. "Did she say anything else to you?"

"Only that she is ready to go," Violet says.

Tears rush to Queenie's eyes again. Spud arrives at her side, a look of genuine concern on his freshly shaven face.

"I can't believe I'm crying like this," she says to him, hoping it isn't the "ugly cry."

To her surprise, it feels good to release the stress and worry she has stored up for way too long. The last time she blubbered like this was when those twin towers came down. It was such a sad day, being aware of all those people who would never get to go home again. Life is more difficult than Queenie likes to admit. The truth is, sometimes crying is the sanest thing a person can do when the world gets crazy.

Crying or laughing. But Queenie isn't feeling that funny right now.

While Queenie's tears are rare, Spud will openly weep during Hallmark and dog food commercials. Not to mention the Olympics—a Championship Cry Fest that happens without fail every two years. Queenie witnessed tears in his eyes more than once at their wedding, and she had some of her own.

Queenie blows her nose on the handkerchief Spud provides. It has been an emotional two days, and she can't believe she is falling apart now. It doesn't help that a hurricane is bearing down on them. A hurricane bearing the name of her dead nemesis.

In the next moment, a gust of wind rattles Queenie's windows, and the three of them jump as if Hurricane Iris has just offered to give Queenie something new to cry about.

CHAPTER THIRTY

Old Sally

Once the dreams start, it won't be long, Old Sally says to herself.

Dreams change when people get to the end of their life. Or so her grandmother told her. During Sadie's final days, Sally sat by her bedside and listened to her grandmother tell her dreams to her in great detail. Long-gone friends and relatives walked through every scene, as well as many people she had unfinished business with. Sometimes the dreams finished things up for her.

Old Sally's latest dreams have Fiddle playing at a wedding on the beach, his music as beautiful as ever. In the dream, the wedding is the one that she and Fiddle didn't get to have. Her daughter Annabelle is alive and well, in her arms and part of the ceremony. Their silver wedding bands were made from a silver spoon taken from the Temple kitchen by her grandmother. Stolen from the Temples because they stole her son Adam and sent him away so long ago.

Sometimes dreams deliver the only justice to be found during this transition from life to death, and the dreams come regardless of whether they are welcome or not. Those who believe in a spirit world have an easier time with these visitations, her grandmother told her. And Old Sally believes in the spirit world. A world where mysteries live. Not just the ancestors, either, but the Creator who set everything in motion and watches over all of them. The Gullah way is to see everything in creation as sacred. The plants, the trees, the animals. Everything on land and sea.

Love is the most sacred thing of all, she tells herself, thinking of the people she loves.

Up from her nap, she looks at herself in the round mirror over the sink in the bathroom. Sometimes she can't believe how many wrinkles she has. Like the rings of a tree revealing her age. But it is her eyes that say the most. The soul's windows, they've been called. If that's true, her soul looks hopeful and sincere, though tired.

The wind is finally picking up outside. Not much. But enough to hint at what's to come. Though the weathermen haven't committed to the exact path the storm will take, Old Sally already knows the outcome. It will come here to the island, and perhaps then Iris will help Old Sally with her transition, just like Old Sally helped her two years before. Except this time, Iris will be in the form of a hurricane.

CHAPTER THIRTY-ONE

Rose

Is it Rose's imagination or has the wind started blowing harder? Max and Jack have stored all the outdoor furniture in the garage and closed the storm shutters on the main house and cottage. Now they stack sandbags on the porch to put in front of the door. Water can do more damage than hundred-mile-an-hour winds, reports say, so whether they stay or leave they need to prepare for a possible storm surge.

Weather fascinates Rose. When they lived out West, she learned to pay attention to it or suffer the consequences. The Rocky Mountains served as a magnet for extreme weather. Tornados. Blizzards. Thundersnow. Twisters that took aim at entire neighborhoods, scattering houses like dice on a board game. And thunderstorms so fierce lightning shot sideways with nothing to ground it.

However, a hurricane appears to be a different beast. Hurricanes don't miss one house and then grab the next in a flash of fate. Hurricanes churn for days out over warm ocean waters to gather strength. High winds team together with a tidal surge to destroy whatever is in its path. Thankfully, they are also slow enough to allow the time for people to get away.

After filling several water jugs in case they lose power and water, Rose goes back to the cottage to rest for a moment. She lifts the faded ledger from her purse and sits on her bed. It smells like the bank vault and paper molecules breaking down and deteriorating. She turns more pages, being careful with the bindings, which look like they could easily break apart. Near the back, she finds notations written in a kind of code. Is it a manifest? She wonders how anything so old could be of any importance today. Yet, something about the book feels valuable.

Max comes into the bedroom and turns on the television. "Look," he says.

The mayor of Savannah is standing in front of town hall suggesting people evacuate Savannah and the surrounding islands.

Max's face has a look that Rose wishes she hadn't seen. Is that fear?

"Are we going to evacuate?" Rose asks.

Max shrugs. The old Max. The one who wears cowboy boots and doesn't share what he thinks unless she pries it out of him.

"But where will we go?" Rose asks. "If we get on 95 going north, we'll probably get stuck in a standstill. Queenie said it was already backed up yesterday when she and Spud were coming back from Hilton Head."

The news of the evacuation spreads fast given the sounds of the voices in the kitchen.

"I guess we'd better go see what the others are thinking," Max says finally.

Rose agrees.

In the kitchen of the main house, everyone talks at once, offering different solutions. It is the first time they've had to make any group decisions other than chore lists. Do they go separately or together? Which cars do they take? How much do they have room for? And—mainly—where do they go?

"Maybe we should vote," Rose says, raising her voice above the others.

"Well, we don't all have to do the same thing, either," Violet reminds them.

"I think we should stick together," Queenie says, looking at Violet.

"No matter what, we've got to keep Katie and the baby safe," Angela says.

Max agrees.

"I was in Charleston in 1989 after Hurricane Hugo hit," Jack begins. "The bridge going to Sullivan's Island and Isle of Palms was destroyed, and people couldn't return to their homes for weeks," he continues. "I don't want to get stuck on the mainland and not be able to get back."

"I agree with Jack," Max says. "We need to be here to fix any damage right away, as well as keep everybody safe. We've collected supplies for two days," he continues, "including a stack of tarps in the garage in case the roof is damaged."

"I appreciate how prepared we are," Rose says to Max. "But we don't want to do anything unwise." Sometimes the cowboy in Max does things regular people consider risky.

At that moment Rose realizes how easy it is to let the men make all the crucial decisions. The thought goes contrary to her Smith College days. Yet, it fits right in with the culture she was raised in.

"What do you think we should do?" Rose asks Old Sally.

Everyone turns. Old Sally is the only person who appears calm in the middle of the chaos. They wait in silence for her to speak, and when she does, her voice is softer than Rose expects, though it is still strong.

"This old house has withstood plenty of storms over the hundred years I've been here," she says. "But we can't afford to put anyone in danger."

Violet's girls interrupt with the latest news.

"They're saying the evacuation is now mandatory," Leisha says. "All barrier islands on the Georgia and South Carolina coastline."

"And anyone who refuses has to leave the name of their next of kin with authorities." Tia's eyes widen, and Violet crosses the kitchen to calm her.

It is agreed. The next hour will be spent getting ready to evacuate. Before the group disperses, Max tells everyone to limit their things to a single suitcase. A suggestion that has everyone talking again.

Back at the cottage, Rose fills one suitcase with a few clothes, an extra pair of shoes, and loose photos she pulled from the family scrapbook, along with a couple of pieces of jewelry her mother gave her when she graduated college. Rose lovingly called these pieces her nest egg. It is a troubling exercise to discern, after a lifetime of collecting things, what to put into a single suitcase.

In a separate, smaller bag she packs dog food for Lucy and Ethel, as well as bowls and two leashes. She returns the Temple ledger to her purse—she doesn't want to risk losing it until she figures out its importance. If indeed it is important at all.

An hour later, they stand at the door ready to leave. Twelve people with twelve suitcases. Three dogs, two cats in a carrier, and a pet turtle in a small dry aquarium. They get outside, and as soon as they lock the front door, Max and Jack pull sandbags in front of it. As they stand in the dunes, Rose looks at the house that has become her home over the last few months. She takes a mental photograph in case it isn't here when they get back.

The night is dark with thick cloud cover. No stars or moon to light the way. The ocean tide can be heard in the distance as they take the walkway through the dunes to the cars. Something about the storm coming at night has Rose unnerved. It is one thing to see a storm coming and wind whipping at trees. It is quite another to only hear it.

In his truck, Max leads the caravan of four cars. They plan to drive inland for an hour and stay at a motel they have booked for the evening. Rose is in the pickup, their two dogs in the back seat already drooling their excitement. In the back are water jugs and the food, along with a chainsaw, a canister of gasoline, and different tools Max might need. She trusts his instincts. He helped them survive many blizzards in Wyoming and a flash flood threatening their home.

The first few blocks the traffic isn't bad, but then everything comes to a stop at the two-lane road that will take them off the island. The road runs along the waterway, with steep shoulders down to the marsh. A steady line of red brake lights leads the way for them to exit the island. At most, six hundred people live on this barrier island. But when they are all in their cars, it seems like more.

Spud and Queenie and Old Sally are in Spud's ten-year-old Toyota directly behind them. Old Sally can be seen holding onto the Jesus bar despite their snail-like speed. Even though Spud could afford something much more expensive, he has not invested in a new car. Queenie is in the middle of the back seat, already talking. It is hard to imagine Queenie taking a back seat to anyone, except for Old Sally.

In the caravan behind Spud are Angela and Katie, followed by Jack and Violet and the girls, with Jake the turtle in the back window.

"Why are we stopped?" Rose asks Max.

"Not sure."

Rose remembers her last trip home to Wyoming after her mother's funeral. Max picked her up at the airport. She would never have guessed when she presented the option of moving back to Savannah that he would have taken her up on it so readily.

As many cars are behind them as ahead of them.

"Should we be worried?" Rose asks Max.

Max shrugs, his eyes staring straight ahead. He doesn't show his fear often, but the look that passed between him and Rose in the bedroom earlier still haunts her.

"What if we can't get off the island?" Rose asks, wishing she had an alcoholic beverage of some kind. Or at least a cup of coffee.

"If we can't get off the island, we'll go home." He sounds slightly irritated. Or maybe that's his worried tone.

"But what about the storm?" Rose asks.

He pauses. "We'll manage."

Rose's worry intensifies. High winds. Storm surge. Katie.

"The last thing we need is for Katie to go into labor," Rose says to Max.

He drums the steering wheel with his thumbs as if this thought hasn't occurred to him. Meanwhile, the line of traffic moves like inchworms out for a leisurely stroll. The truck finally comes to a stop.

The truck idles. Ten minutes pass. People start to turn off

their cars. Max puts on the parking brake, although the terrain is perfectly flat, and turns off the engine.

"I'm going to walk up there and see if I can see anything."

"I'll come, too," Rose says.

Windows down, they get out of the car, telling Lucy and Ethel to stay. They drool their disappointment. Then Rose walks back to tell Spud and Queenie what they are about to do.

"Catching another ride?" Queenie asks when Rose shows up at the window. Despite her joke, she looks concerned.

"We're going to walk up ahead and see what we can find out," Rose says.

"It be too late for that," Old Sally says, looking toward the horizon as if seeing the future. She appears both diminutive and formidable.

"You know something you aren't telling us, Mama?" Queenie asks from the back.

"Just that we be staying here on this island, storm or no storm."

Rose and Queenie trade looks. Neither are willing to question her.

"Well, we might as well stretch our legs anyway since we're stuck in this line," Rose says.

Everyone mills around among the long line of parked cars. The only person in their makeshift caravan who is still in the vehicle is Old Sally. Violet joins Rose to go check out what is up ahead. They have barely talked since the evacuation began. As they walk, the warm breeze coming off the ocean has a sudden chill to it. Rose zips up her light jacket as though her mother—in the form of Hurricane Iris—has suddenly brushed against her.

CHAPTER THIRTY-TWO

Violet

During the evacuation, the lane coming onto the island is closed, and they walk down that side of the road. Violet holds her left shoulder, questioning its silence. This has never happened before when she has wished her shoulder would give her a sign.

The air is filled with the smell of salt marsh. A pungent mixture of land and sea that makes Violet's nose itch. The marsh creates an ecosystem unique to this area. The salt marshes are regularly flooded with seawater during high tide, servicing the clams, mussels, and snails, as well as various fish that come and go with the waves. Fiddler crabs, ghost crabs, and blue crabs feed on the bacteria in the muds, creating a feast for the seagulls, snowy egrets, and great blue herons. A banquet put on every day by nature.

Along the edges of the marsh are salt-stunted oaks, a few loblolly pines, and scrubby saw palmettos. At low tide, the water gives way to pluff mud and seven-foot-tall spartina grass. But water is coming in with the tide, and all that mud will soon disappear. Later the sea will shift again and call her salty presence home.

Rose points and Violet turns to look. A giant egret flies by on ghostly white wings, its coarse call spreading the word of something coming.

Meanwhile, Violet nods a greeting to people standing by their cars as they wait for the limbo to lift.

"I never noticed what an interesting mixture of people live on this island," Rose says.

Violet agrees. "The diversity is one of the things I love about living here," she begins. "As many blacks as whites. As many rich people as poor and everything in between," she continues. "All ages, too, ranging from newborns to Old Sally, the only centenarian on Dolphin Island."

"It has a totally different feeling to it than Savannah," Rose says. "I love living here."

"I love that you love it," Violet says, as they lock arms.

Violet's Gullah ancestors settled this island and named it after the dolphins living in the waters off the coast. White masters didn't want to put up with the mosquitos, the heat, or being so far away from the luxuries of civilization, so they let the Gullah people live here mostly undisturbed. Her ancestors made their own fishing nets, wove sweetgrass baskets, made their own clothes. Grew indigo, sugarcane, and rice, as well as all sorts of vegetables.

Many of the stories that Old Sally has shared with Violet include Gullah superstitions and the use of folk magic—potions and spells—to protect and heal. She wonders how much Gullah history Rose knows. Someday she will tell her, and maybe the island will come even more alive for her, too.

Without the occasional streetlight, they would have trouble

seeing along this stretch. The island didn't have electricity until Old Sally was a grown woman. She told Violet stories about how strange it was to have a light bulb that lit a room instead of a lantern. Her mother and grandmother sometimes stared at the bare bulb in the evenings like they were witnessing someone walk on water. Miss Temple took pride in the fact that the Temples were the first family in Savannah to get electricity. It came to the island years after that.

An orange traffic cone is placed in the middle of the road where Max has stopped, giving Violet and Rose time to catch up. They unlock arms. On the edge of the marsh, a tree has fallen across the road, bringing down a power line with it. A sheriff's deputy is on his radio. When he finishes, Max asks him how long it will be before the road is passable again.

"Two hours," the deputy says. He is a young black man who Violet doesn't recognize. His uniform is perfectly pressed. He is someone who takes pride in his appearance.

Max thanks him. "We might as well go home and try again later," Max says to Violet and Rose.

"We can't evacuate?" Violet asks, aware that Old Sally already predicted this.

"Not for at least two hours," Max says.

Violet looks at Rose. Are they thinking the same thing? There is no other way off Dolphin Island. For years, islanders petitioned for a second bridge so what happened up the coast on Sullivan's Island and Isle of Palms during Hugo didn't happen here, too. But government funds are slow to come to this part of the country.

Walking back to the car, people ask them what they found out. "Two hours," Violet says.

Various moans come from the cars, and engines start.

Exhaust fumes mingle with the smell of the salt marsh, making Violet feel a tad nauseous.

"Let's go home," Violet tells Queenie and Spud. "A tree and a downed power line are blocking the road. They hope to have it cleared in a couple of hours."

"Sweet Jesus," Queenie says, her eyes wide. "Does that mean we can't leave the island?"

Violet reassures her that everything will be fine, though at this moment, she has doubts.

"What does your shoulder say?" Queenie asks Violet, as though consulting an oracle.

Violet gives Queenie a quick shrug. "Nothing to report."

Queenie exhales as though this is good news.

Cars begin making three-point turns, which Violet practiced here on the island before getting her driver's license and has never used. She is relieved that it is Jack who turns the car around, not her, as they head back toward home. Now the traffic jam faces the other direction. She doesn't often view their island at such a slow pace. It is interesting to note how things haven't changed much since she was a girl and rode the school bus to the mainland and observed her world.

The main intersection on the island contains a convenience store that also houses a tiny post office in one corner, as well as a back wall that carries beach balls, flip-flops, and T-shirts with DOLPHIN ISLAND written on the front and either a dolphin or a lighthouse on the back. A seafood restaurant called Dolphin Shrimp is next door and is only open from Memorial Day to Labor Day. Alongside the restaurant is a gas station with two pumps that are currently out of gas. Violet goes to Savannah for groceries, gas, and the post office, as most islanders do.

Back at the house, they gather again to talk about Plan B. It feels anticlimactic to be here.

"Do we try again?" she asks Jack.

"Two hours was probably a best-case scenario," Jack says. "I'd be surprised if they get that mess untangled by morning."

Max agrees.

"But isn't the storm supposed to make landfall before then?" Queenie asks, holding onto Spud's arm.

No one answers.

Violet turns to Old Sally. Every time Violet looks at her, she seems smaller somehow, and older.

"That storm be the least of our worries," Old Sally says.

A moment later Katie lets out a loud moan, doubling over from the pain.

A flash of panic crosses Angela's face, and Rose steps to Katie's side. Meanwhile, Katie looks down at her belly as though an alien is about to burst out of her skin.

"Maybe it's false labor pains," Violet says, purposely sounding calm. "I had those a lot with Tia."

Katie looks instantly relieved, as does Rose, and the relief passes to Angela.

"That's what it is," Angela says, giving a convincing look to Katie. Nobody mentions the fact that they couldn't get off the island if they wanted to. Not to a hospital or a birthing unit. It is a time to stay calm and endure.

"Heaven help us if that sweet baby comes during a hurricane," Queenie says.

"We'll be fine," Violet says, turning toward Queenie, her expression relaying the message to not alarm Katie and Angela. It is Violet's opinion that babies need to come into this world with love surrounding them, not fear, and the concern in the room is growing.

How people enter and leave this life fascinates Violet. Old Sally calls it a threshold. She regrets she missed Miss Temple's passing. She would have liked to be a part of Old Sally helping Miss Temple transition. Old Sally describes herself as a midwife for the dying. Perhaps she can be one for the living, too, and deliver this baby if it decides to come.

Violet remembers the bluebird on the rocker. A sign that company was coming. At first, Violet thought the bird was announcing Heather. But could it have been announcing the baby, too?

Katie rubs her belly, Harpo at her feet looking up. At least if they are real labor pains, they aren't close together yet. Hopefully, the road to the mainland will be open soon.

Violet catches Old Sally watching her, perhaps reading the tea leaves of her mind.

What? Violet asks her. Their unspoken conversations are a kind of underground railroad. Thoughts safely transported to their destination.

We must keep everyone calm, Old Sally answers.

How do we do that? Violet says.

We be examples, Old Sally says.

Whether a baby is coming or a hurricane—or both—they are in for a long night.

"Anybody hungry?" Violet asks.

The response is animated.

Violet unpacks the sandwiches she made before they left to eat when they reached the motel. They forego formality and eat standing at the island in the kitchen.

After eating, Old Sally suggests that everyone get some rest, even though it is only eight o'clock. Tia and Leisha look at their mom, questioning if this could possibly pertain to them, too. The thought of going to bed now doesn't appeal to Violet, either, but she knows Old Sally is right. If the storm is coming at three or four, it would be nice to have slept some before the night gets interesting. Violet yawns with the knowledge that her body could actually use the rest. It has been an unusually busy weekend.

Meanwhile, Old Sally is already in her bedroom. Whatever is coming, she appears to know she needs her full energy. Violet trusts she is right. Others leave, thanking Violet for the sandwiches. Finally, it is only Violet, Queenie, and Spud in the kitchen.

"There's no way I could sleep now," Queenie says. "Anybody up for a game of Twister in honor of the hurricane?"

Spud laughs. "How about a game of Hearts in the bedroom?" he suggests with a wink.

With this storm on the way, Violet has forgotten that there are newlyweds in the house. She kisses each of them on the cheek as they say their goodnights and go upstairs.

Left alone in the kitchen, Violet washes and dries the last of the dishes and puts them away. This is her favorite time of day, the hour before bedtime when she can look back and see what she accomplished that day. But this hasn't been an ordinary day.

Being turned away at the bridge was distressing, knowing that they are trapped on the island. At least temporarily. Then Katie's false or possibly real labor pains. Violet can't imagine what is to come. A sudden gust of wind rattles the shutters as if to confirm that the night has only just begun.

CHAPTER THIRTY-THREE

Queenie

Queenie watches in disbelief as Spud puts on his pajamas and gets in bed like it is any other night.

"How in the world can you think of sleeping with Iris rattling our windows?" Queenie asks.

"Old Sally is right to tell us to get some rest," he says. "It's going to be a long night."

"This is not how I thought I'd be spending my honeymoon," Queenie says, a pout threatening to form.

"Come lay down next to me, Buttercup." Spud opens the covers and pats the bed.

"Where in heaven are you getting these names?" Queenie asks. "Is there a book somewhere called *Lame Nicknames to Call the Woman You Love?*"

As soon as she hears the words, Queenie regrets saying them. Queenie doesn't know much about relationships, but it seems that apologies are a big part of them. She tells Spud she's sorry. Sarcasm has never looked good on her. In fact, she has never known anyone it looked good on. Iris Temple perfected it to the point that she could cut you wide open with a few choice words, leaving you to bleed out on one of the Oriental carpets, the blood not even clashing with the design.

During the thirty-five years Queenie lived with Iris, there were a million things done to Queenie that would have warranted an apology. The correcting. The criticizing. The condescending looks. Sometimes downright meanness. Scheduling events on Queenie's birthday so Queenie couldn't take a day off. Making Queenie take multiple trips to the bank or post office on any given day, instead of letting her combine trips. The fact of the matter was that Iris Temple loved ordering people around.

But she would never have apologized even if her life depended on it, Queenie thinks.

It takes a certain amount of humility to know that you can be wrong about things or to admit that you can hurt people, even if you don't mean to. Iris, however, seemed to enjoy gutting people on occasion. Nothing accidental about it.

Spud accepts Queenie's apology, and they kiss. Love at sixty is the best kind of love. No time to waste or take things for granted. And who cares if they don't have the bodies of twenty-year-olds. The biggest surprise is how much passion Queenie stored up for so long. Thankfully, Spud doesn't seem to mind making up for all those years they weren't together.

Queenie remembers the weekly trips she took with Iris to the Piggly Wiggly where Spud worked. She not only judged that book by its cover, but she put him in the wrong section of the library, too. A section called *Not Interested.*

Boy was I wrong, Queenie thinks.

They kiss again. When Spud unhooks her plus-size bra to view what he calls her "chocolate truffles," she gets a hot flash unlike any before. The heat forces her to rush to the balcony and step outside, but not before grabbing the light robe on the back of her chair to cover her nakedness. The warm breeze greets her, and Queenie fans the flames prickling up her arms and neck.

Spud steps out onto the balcony with her, his pajama top blowing in the wind and revealing his pale chest, her kimono revealing a glimpse of her untethered breasts. A photo opportunity for the cover of a geriatric, interracial romance novel if ever there was one. Queenie silently scolds herself for comparing him to Denzel in a moment like this. Who cares if the man of her dreams is a different color? It is what's in his heart that matters.

"You okay, honey bun?" Spud asks.

"I can't believe how riled up I am over this storm," Queenie says, fanning herself with both hands. "Can you believe the day after our wedding we are dealing with a hurricane? A hurricane with the same name as your ex-girlfriend and my deceased half sister?"

Queenie knows she is bringing up Iris and this storm a lot, but she can't seem to get over the coincidence of it. If Iris somehow found a way to transform from a ghost into a natural disaster to destroy Queenie's life she would do it.

"Don't panic," Spud says.

"I'm not panicking," Queenie answers. Heat climbs up her face and neck, and she bites her lip.

A gust of wind grabs at her robe and the porch light illuminates the dune grasses swaying in the breeze. A figure in white stands on the walkway below.

Is that Iris's ghost visiting to rub it in? Queenie wonders.

She has no patience for apparitions at this moment. Real or imagined. She retrieves her glasses from the pocket of her robe and puts them on, letting her vision focus. Thankfully, it isn't a ghost after all. It is Old Sally standing on the walkway, looking out at the dark sea. Her long white nightgown blows in the wind, as well as the shawl that is wrapped around her shoulders, giving her an ethereal look. No wonder Queenie thought she was a ghost.

"Mama?" Queenie calls from the balcony, but Old Sally doesn't hear her.

"What's she doing?" Spud asks Queenie.

"Standing on the walkway looking out at the ocean," Queenie says. "I doubt she can see a thing."

"Maybe she's listening," Spud says. "Should I go check on her?"

"Wait. It looks like she's talking to somebody," Queenie says, squinting her eyes behind her glasses.

"Who would she be talking to?" Spud asks.

Queenie leans over the small balcony. "Nobody I can see."

Old Sally is always doing peculiar things. Peculiar, at least, to someone who isn't familiar with the Gullah ways.

A chill climbs Queenie's arms that feels wonderful after so much heat. She can't shake the feeling that something big is about to happen. Big, as in life-changing. A plus-size adventure.

"Let's go back inside and go to bed," Spud tells her.

"Spud, honey, do you think we'll be okay?" She turns to face him.

"Yes, my dearest."

Dearest, she can handle. It's all the food nicknames she has a hard time stomaching. Plus, they make her hungry.

"Are you sure?" Queenie asks.

He puts an arm around her. "In all probability, we'll be fine," he says.

"In all probability?" Queenie doesn't like the sound of that. "What do you mean by fine?"

Spud looks confused.

Voices rise from the kitchen. Their housemates must be gathering again, and it sounds like the television is on. Soon, Queenie will talk to her mama and get her inside, but first, she and Spud will join the others. Animated voices mean something is going on.

Downstairs they watch the latest coordinates of Hurricane Iris, which are being given on the television screen. Iris has been upgraded to a Category 4 storm with the potential to be a Category 5, which could have catastrophic results. Hugo was a Category 4, and it took years for people to recover from the destruction. If they ever did.

Graphics show the latest predictions of where Iris will come ashore. Bright red arrows point to her destination like a bull's-eye on the map of the southeastern United States. Dolphin Island is ground zero.

CHAPTER THIRTY-FOUR

Old Sally

The storm makes Old Sally agitated. It has been impossible to sleep. She stands outside, her nightgown flapping in the wind. The waves crash against the shore in the darkness. The chaos from the sea churns inside her. She holds a hand over her heart and can feel it beating faster than usual. Forces are aligning that she has never experienced. This may be the type of storm that comes once a century. Or maybe once every two hundred years. Perhaps Old Sally's ancestors never saw a storm like this in their lifetimes. But it is Old Sally who is called to witness it now.

If the road leading off the island is clear, perhaps they should drive inland as quickly as they can, ignoring speed limits as they try to outrun Iris. Yet, at the same time, she realizes that everyone will be trying to do that. Best to be in a stronger structure. Old Sally has never felt safe in a car given how Fiddle died, as well as her daughter Maya who was killed here on the island.

In the time Old Sally has been standing here, the wind has ratcheted up its power another notch. These aren't the calm ocean breezes that air out a soul. These are winds that come to destroy. Not because it is angry, but because it is what nature does. It destroys and renews. Even the strongest Gullah folk magic must bow to nature.

An owl hoots in the live oak next to the porch and Old Sally turns toward it with alarm.

To the Gullah people, a hooting owl is a bad omen. A bad omen is the last thing they need on a night like this. Old Sally pulls from her memory what her grandmother taught her. If she is outside and barefoot, she can counteract the evil by pointing a finger at the owl to cancel out its power. Old Sally tosses off her sandals, doing as her grandmother taught her. With silent wings, the owl flies away. She relaxes her shoulders.

Meanwhile, the sea smells different somehow. Saltier. A more pungent version of itself. Tiny particles of sand cling to Old Sally's lips. The dune grasses begin to dance, while the clouds periodically reveal the stars and moon behind. Celestial witnesses to a tempest that from their perspective is a grain of sand. The wind lets out a low growl like a lion cub finding its voice. A voice with plenty of room to grow.

When faced with a storm of this magnitude, her ancestors would have sought refuge on the other side of the island. The highest point is a rise near the cemetery where the old abandoned church sits, falling in on itself, among the live oaks. It is where their old village was before people left for the mainland. Not because of storms, but to find work and raise families because the island could no longer support them. The second highest point is the lighthouse.

Ancestors clamor for Old Sally's attention. Spirits, not

ghosts. Never ghosts. Or hags. Hags possess you and don't let you go. They are like the past that you can't get rid of. Guilt and shame ride a body until it is tormented thoroughly. All used up.

Spirits are good. Benevolent. Helpful. Old Sally could use help now. The others look to her for wisdom, though she doesn't feel that wise.

An ancient weariness comes over her. Exhaustion that comes from living a long time and being ready to go. Life is precious. Yes. But life isn't all there is. The time spent with the ancestors is sacred, too. With death also comes renewal. A different part of the same journey.

The past comes in like the tide. Old Sally remembers when she was a girl and sat by the deathbed of her Grandpa Joe, Granny Sadie's husband. A roomful of relatives and friends waited by his side, singing softly, sending prayers to get heaven ready for him. It was high summer. With candles burning, it was stifling hot in Grandpa Joe's room. This was in the house her grandmother used to live in before she moved in with Sally's family.

The night he died, everyone held paper fans that moved the air around to little good. Paper fans that to Sally looked like butterflies filling the room. Every now and again Sally would feel the wind from their wings. Her grandmother held a young Sally in her lap. Sweat mixed with tears rolled down her grandmother's face. Sally traced their path and tasted their salty essence. Tears were nothing to be afraid of, her grandmother told her. Nor was grief. Grief meant you had loved well. Grief meant you were alive. Mourning was a regular part of living. A necessary part of being alive.

A hand on her shoulder pulls Old Sally away from the past

and back into the here and now. She turns to see Queenie's new husband.

"Queenie sent me to check on you," Spud says, standing close enough to be heard. "Anything I can do for you?"

Old Sally shakes her head no. "Tell my daughter not to worry."

"She's worried about everything right now," he says. "But mainly this storm."

His gray hair lifts with the wind like wings that might lift him into the night.

"Tell her I'll be right in," she says, patting his arm.

Spud nods and then leaves.

People treat her like a child these days. Always checking in on her to make sure she's okay. Checking to make sure she hasn't fallen out of bed, or some such nonsense. Old Sally has been getting up and out of bed for over a hundred years. They need to trust that she has gotten the hang of it by now. Old age doesn't make a person automatically senile. Though it does make a person frail when bones get this old. She understands their concern. But people get caught up in the number of years she's been on this earth instead of their experience with her. They mean well, she knows. And with this storm coming she must admit she feels vulnerable, too. A strong wind could blow her over, that's true. But if she is to leave this world by way of a hurricane, then so be it. She will move on any way she can.

When her grandmother died, many years after Grandpa Joe, people said it was the most peaceful crossing they had ever witnessed. Like Old Sally, her grandmother was ancient and ready to go. In the last year of her life, she passed on everything she could to Old Sally.

A tear rolls down her face, the wind catching it and tossing it away. Human tears are powerful in potions. But now isn't the time for making spells. It is time to let life do as life does.

Can you hear me, Grandmother? Old Sally asks.

Goosebumps come. A sign that a spirit is near. A vision comes, too. Her grandmother stands in the dunes, untouched by the wind.

Remember what I taught you, she says.

Old Sally pauses. Is this real? Or maybe she hears what she wants to hear. Needs to hear. Her grandmother's scars from the out-of-control fire in the Temple kitchen so long ago are illuminated by the moonlight. They look somehow beautiful.

You taught me so much, Old Sally says. *What part do you want me to remember?*

You be solid. It's the ground that be shaky, her grandmother says.

Old Sally narrows her eyes, reaching for understanding. Leave it to her grandmother to pose a riddle from the Afterlife.

What do you mean? That makes no sense, Old Sally says.

Her grandmother doesn't answer, and in the seconds that follow, her image fades away. What is she to remember? Looking out over the dark landscape, Old Sally feels utterly alone.

CHAPTER THIRTY-FIVE

Rose

Though Rose hasn't had a drink for over a decade, she wants one now. Perhaps a glass of red wine, or a vodka tonic with a slice of lime. It is hard to say what beverage is better suited for a hurricane. Perhaps both. One after the other. Instead, she goes into the kitchen to make a pot of coffee. The digital clock says it is after midnight, 12:34 to be exact. Spud waves from the stairway as he returns to Queenie's room. She imagines Queenie has sent him to check on Old Sally. Something they all do these days.

They are opting to stay in the big house tonight instead of their cottage to keep everyone together. They are on the pull-out sofa, the dogs on the floor nearby. The house is quiet except for the sounds accompanying the storm. The wind is steady and slowly growing in power. Palm fronds beat against the side of the house like a drumroll announcing the main event. Every now and again Rose hears something hit the house. Things left unsecured on the island. A plastic bucket clatters through the back patio. When she looks out back, an aluminum lawn chair flies through the air, looking like something from the tornado scene in *The Wizard of Oz*. Will she see her mother riding a bicycle next, a basket on the back for when she steals Toto?

In the past, Max has slept through blizzards and crackling thunderstorms that had Rose on her knees praying to the saints of her childhood. However, something is different with this hurricane. He is wide awake and wanting coffee, too.

Rose pours two cups and retrieves the faded ledger from her purse, handing coffee to Max and then curling up in a side chair. With all the excitement of the storm and Katie's false labor pains—at least they hope they are false—Rose hasn't had time to further explore the old journal. The musty smell causes her to rub her nose and Ethel the dog sneezes. Rose opens the book somewhere in the middle and tries to read the ornate cursive writings from the 1820s, written by Rose's great-great-grandfather, give or take a "great." A portrait of him was at the end of the hallway near her room in the Temple mansion. A stern-looking patriarch if there ever was one, who had the Temple nose. In the portrait, he wore one of the swords Edward played Cowboys and Indians with when they were young. Not that cowboys carried swords usually, but to Edward, anything that let him have power over her was fair play.

Rose thinks of Heather, who also possesses the Temple nose. The more Rose reflects, the more Heather showing up this weekend doesn't seem like an accident. Like the storm, it feels like a convergence. Or in the case of the ledger, a kind of reckoning. A time to take stock of the Temple wreckage.

Rose turns another page, reading a mystery set in the past. A more readable script follows. Lists of numbers. Notations about property deeds, including a rice plantation in Charleston and a property in Richmond, Virginia. Another page lists investments into tea farms in India. More numbers. More names of people who were property.

Rose's face turns warm, but already she is less shocked. Did no one think that slavery wasn't a good thing? Or that in a hundred years or so it might be considered evil? These were her ancestors. Elite southerners. Owners of slaves. Who for whatever reason crossed a vast ocean to forge their way in a new world. *And make money,* she thinks. The Temples have always been good at making money and keeping money. Old money.

When Rose left Savannah after marrying Max at twenty-one years of age, she didn't want any part of the Temple money, and her mother was happy to oblige. At various times, Rose and Max struggled to keep their ranch in Wyoming going, and Rose had a certain amount of pride about their struggle. But in the end, it was her mother's last will and testament that enabled them to come back to Savannah. Would she have ever returned otherwise?

Rose closes the ledger. What exactly is she searching for? If the book contains more secrets, she hasn't found them. To what good are the secrets of dead people, anyway? At some point, the scandals don't matter anymore. Rose wonders now why she went to that old bank vault anyway. Then she remembers what Red told her. Edward was looking through these same papers a few days before he died. Why? What was he looking for? And what is the significance of Edward's daughter showing up literally on their doorstep?

Queenie enters the kitchen, looking wide awake. "I thought you were going to try to get some sleep like the others," she says to Rose.

"It didn't work. You, either?"

"Not a wink," Queenie says. "And Spud is sawing logs like he works at a lumberyard."

"Coffee?" Rose asks.

"No, thanks." Queenie points to the journal. "What's that?"

"I thought it was another Book of Secrets," Rose says. "But it appears to be a list of assets and property."

"Sounds like something that could help you sleep," Queenie says.

"You'd think," Rose says, "but this storm has me wired."

"Me, too." Queenie sits on a kitchen stool.

"So, how's married life?" Rose asks, giving her coffee another stir.

"Too soon to tell," Queenie says. "At least I haven't killed him yet."

"Nothing like a hurricane to put stress on a new relationship," Rose says.

"No kidding," Queenie says, her face serious.

"What's up?" Rose asks.

Their dog Lucy has a fondness for Queenie and ambles over to greet her in the kitchen. At first, Queenie didn't welcome her attention, but now she seems much more at ease. She bends down to pet her.

"Have you ever noticed that I've never owned a dog or cat?"

Rose pauses. Considering everything else going on, this seems an odd question. "You know, to be honest, it never occurred to me."

"Of course, your mother would have never allowed a pet, anyway," Queenie says.

Rose agrees. Her mother wasn't fond of animals. It seemed she wasn't fond of anything living. People tested her patience. Animals served no purpose except to be eaten. It wasn't until

Rose moved out of the house that she had her first cattle dog at the ranch. Lucy looks up at Rose, as if hearing her thoughts.

"But even if I had wanted a pet," Queenie begins again. "I could never get past knowing that I would probably lose them at some point. I didn't think I could bear losing something that I loved."

"Is that what this is about? Are you afraid of losing Spud?"

Queenie's eyes fill with tears.

Rose doesn't expect such a robust show of emotion from Queenie and immediately stands and hugs her broad shoulders.

"Oh, Queenie. It's okay," she says, thinking how interesting it is to know someone your entire life and never know them at all. Not the most vulnerable parts, anyway. "It's better to love someone," Rose says, "even with the risk of losing them. Honestly, it is."

Queenie pulls a clean tissue from her robe pocket. Her crying sounds a little like her laughter. Big, bold, and full-bodied. Rose keeps talking, despite not knowing what to say. "Sometimes I think simply living our lives fully is one of the bravest things we can do."

"You sound like Mama," Queenie says. "And in case you haven't noticed, I'm not a very brave person, Rose." She lowers her eyes.

Rose isn't feeling that brave herself with a hurricane building outside. And she, too, has noticed how they are all beginning to sound a little like Old Sally.

"I wish I could be like you," Queenie says. "You're the most courageous person I know."

"Don't be silly." Rose has never been called brave in her life. In fact, her mother reminded her on a consistent basis what a coward she was when she was growing up.

"I'm serious," Queenie says. "You moved out West when you got married after college, and then you moved back here. You stopped drinking when you realized it was becoming a problem. My God, that takes the heart of a lion. All that and you've been married to the same man all these years and raised a child." Queenie pauses to think of more things, and Rose stops her.

"I guess it's a matter of perspective," Rose says. "According to Mother, I was too lazy to ever reach anything close to my potential."

"Well, your mother was an ass," Queenie says, "and I speak from personal experience. I knew her. Iris wasn't even one-fourth the person you are, Rose Temple."

Now it is Rose's turn to tear up. She thanks Queenie for saying that, even if she has trouble believing the last part.

The lights flicker and then flicker again.

"You think we made Mother mad?" Rose asks.

Queenie cackles. "Well if we did, then Lord help us. Especially if she has anything to do with this storm."

In the next second, the lights go out with a clap, leaving Rose and Queenie in total darkness.

CHAPTER THIRTY-SIX

Violet

Violet wakes suddenly when someone shakes her shoulder. Her first thought is of the old Temple ghosts who used to startle her on occasion when she worked at the Temple mansion. Her second thought is Old Sally. However, it is Tia standing next to the bed with a lit candle.

"Mom, the lights went out."

Jack wakes up as Leisha shows up behind Tia with another candle lit, her eyes wide.

"Do you hear that wind?" Leisha says.

Storms scare her, even relatively tame ones. As a little girl, she would hide under the dining room table after a thunderclap, covering her ears.

"Nothing to worry about." Jack sits up in bed and rubs his eyes. "We're safe here."

Violet wonders if he truly believes they are safe this close to the sea, the house so exposed to the wind.

"We should have evacuated," Tia says.

"We tried," Leisha says. "Remember?"

"Maybe we should try again," Tia says.

They are close to bickering. Everyone is stressed.

"Well, the road is probably still closed," Violet says. "But we'll be fine. You'll see."

The girls sit on the end of the bed, looking toward the windows.

"I wish we could see what's happening," Leisha says. "It's like having a blindfold on."

"The wind gives me the creeps." Tia's hand trembles, making the candlelight dance.

"What should we do, Mom?" Leisha asks, resorting to biting a nail.

"Storms are temporary, honey. They move in, and they move out. That's their job."

"I'd better get up and see if there's anything I need to do," Jack says to Violet.

As soon as he gets up, Tia and Leisha put their candles on the nightstand and climb in with Violet. She has missed snuggling with her girls. Even though they are practically grown, they still act like children sometimes. The hurricane looming out over the Atlantic is making Violet feel shaky, too.

"You coming?" Dressed now, Jack grabs a flashlight from their dresser.

"In a minute," she says, stroking Leisha's hair.

Violet hates to admit how much she has missed the closeness she had with her daughters before adolescence hit. They are still close, but she doubts it will ever be the same as before.

"Mom, what if the hurricane blows our house away?" Leisha says.

"You mean with us in it?" Tia scoots closer.

"We'll be fine," Violet says again, her throat tightening.

Nature is never to be underestimated. Two scared teenagers are not to be underestimated, either.

After some coaxing, the girls go back to their rooms to get dressed. Violet dresses in candlelight and makes her way down the dark hallway and into the kitchen where Max hands her a flashlight. Rose sits in the living room with Katie and Angela, who are also up. Tia and Leisha are now with Jack in the kitchen. Queenie, Spud, and Old Sally are the only ones not here. However, Rose tells Violet that Queenie was just here and went upstairs after the power went out to try to get some rest.

Violet asks if anyone has seen Old Sally and no one has. She retraces her steps down the hallway and knocks on Old Sally's bedroom door. When Violet opens the door, the bed is empty. The wind rattles the side door that leads out to the deck. Jack and Max had put sandbags against the door, but they have been pushed aside.

Where are you? Violet asks, using their underground network.

Old Sally doesn't answer.

Violet steps out onto the dark deck and instantly regrets it. Though the storm is still young, the wind is already strong. Sand burns her eyes. She steps back inside to find something to cover her face and grabs Old Sally's summer robe on the back of the door and puts it on. It smells of her and reminds Violet of their early-morning talks, before Violet leaves to go to her tea shop.

With the robe pulled up over her nose and mouth, Violet goes back outside. Her flashlight highlights the grasses on the dunes frantically waving like they are warning her away. If this is only the beginning of the storm, what will it be like later?

"Old Sally?" Violet calls, her words quickly tossed aside by the wind. She holds onto the railing and follows it around to the front of the house. A bigger pile of sandbags blocks the front door, a flimsy fortress against the storm surge predicted to come. Though it does no good, Violet calls out Old Sally's name again and then walks down the front steps toward the ocean. The wind in her ears reminds her of flapping sails.

How would Old Sally ever be able to stand up against this wind? Violet is more than fifty years younger, and she can barely navigate it. The wind steals Violet's breath away. Her shoulder begins to throb. But is it phantom pains like Katie's false labor?

Where are you? she asks Old Sally again. She imagines the channel opening between them but hears nothing in response.

Violet shines her flashlight up the beach toward the abandoned lighthouse, the destination of many of Old Sally's walks. She has never understood her grandmother's fascination with the place. It's like an altar she visits every day to worship some unseen god.

Surely, you wouldn't have gone there, Violet thinks, looking up the beach. *Not with a storm coming.*

Turning her flashlight back toward the house, Violet sees Jack waving at the top of the stairs for Violet to come inside.

When she joins him, he hugs her close, and they walk together around the side of the deck to Old Sally's room. Once they are inside, he pulls the sandbags as close as he can and closes the door.

"What were you thinking?" he asks, though she can tell his question is more out of concern than anger.

"I can't find Old Sally," Violet says.

He looks at the empty bed, as though not noticing it before.

"Let's go back to the kitchen and see if anyone else has seen her," Jack says. He leads the way back to where everyone is now gathered.

In candlelight, they listen to the wind. It is 1:30 on a Monday morning and the full force of the storm isn't even due to hit until 3:30 or 4 A.M. Violet asks if anyone has seen Old Sally. They go from silence to everyone talking at once, but the consensus is that no one has seen her.

"Let's search the house just in case," Jack says, giving instructions on who is to go where.

They each take a candle or flashlight and head off in different directions. Rose and Max go back to search their cottage. Katie and Angela search the garage. Queenie and Spud, who until recently were napping, join them and look in every bedroom and bathroom upstairs. When they all meet back in the kitchen, their concern has reached a new level.

"Lord in heaven," Queenie says, "I just saw her a while ago from the balcony. Spud checked on her. Where in the world would she go? Doesn't she know a hurricane is coming?"

Spud puts an arm around Queenie and tells her to stay calm. It doesn't work.

"Maybe it's nearing her time," Violet says, and then questions the wisdom of saying that now.

"Her time?" Queenie asks, picking up on Violet's fear.

Tia and Leisha look at Violet. "What are you saying, Mama?" Tia asks.

"Never mind," Violet says, refusing to alarm them any more than they already are.

A lightning bolt of pain shoots through Violet's shoulder. Definitely real this time. In the next second, Katie grabs her stomach and leans over with a half grunt, half scream. Holding the edge of the countertop, her knuckles are white from the strain.

Tension crackles through the kitchen as looks are exchanged. Who will deliver this baby if they can't get to a hospital? Only Old Sally has done this before. In fact, she delivered Violet. Now they have even more reason to find her.

"That sure didn't feel like false labor pains," Katie says, no longer leaning over.

"You are not allowed to have this baby during a hurricane. Do you hear me?" Angela's panic feels almost contagious.

"It could still be Braxton-Hicks, right?" Rose turns to look for Violet to agree with her. But Violet isn't so sure.

With Old Sally missing, Katie possibly in labor, and a hurricane approaching, nobody speaks. Violet feels almost paralyzed, not knowing which action to take.

"It's a first baby," she says finally to reassure everyone. "First babies take their time coming. I was in labor with Leisha for almost twelve hours."

Angela sends a grateful look in Violet's direction, and Katie appears visibly relieved.

"Just in case, we need to find Mama," Queenie says. "She is the only one who has ever delivered a baby before."

"Should we look on the beach?" Spud asks.

"Have you heard those waves?" Rose says. "Why would she risk life and limb to go to the beach?"

"I think she may have gone to the lighthouse," Violet says.

"But why would she go there?" Rose asks.

They all talk at once with different theories until Katie lets out another long moan. All the while, Angela reminds her to breathe.

"Better start timing those," Violet says, and Angela nods.

"Do you know something about this lighthouse that we don't?" Queenie asks.

"It's like a touchstone for her," Violet answers. "She walked there every day until a few months ago."

"Actually, that makes sense," Queenie says. "It holds special memories for her."

"I'll go see if she's there," Jack says.

"I'll go, too," Spud offers.

"Not without me, you won't," says Queenie.

"Have you forgotten a hurricane is coming?" Violet says to Queenie, concern in her voice. She is not about to lose her mother again, having only recently found her.

"She may need us," Queenie says, which is hard to argue with. "And we sure need her," she adds, looking at Katie.

Meanwhile, Violet's shoulder appears to be waking up with a clear and steady warning of what is to come.

CHAPTER THIRTY-SEVEN

Queenie

"Sweet Jesus," Queenie says to herself. "The last thing I expected was for Mama to go missing during a hurricane."

She doesn't know whether walking to the lighthouse during a storm is the smartest thing to do, but she trusts Jack and Spud to keep them all safe.

Before they go in that direction, however, Queenie and Spud circle the house with flashlights to make sure her mama isn't somewhere outside and has fallen and can't get up like those television commercials that advertise medical alert systems.

The wind increases in power, making Queenie glad she has some substance to her. Otherwise, Iris might knock her over. It helps that Queenie and Spud are in an armlock, each carrying a flashlight so they can see ahead of them.

For better or worse, her marriage vows said. But she didn't expect the *worse* to come a day after the ceremony.

The first thing they notice from circling the house is all the debris. Plastic bags cling to the trees like SOS flags. Palm fronds are everywhere. Drifts of sand have blown against the house. The patio has disappeared, covered with sand, with no possibility of finding footprints to confirm where Old Sally might have gone.

Within seconds of being outside, an airborne milk jug causes them to duck. An excellent test of aging reflexes. Then an empty soda can nearly hits Queenie in the head. She jerks sideways just in time. She feels like she is fielding foul balls at a World Series between the Hurricanes and the Newlyweds.

There's no way Mama is out in this, Queenie thinks. *If the wind doesn't blow her away, a soda can might take her out for good.*

Heaviness sits in the center of Queenie's chest. Why would her mama risk her life to go out in this storm? How could she even find the lighthouse in this darkness? It would help if the beacon still worked, but that hasn't been turned on in decades.

When they turn the corner of the house, the wind is so strong they struggle to move forward. Spud turns them around to go back the way they came, the wind at their backs. At least they can breathe again. The wind pushes them back to the house. Once inside, they shake the sand from their shoes, clothes, and hair. Now that they've gone around the house, they have a sense of what it will be like to get to the lighthouse.

Rose sits next to Katie, waiting for the next real or fake contraction. Meanwhile, Angela looks like she could use a strong sedative. Katie—distracted as she is by potential motherhood—asks if there are any signs of Old Sally. The two have become close over the last few months.

"Nothing?" Violet asks Queenie when they return.

"Nothing," Queenie repeats.

She remembers Old Sally's story of the love of her life. Would that be enough to get her to walk through a hurricane?

"I think we need to check the lighthouse," Queenie says. "If she's not in the house, it's the one place she might go."

"The other day she told me that her father helped build that old lighthouse in the 1920s," Spud says.

"She told me that, too," Leisha says, and helps Queenie brush the sand out of her hair.

"She hated that it was abandoned," Tia says, as she helps her sister.

"It's supposed to be locked," Spud says, "but when I checked it last fall, the lock had rusted off the door."

"So, she could go inside?" Queenie asks.

"I think so."

"Max and I will check it out," Jack says, asking Spud to stay at the house and watch out for everybody.

Queenie could kiss Jack for giving Spud a reason to stay behind. She doesn't want to lose her new husband in this storm along with her old mother. Was her wedding only yesterday?

Iris is due to come ashore in two hours. Her mama is missing. Katie is in labor. Or not. Her one and only honeymoon has been rescheduled like it is only a dental appointment. Could it get any worse?

A pounding on the back door is her answer.

CHAPTER THIRTY-EIGHT

Old Sally

Old Sally stands on the beach below the lighthouse. The wind rips at her raincoat, wanting to tear it from her body. Hurricane Iris is already a formidable presence, just like Old Sally's former employer, who asserted her stubborn power up until the last moment of her life. She knows this because she helped Iris transition. Or tried to. Old Sally doesn't begin to understand the forces that call together a storm of this magnitude. For all she knows, the spirit of Iris Temple is riling this hurricane up. If anyone could, it would be her.

The power Old Sally possesses isn't the harsh power of lording over, but the soft power of her Gullah ancestors. It is the power of knowing the land, as well as medicines and charms. Some might say her beliefs are based on superstition. However, it is much deeper. She also believes in the white man's religion, and the idea that help is everywhere. Not just in the spirit world but here on earth.

It isn't like her to leave the house in the middle of the night.

But the dream that woke her was so vivid, more real than real, she felt like she didn't have a choice. The visions of her ancestors that have been coming for weeks now mostly have to do with going on a long journey or getting things ready. Preparations. The destination being a hard-earned peace.

In her most recent dream, her grandmother told Old Sally to meet her at the lighthouse to build the courage fires. Her grandmother looked like she did when Old Sally was a girl, with her dark skin and solid white hair. She was a strong woman. A strong woman who taught Old Sally everything she knows.

The wind wails that it doesn't care about dreams and ancestors, and especially not strong women.

But Old Sally does, and she will honor them as long as she has breath in her body.

You coming, girl? Her grandmother's spirit stands a hundred feet away, at the top of the lighthouse steps, unaffected by the wind. The concrete lighthouse looms behind her.

Old Sally hasn't been called *girl* for close to a century. It makes her smile, despite a hurricane bullying her.

I'm coming, Old Sally tells her. She steps from the solid sand of high tide into the deep, soft sand of the dunes, struggling until she reaches the concrete steps that lead up to the lighthouse. She questions the wisdom of leaving the house as a storm approaches, but Old Sally has spent most of her lifetime visiting this lighthouse.

In a way, she feels like she is still dreaming. She has no idea how she got here through the growing winds, the waves crashing ever higher on the beach, and the salt spray reaching for her with every wave. The moon gave her very little help in finding her way. If not for the large flashlight Jack left on her nightstand earlier that evening, she might never have made it.

But at the same time, she could find her way to this lighthouse with her eyes closed, her body over the years having memorized every step.

At the bottom of the steps, a sun-bleached sign warns people that the lighthouse is closed. No trespassing allowed. The wind howls around her. Old Sally closes her eyes to rest them. The wind has dried them out, and the sand makes them burn.

What do you want with me here? she asks, looking up at her grandmother. But when she opens her eyes, the image is gone.

The lighthouse continues to loom up ahead. She has a history here. A past that haunts her, as well as sustains her. After she got too old to work for the Temples, her visits to the lighthouse increased. She needed rituals to fill her days that didn't involve dusting and running a vacuum cleaner. For many years a walk to the lighthouse was what she did first thing in the morning when the sun came up. She rarely missed her daily walk unless the weather refused to cooperate, but sometimes she even walked in the rain. All this training must have helped her get here.

The beacon was turned off sometime in the 1980s. Decommissioned, the officials said. Another NO TRESPASSING sign went up by the only door. A lock added. For twenty years it has made her sad to think of a lighthouse not shining its light. Not fulfilling its purpose for being. Too many people don't know what their light is, either. They convince themselves they don't have one. Or other people convince them. Or they say their light isn't good enough, bright enough, or is too bright when all that's required is to stand in their Truth. Thankfully, Old Sally can see her light.

However, the lighthouse is also a monument to her biggest regret. A memorial to youth and a life she could have had if

things had gone differently. After Fiddle died, she felt
unmoored, like a boat on a vast sea in danger of crashing
ashore. Grief does that to a person. The ground gives way, and
people are set adrift. The lighthouse saved her. It gave her a
way to honor the past and finally make peace with it.

Old Sally rests. She must garner her strength to climb the
concrete steps. A long life carries so much grief. Not only from
her own life but also the losses passed on to her from her
ancestors. Sorrow from those days of not being free and not
getting to choose what to do with their lives. Old Sally carried
this history with her to the Temple mansion every day she
worked there. She scrubbed grief into the floorboards as she
cleaned the Temple mansion. Old Sally cooked grief into every
meal. She polished grief into the silver until it shone like a full
moon. That is why that old house burned down. It was a
necessary sacrifice. All the grief needed to burn away and turn
to ash, so her people could finally be free. And so the Temple
grief could be set free, too. Sadness from knowing what they
did, even if they never acknowledged it.

Not much longer now, her grandmother says, reappearing at
the top of the steps near the entrance of the lighthouse.

Why did you bring me here? Old Sally says, now concerned
that it was too much to ask. *To get my old heart to finally stop
beating? To push it beyond what it can do?*

Fear hits, nearly staggering her. When she doesn't resist it,
it moves on with the wind.

After working in the Temple mansion for so many years
and going up and down the spiral staircase thousands of times,
Old Sally kept up her exercise by climbing these concrete steps
stretching between the beach and the lighthouse. Forty-two of
them, to be exact. She started counting them after reading an
article in *Reader's Digest* about how to keep her mind active by

counting things and working on crossword puzzles. The old iron railing still stands, except for one section about halfway up. There, she must rely on balance to keep herself upright.

One at a time, she takes the steps now. Every five steps she rests. Where the railing disappears, her grandmother takes her hand. Real or imagined, it is a great help.

When the lighthouse was being built in the early 1900s, the government hired Gullah men to be the laborers and paid them less than white men. Her father was one of those men and was proud that he had a part in the lighthouse being here. When she was a girl, he walked with her up the beach to show her his handiwork. He told her stories of mixing concrete to make the floors and walls inside, as well as the steps outside that hold her now. Back then, you could see the beacon from their house, which was the closest thing to having God looking over her in the darkness that she could imagine.

You did good, Daddy, she says to his memory.

It feels strange saying "Daddy" as a hundred-year-old woman. It has been decades since she uttered the word. Just like it has been decades since she has been called a *girl*. But the girl still lives inside her even now, and Old Sally remembers her often these days. Her endless curiosity. Her delight in simple things. Sunshine. A beautiful seashell. A sweet breeze. The sound of laughter and the playful chatter between family and friends. Like school photographs causing her to recall specific memories, every year of her life is documented inside her. She is the girl she once was, even as an old woman. Remembering that makes her life evergreen, even during the bleakest winter.

The Gullah menfolk tended to die off early, leaving the women—her mother, grandmothers, and aunts—to keep things going. Even in her dreams, it is the old women who visit her, rarely the men. Maybe it is true what she has thought for years, that women are the stronger ones. Raising children and tending homes. Midwives for births and deaths. Storytellers. Magic keepers.

Her father died when she was nine. She remembers his massive arms and how he would lift her up as a young child and carry her on his shoulder like she was as light as a seagull's feather. He smelled of tobacco and taught her how to have a poker face and not reveal—with wide eyes or a sudden gasp—what cards he held in his hand when he played blackjack with his friends. These memories live in the past and feel further away than the recent dreams of her ancestors. One is a remembrance, the other a visitation. Whenever her grandmother shows herself, it is like she is standing in the room with her. Flesh and blood. Sometimes she can even feel the weight of her sitting on the end of Old Sally's bed.

At the top of the outside concrete steps, Old Sally stops. Her knees quake with the task. Finally, she touches the familiar coolness of the metal door, corroded from age and salty air. Her hands shake as she pushes against the door. A door that will not open.

Her grandmother now stands next to her, a calm presence in the growing chaos.

I need help, Old Sally tells her.

Her thoughts create the opening between the worlds. The threshold Old Sally and Violet have begun to explore.

Be gentle, and it will come, her grandmother says, regarding the door.

This makes no sense to Old Sally. This door does not need a soft touch, but a man-sized shove. Or two. Or three.

But Old Sally heeds her advice. A harsh wind at her shoulder, she turns the handle and gives it a gentle push. The door swings wide open with the help of the wind, nearly pulling her inside.

Steady, her grandmother tells her. *You must save your strength to build the courage fires for the others.*

If only someone would tell her what that means. It is June in the South. Humid and hot. No need for a fire of any kind. Not a literal fire at least.

As Old Sally steps through the threshold, the past greets her with a metallic, musty smell. She blinks, shining her flashlight into the dark room, her eyes adjusting to the new darkness. The absence of the wind is a blessing. Yet, the sudden silence disorients her. She falters as past and present collide, steadying herself to keep from dropping to the concrete floor. To reorient, she aims the flashlight at the old metal cot still in the corner, and the metal desk chair nearby, companion to the metal desk across the room. An old gray army blanket covers the bed with its edges tucked in over the narrow mattress.

No one has ever lived here full time. For decades, old Mr. Harrison stayed on stormy nights to make sure the light stayed lit for passing vessels. A set of metal stairs winds up the center of the structure into a small observation deck, where the great beacon holds center stage. For something so old and so close to the sea, the moisture has done little damage. Everything inside is remarkably well preserved.

This is where she met Fiddle on their one night together. The closest she has ever come to loving someone with her whole heart. From the pocket of her raincoat, Old Sally takes out the only thing she brought with her when she left. A piece of worn pink fabric with an *A* embroidered on it. *A* for Annabelle. Her sweet baby girl who died after only six days of living on this earth.

Dark and sweet as night, Old Sally says to herself as she

fingers the cloth, remembering the warmth that at one time lived beneath the fabric.

The wind wails outside and reminds Old Sally of her howling grief when Annabelle died. If only she could have traded some of her time here on earth so that Annabelle could have lived longer. No need for Old Sally to have so many days, years, and decades when a tiny creature so pure and beautiful gets only six days. It doesn't make sense to her how life-and-death things are decided. So many things just don't make sense. Automobile accidents. Slavery. Random blessings and curses everywhere.

Meanwhile, she can't remember a time when she was more tired. She lies down on the old cot and closes her eyes, feeling she could sleep for another lifetime. Every bone in her body confirms her journey through the hurricane.

Seconds later, the spell of the past is broken, and she realizes for the first time why her grandmother has brought her here: to get the others to follow.

CHAPTER THIRTY-NINE

Rose

The pounding on the back door brings everyone to see who it might be. When Queenie opens the door, she shakes her head and says, "What are you doing here?" as though the storm has decided to introduce itself.

When Queenie steps aside, Rose hides a grimace. In the back doorway stands Heather, windblown and breathless from the storm.

"I thought the road onto the island was closed," Rose says, a flashlight the only light between them. "A power line had fallen."

"They moved it," Heather says. "The road had just opened again when I drove up. I was the only person not heading off the island. But those people won't get far," she continues. "The interstate is at a total standstill. People are stranded and running out of gas."

While Rose takes this in, Heather steps past her into the dark kitchen. She takes off a hooded windbreaker and throws it on the kitchen counter. Rose's jaw tightens with the familiarity Heather assumes.

"What did you find out at the bank?" she asks Rose.

Rose pauses. "That's an odd question given what's going on outside."

"Is it?" Heather shrugs in the shadows of the kitchen.

"Wait, how did you know I went to the bank?" Rose asks.

"You told me you were going to the bank," Heather says. "Remember?"

"No, I don't remember that." Rose is confident she didn't share this bit of information with Heather. A person she doesn't know or trust.

"Yes, you did." Heather smiles and cocks her head, looking almost pleased with Rose's agitation.

However, Rose refuses to bite the wormy hook Heather dangles in front of her. She has more important things to deal with.

"What's going on?" Max approaches, his flashlight spreading more light into the foyer.

"You remember Heather," Rose says to Max.

Max nods at Heather and looks back at Rose like a bouncer in a bar waiting for instructions to bounce. But Rose's lifelong goal has been to avoid conflict, not engage in it. As a girl, if she had ever questioned her mother's criticisms, she believed the earth might open and swallow her. Back then, Rose stayed in the kitchen with Old Sally or played with Violet in the courtyard. Even today it challenges her to confront anyone, even if they deserve it.

"Is the road open again?" Max asks Heather.

She says it is and repeats what she reported to Rose. "Have you decided to stay on the island?" she asks Max.

"Sounds like we don't have a choice," Max says.

Like all previous encounters with Heather, something about it doesn't make sense. When they tried to evacuate before, both lanes of the road leading off the island were being used for evacuation. How would Heather get back on the island? And why would someone drive directly into a storm when the island is being evacuated? Was she hoping to find the house empty? Also, how did she know Rose went to the bank?

Violet returns to the kitchen and looks at Rose as if to ask, *What the hell is she doing here?*

Rose answers with an *I have no idea* shrug of her shoulders.

Violet holds a piece of paper. "It's a note from Old Sally," she says to Rose. "I found it next to her bed. I'm not sure why I didn't notice it before."

"The old lady is missing?" Heather asks.

No one answers.

The windows rattle with stronger gusts, and the thought of Old Sally out in this storm somewhere makes Rose tremble.

"What does the note say?" Rose asks Violet.

They gather around the kitchen island, which looks somewhat romantic with all the candles burning. "The only thing it says," Violet begins, "is how important it is for us to meet her at the lighthouse."

"The lighthouse?" Rose looks at Max, worry etched in her eyes.

Violet nods, mirroring Rose's concern.

It was only last week that Rose and Max walked up the beach and explored the old lighthouse. The outside steps were crumbling. Part of the railing was gone. Not the safest place for an old woman to go.

"Was the note to all of us, or only you?" Rose asks.

"I have no idea," Violet says. "It isn't addressed to anybody."

"Sounds like she means all of you," Heather says.

Rose and Violet turn toward Heather. Does she want them out of the house? Does she think they keep the Temple jewels in their closet or something? Although her closet was precisely where Rose kept her nest egg for years.

"Why the lighthouse?" Max asks.

"I'm not sure," Violet says.

"How did she even get there in this wind?" Rose asks.

"Maybe the old lady is losing it and just wandered off," Heather says.

"She left a note." Rose shoots Heather a look that says, *How dare you.*

"Old Sally is a lot sharper than most of us," Violet says.

And definitely a lot sharper than you, Heather, Rose wants to add, her anger rising.

In the next moment, hairs raise on the back of Rose's neck, and it's not from her anger at Heather. A loud creaking noise quickly crescendos like a giant rusty nail being pulled out of an equally giant piece of lumber.

A crashing sound follows, and the entire house shakes. Violet's girls scream like extras in a horror film and the dogs bark. For a moment nobody moves.

Rose grabs Max's arm and tells him to check on Katie and Angela, whose bedroom is upstairs. He points his flashlight into the darkness and dashes away. Rose follows Queenie and Spud up to Queenie's bedroom, where the sound appears to have originated.

When Queenie opens her door, she screams something that evokes the entire Holy family: Jesus, Mary, and Joseph. The live oak that had been growing for two centuries next to the garage has fallen into Queenie's room. Most of the roof went down with the tree, as well as a considerable chunk of the porch and wall. Queenie's bed is crushed underneath massive limbs, where only a short time ago Queenie and Spud were lying. The strong wind rattles the leaves and whistles through where a wall once stood. Spanish moss clings to the limbs like ghosts hanging on for dear life.

The tree was one of the oldest on the island and has withstood storms for hundreds of years. The oaks on the island are second in age only to the Angel Oak up the coast near Charleston, which dates to the Revolutionary War.

When Rose questions how the situation could get any worse, it begins to rain.

CHAPTER FORTY

Violet

The rain forces everyone into action. Violet grabs anything in Queenie's room that she can lift that is not destroyed and takes it to a dry part of the house. Jack and Max disappear to get tarps to nail over the gaping hole in Queenie's wall and ceiling. Within seconds, everyone is soaked, as the rain comes down harder.

When the men return, Jack reports to Violet that most of their cars are crushed under the giant limbs of the tree. Max's truck is the only one that appears to be drivable. His look confirms that there is no way they can evacuate now.

Panicking is not helpful, Violet reminds herself.

She has attempted to reach Old Sally via the underground-between-worlds-radio, and Old Sally is not answering. To make matters worse, Violet's left shoulder has finally woken up with a hurricane warning of its own.

"What will we do?" Violet asks Jack.

He pauses. "I have no idea," he says.

The thought of Jack not knowing what they should do unnerves her even more.

Violet helps Queenie spread a smaller tarp over her dresser, and Queenie wipes tears and rain from her eyes. Violet hugs her, telling her everything will be all right. But she doesn't know if that's true. This could be only the beginning.

"They're just things," Violet hears herself say. She said something similar when Queenie lost everything in the Temple fire. However, Queenie helped her understand that losing things can be devastating, too. In a way, it's like losing your identity and a feeling of safety in the world.

We need you, Violet tells Old Sally, trying again to reach her.

She wishes this mysterious communication system of theirs also had an answering machine. Violet would leave a frantic message asking her to come home immediately.

"My wedding dress is ruined," Queenie says, pointing to the chair where it was draped, now crushed by the tree.

"Maybe it's still salvageable," Violet says.

Was it only yesterday that her mother and Spud spoke their vows to one another? It seems like weeks ago.

"I thought Iris might *crash* the wedding, but it seems she waited until the honeymoon," Queenie says.

From the floor, she picks up the red hat she wore at her wedding and puts it on to keep the rain from her eyes. Leave it to Queenie to be colorful even during a hurricane.

"After this storm blows over we'll see what we can do about your dress," Violet says, making her voice sound hopeful.

"It's not like I'll ever wear it again," Queenie says. "I'm just hoping it's not a sign."

"Since when do you look for signs?"

"Since Iris crashed a tree into my bedroom," she says, water dripping from her brim. "Is Mama still missing?"

"She's at the lighthouse," Violet says. "I found a note. She wants us all to meet her there."

"How did I not know this?" Queenie asks, pulling Spanish moss from her lampshade, delivered by the tree.

"I have no idea," Violet says.

"Why is she at the lighthouse?"

"I have no idea about that, either."

Pain pings Violet's arm. She can't believe just a few hours ago she was convinced her sixth-sense shoulder had somehow given up the ghost, so to speak.

While the others work to salvage more of Queenie's things, Violet returns to her bedroom. She can't just do nothing. The lighthouse is only a ten-minute walk if she runs some of the way. She can get there and back with Old Sally in half an hour. That is, if she can convince her that she should come home. Violet puts on her raincoat. She has taken this walk a thousand times or more, although not in the dark, and not with a hurricane offshore.

Violet leaves a note on the dresser telling Jack what she's going to do. He will try to talk her out of it if she speaks to him directly. Either way, he will be upset with her for wanting to do this. The first rule if someone gets lost is to not go looking for them, or you might get lost yourself. But what if Old Sally needs her? What if this is her time to transition and Violet isn't there?

Violet leaves the house with one of the bigger flashlights. She keeps her raincoat and hood pulled close and wraps a scarf around her nose and mouth. Seeing the downed tree is like seeing an old friend struck down. It takes her breath away as much as the wind. Their cars are indeed crushed underneath. The wind pushes her through the dunes and down the beach, a giant hand on her back urging her to get to the lighthouse. The waves are like an advancing army inching their way up the beach. But it is the wind, by far, that is a different beast than anything Violet has ever experienced. It has teeth and a bite to it. Yet, it is only an infant compared to what it will grow up to be.

How did Old Sally walk in this? It was earlier in the evening, but it would still be difficult. And why would she go to the lighthouse, anyway?

The ancestors, Violet thinks. It is the only explanation that makes sense. Old Sally must have had another dream.

Increasingly, Old Sally has lived in both worlds. The everyday world marked by days, months and years, and the timeless world of her ancestors. Ancestors, Old Sally told her only a day or two ago, who seem as real to her as Violet.

When Violet visited the lighthouse as a girl with Old Sally, its presence felt unlike when she went up into the attic at the Temple mansion. At the mansion, Violet dealt with a whole house full of dead Temples that rattled her with their creepiness. At least at first. However, her Gullah ancestors are more benevolent spirits. Preferring to be helpful, instead of obnoxious.

Violet stops walking. Her thoughts have been racing, and she hasn't kept track of where she is in relation to the old lighthouse. Thick clouds cover the moon, which doesn't help.

Thanks to Old Sally, the island's history is alive to her now. It isn't just the place she grew up, but a place with a past. A past with hidden treasures. With the distraction of modern life, Gullah traditions are more threatened than ever before. The winds of change want to clear the coastline of all evidence that the Gullah culture ever existed. Old Sally's primary concern is that everything will be forgotten.

At times, it feels to Violet like an overwhelming mission to be the person who remembers. The person working to preserve an entire culture. Yet, without Old Sally, Violet would never have recognized the imprint her people have made on this island, as well as the mark they have made on her own life.

Using her flashlight, she searches for familiar landmarks. She finally sees the shape of the lighthouse up ahead. Between the beach and the structure are the dunes. Beyond the dunes is a forested part of the island with a cluster of live oaks and underbrush.

The only remnants left of the Gullah culture are a one-room schoolhouse on the far end of the island, stone ruins around their cemetery, and the small praise church Old Sally went to when she was a girl, now covered from floor to rafters with wisteria. These structures blend in so well with their surroundings they are almost hidden.

This area is always where the wild indigo grows, another reminder of the past. A crop that was cultivated and used to dye clothes for hundreds of years. The roots of the plant are used for medicines. Last week Violet and Old Sally collected and dried some of the roots for indigo root tea, known to be good for digestion and kidney ailments.

Violet's mind remains active as the wind continues to push her up the beach. It is slow-going; she can only see two or three feet ahead of her with the flashlight. It is her intuition that reminds her to turn where the island juts left.

When she goes in this new direction, the wind pushes her sideways. She steadies herself to keep from falling. What propels her forward is the thought that Old Sally might need her. In a way, her grandmother is like the lighthouse. A beacon to future generations, yet also somehow abandoned and not appreciated for the history she holds.

Aiming the flashlight upward, Violet sees the lighthouse

looming above her. She heads into the dunes that lead to the steps. Climbing the steps from the beach, her left hand clutches her raincoat and flashlight while her right uses the railing to pull herself forward. The wind tugs at her clothes while burning her eyes and stretching her skin wherever it is exposed.

Violet can't imagine what the full thrust of this storm will be like in two hours, when it is supposed to finally make landfall. Surely, no one will be able to stand, much less walk in this wind and driving rain. It is a challenging climb in a storm. She pulls herself up each step until she reaches for the railing and nothing is there. Her body lurches forward, and she screams as she tries to not fall headfirst into the dunes. Her heart takes a quick elevator to her throat until she steadies herself. For the next few steps, she places each foot solidly before moving it to the next level. Finally, the railing returns. She stands for the longest time, not moving, appreciating the railing's support. Her heartbeat calms as she stands on the landing in front of the lighthouse. She made it.

When Violet tries to open the large metal door, it doesn't budge. With one fist, she beats on it. If Old Sally is inside, she doubts she will hear her.

If, she hears herself say.

What if Violet has come all this way for nothing?

Shining the light on the handle, she pushes against it with her right shoulder. Someone pulls from the other side, and Violet stumbles into the lighthouse. An instant later, the wind grabs the door and slams it behind her.

CHAPTER FORTY-ONE

Queenie

Queenie's bedroom is soaked with water and filled with the pungent destruction of live oak and unearthed soil. For a moment, she feels much sadder about the tree than her bedroom. A bedroom can be rebuilt.

"It's a good thing we weren't celebrating our honeymoon when it happened," Spud says, with a wink she assumes is meant to reassure her.

Queenie leans into him as they survey the damage, a large puddle forming on her oval rug. "This is serious, Mister Grainger. Please don't make light of it. Where are we going to live now?"

"My place, Mrs. Grainger, until we get everything fixed good as new."

The *Mrs.* catches Queenie by surprise. She prefers *Ms.* to *Mrs.* Besides that, she hasn't told him yet that she plans to keep her old name—Queenie Temple—given that's how everyone in Savannah and on the island has known her for the last forty years. She claimed the Temple name after working for Iris for only a year. If she was going to be treated like someone lower than the graveyard dirt her mama keeps in the flour bin, she decided to legally change her name. Since she resided in South Carolina, nobody in Savannah even knew about it until it was official. It was an act of pure defiance, and something she has not for one instant regretted. The Temple name gives her a little prestige, like driving a new Mercedes instead of taking the city bus.

When Iris married, she refused to change her last name, too, to keep the power that came with the Temple title. It doesn't matter to Queenie that she is a Temple by way of the back door, as the illegitimate child of Iris's father, the second or third Edward Temple in a long line of Edwards that Queenie can never keep straight.

Meanwhile, all this chaos and debris has stirred up Queenie's past. Besides Spud, the only other man Queenie ever slept with was Iris's husband, Oscar—Violet's father. Not that it was Queenie's idea for one second. Although she did develop feelings for him. Complicated and confusing feelings. None of which she has for Spud.

Come to think of it, natural disasters don't offer a whole lot of choice, either, she reasons. Maybe that's why she is all of a sudden thinking of these things again.

Oscar had his demons, too. The only time Iris showed him any respect, as far as Queenie observed, was to change her will at the last minute and honor his wishes that Violet inherit the mansion. Oscar knew that Iris's only weakness was deathbed requests and the fear of what might happen if she didn't fulfill them. Queenie still can't believe Iris did it. If not for her falling into a coma soon afterward, she probably would have changed the will back lickety-split.

"What are you thinking about, sweet-tart?" Spud kisses Queenie on the cheek.

Queenie doesn't comment on his latest confectionary nickname, except to note that it could be taken in the wrong way. She is not a tart or a loose woman by any imaginative stretch. However, she is certain Spud didn't intend it as anything bad. She also doesn't answer his question. He might not understand her flirtation with prestige. She will wait for the ideal moment to broach the subject of keeping the Temple name.

"Maybe the good Lord wanted to teach me a lesson that it's not good to get attached to things," Queenie says.

"Possibility," Spud says, "although it could also be about an old tree doing battle with a strong wind and losing."

"True." Queenie appreciates Spud's practical nature. "Let's hope we don't lose the battle, too."

"Indeed," Spud says, reaching to straighten a bow tie that isn't there. He asks if she is okay and she says she's been better. She assumes he knows how much this house means to her. Not only was it her childhood home in its previous rendition, but it has also been her first real home since Edward burned down the Temple mansion. At least everybody thinks it was Edward who burned it down, given he was walking around in the mansion that night and didn't get out alive.

To this day, it perplexes Queenie why Edward would do such a thing. She knew he could be a pompous jerk, but she never thought he would try to murder her in her sleep by committing arson. Something about all that didn't make sense. Anybody in Savannah who had a secret would have a motive. But instead of scrutinizing the whole city of Savannah, investigators determined Edward did it, and it's not like he could object.

Queenie was the only person living in the mansion at the

time, though Rose and Max had just arrived from Wyoming and were spending the night, too. However, it was Queenie's bedroom and all her possessions that were destroyed in that fire. As far as personal items, she had to replace everything from underwear to books. What she couldn't replace were her journals from the last twenty years, and Rose's letters she had kept for decades. The loss still makes her tear up if she thinks about it long enough. In their new house here on the beach, she finally had everything to her liking. And now this.

Queenie sighs. It never occurred to her that a tree could crash into her bedroom and do this much damage. That old oak was thought to be the oldest on the island. As a girl, Old Sally told her trees are our elders and should be respected as much as people. This old tree provided shade during the boiling summers when Queenie was a girl. She sat under it while Old Sally braided her hair. She played with her dolls under it. In a way, it is like an old friend. An old friend pushed over by a playground bully named Iris.

When Queenie and Spud ventured outside a little while ago to see the damage from the other side, the entire root system of that sweet old tree had been unearthed and was dangling above the ground. All its secret parts exposed for the world to see.

Queenie thinks again of her wedding dress. It was in the garment bag it came in, the bag lying across the big armchair in her room where she did her journaling. The new chair was never quite as comfortable as her old one that burned in the Temple fire, but it didn't deserve to be destroyed.

Tears cling to her eyelashes as she takes stock of her current losses. Yet, like Spud said, it could have been a lot worse. What if they had been in bed celebrating their nuptials, or Queenie had been reading or journaling in her chair?

She imagines the headlines in the Savannah newspaper the next day:

ELDERLY NEWLYWEDS MEET TRAGIC FATE DURING HURRICANE IRIS

Well, I'm not dead yet, Queenie thinks, *and I'm not willing to meet a tragic fate.*

In typical fashion, Queenie asks herself, *What Would Oprah Do?* The answer is easy. Oprah would err on the side of gratitude. There would be no room for feeling sorry for herself. No spending time with the thought that she might be somehow cursed with bad luck. Nothing is required but gratefulness.

Queenie will have to start over again, at least regarding a few items, but the one thing she knows for sure is that she is resilient.

Queenie and Spud return to the candlelit kitchen. Only Jack is there.

"Who died?" Queenie asks, seeing his face.

"Vi is out in this storm somewhere looking for Old Sally."

Queenie gasps. She can't believe she has been worrying about a stupid wedding gown when Violet may be in trouble. "What should we do?"

"I'm not sure," Jack says. "They may be on their way back already. That's what I'm hoping, anyway."

Queenie has never seen Jack look this worried. "Where is everybody?" Queenie asks.

"Tia and Leisha are in their room," Jack begins. "Rose is somewhere with that Heather woman. Max is taking a quick nap, and Katie and Angela are in their bedroom resting up for the big event."

"Which big event?" Queenie asks. "Baby or hurricane?"

"Hurricane, I guess. The latest word is that the earlier contractions were a false alarm."

"Thank goodness," Queenie says with a relieved sigh.

Queenie remembers very little about giving birth to Violet. She was incredibly young, for one thing. But she does remember that having a baby feels as life-changing as a hurricane coming. No one can stop a force of nature. Just like no one can predict where exactly Iris might come ashore. Queenie wishes now that they had made it off the island. She and Spud could be sleeping soundly at a Days Inn without a single worry except what they might come home to. Instead, they are right in the middle of a disaster waiting to happen.

"Are you sure we shouldn't go after Violet and Old Sally?" Queenie asks Jack.

"No, I'm not sure," he says. "But for now, it makes sense to stay put. They both know how to take care of themselves."

Queenie is not so sure non-action is the course to take. Spud sends her another reassuring look. But how could she not worry? Two of the most important people in her life are somewhere out in a hurricane. Or at least the beginnings of one.

Do Max and Jack believe that a few storm shutters and sandbags are going to keep an ocean out of their house? Nothing prevented the poor unfortunate tree from falling into her bedroom and taking half the porch and several cars with it.

Queenie can usually laugh her way through anything, but she finds nothing at all funny about their current danger. As if to prove her point, one of the tarps rips away from the roof, and the wind whips through the house. If she could get on her knees with any ease, she would be on the floor praying by now.

A shiver climbs Queenie's spine as she thinks of Violet and Old Sally out in the storm. A storm that seems determined to challenge them in every way possible.

CHAPTER FORTY-TWO

Old Sally

Old Sally wakes to find Violet sleeping in the chair next to her. Then she remembers Violet's arrival and her disappointment that Violet didn't bring the others. The steady drone of the storm outside sounds like a wild lullaby. She recalls the dream where her grandmother told her to build the courage fires for what is coming. Old Sally thinks now that the dream was telling her to get everyone to the lighthouse and light the beacon. It will be the safest sanctuary for them.

Violet's head tips forward, and she startles awake. "I must have fallen asleep," she says. "Are you okay?" Violet moves to the cot and Old Sally's side.

"I be fine," Old Sally tells her, but even to herself she doesn't sound fine. Her voice has a quiver to it that is new since her walk to the lighthouse.

"We didn't talk about it after I arrived. Why did you come here?" Violet says this gently, as if speaking to a cherished child who was lost and who is suddenly home.

Old Sally has noticed how the young and the old change places at some point. Old Sally took care of Violet. Now it is the other way around. A mantle passes there, too.

"My grandmother told me to come here and light the courage fires," Old Sally says. "Our ancestors were sending me a message through the dream."

If anyone can comprehend the urgency, it is Violet. Yet, she doesn't wear the expression of someone who understands.

"Well, we've got to get back to the house," Violet tells her. "Everyone is so worried about you."

"I left you a note, so you could bring everyone here," Old Sally says.

"We can't stay here during a hurricane." Violet looks around the inside of the lighthouse as if gathering reasons why this won't work.

"It not be safe at the house," Old Sally says. "The storm is angry, and the ocean, too. This is the safest place we can be if we stay on the island."

Violet pauses and takes another look around. "That live oak next to the house came down after you left," Violet says. "Everybody is fine, but it fell into Queenie's bedroom and smashed several cars."

A wave of loss crashes over Old Sally. That tree kept her small house shaded during the hottest summers and protected it from the wind all year long. Not to mention its beauty and the number of creatures it supported. Birds. Chipmunks. Squirrels. Insects. Even that old owl she scared away earlier. The live oaks on the island have long outnumbered the people here. The roots of the live oaks grow shallow and cling to the sandy soil, weaving an immense tapestry just beneath the surface. Being rooted is vital for humans, too. No matter how long they live in a place. This particular tree has grown alongside Old Sally for a century. It is an ancestor, as well.

"So sorry to hear that," Old Sally says, a wobble of emotion in her throat, along with the quiver.

"I loved that old tree, too," Violet says. "Remember how I sat under it to eat my breakfast?"

"You fed it oatmeal," Old Sally says. "I had to teach you that a tree's food was the sun, rain, and nutrients in the ground."

"You were teaching me even then," Violet says.

"Yes, I was." Old Sally thinks again of how the tree was already ancient when Sally was a girl. A storm this size will topple many trees. The pines may stay rooted—most of the damage will be to the branches and upper parts of the trees. But the wind will do different injury to the oaks. The live oaks are top heavy, with roots that don't go that deep in the sandy soil. The most vulnerable ones will be pushed right over, roots and all.

Violet looks at her watch. "We don't have much time left before the full brunt of the storm is here. What are you suggesting?"

"You need to get the others here as quickly as possible," Old Sally says. "We must keep everyone safe. My grandmother has never been wrong about anything like this."

Violet takes a deep breath, as though her belief in Old Sally is faltering.

"I wouldn't want to walk back in this storm, either," Old Sally says, "and I wouldn't even suggest it if lives weren't at risk."

Violet nods.

A few days ago, Old Sally's tea leaves predicted a great disorder would occur before order returns. She didn't realize the full extent of the danger until now. Sometimes in the dark of night, things become clear as day. Her people have survived many storms on this island, but the coming storm is more extensive than any of her ancestors have ever seen before. One that will be documented in history books. One that will change everything.

CHAPTER FORTY-THREE

Rose

Rose excuses herself to go out to the cottage to check on things, but the real reason is to get away from her newfound niece. Unfortunately, Heather doesn't take the hint and follows Rose to the cottage. Now Rose must look busy and like she has a reason for being here.

A hurricane is hard enough without a stranger hanging around. A stranger with hidden motives. Rose has never figured out Edward's hidden motives for burning down the Temple mansion with Rose in it, and she can't help but wonder if that same family trait has passed to Heather. A character trait that destroys instead of preserves. A trait that could be true regarding Rose's mother, as well.

"Do you mind if I ask you something?" Heather has cornered Rose again, something she seems quite good at.

"I guess not," Rose says, a thin veil hiding her irritation.

"What kind of man was my father?" Heather asks.

Oh, good God, Rose thinks. *Now?*

The storm is due to hit in two hours. Now is not the time to give Heather a character analysis of her brother, and yet the question causes her to pause. Hasn't she asked this before? Should she offer a feel-good version of Edward, so Heather can walk away thinking he has contributed something endearing to her gene pool? However, there is also something to be said for knowing the truth.

"If he hadn't been my brother, I probably wouldn't have spent any time around him at all," Rose says.

This admission bolsters her. Yet, the candle in their small cottage kitchen illuminates Heather's disappointment.

"He was older than me by a few years," Rose continues, feeling a bit stormy herself. "I irritated him simply by being alive, and sometimes he tormented me, too."

There, Rose thinks, *let her chew on that for a while.* Maybe it will stop any further questions.

"When my mom was dying, she told me he was a real jerk," Heather says. "She said she didn't like him that much."

And the truth shall set you free, Rose thinks.

For years she tried to understand why her brother was the way he was, attributing all sorts of childhood wounds and Temple family karma. But the truth is whether you were family, friend, or stranger, Edward was an alpha dog who played dominance games. You never knew when he might try to pee on you, hump your leg, or toss you to the ground.

"But I thought she told you that your father was a sperm donor," Rose says.

"Yes, she did," Heather says. "Initially. Then when she was dying she told me the truth."

Rose pauses. Didn't Heather tell her that she found out while looking at her mother's documents?

"We were very close," Heather adds. "Like friends instead of mother and daughter."

Rose can't imagine being her mother's friend. As far as she knows, her mother didn't have friends. She had connections to assert her influence. People who witnessed her wealth and status. Not close friends like Rose is with Violet.

Violet. How could she forget her best friend is out in this storm? She left a while ago to look for Old Sally. Has she even come back? Heather has distracted Rose from what is essential. Two of Rose's chosen family members are in danger: Violet and Old Sally. Two people who helped Rose survive her mother's dominance and are directly responsible for the person she is today.

Rose leads the way back from the cottage to the big house, her light jacket doing little to protect her from the wind and blowing sand. Heather is even less prepared for the elements and uses Rose's back as a buffer. Once inside, the ongoing weather report now has the forecasters calling the storm a potential hundred-year-event. A destructive storm, like her mother could be, who if crossed had no problem destroying lives and making you wish you had never met her.

Seconds later, Violet bursts through the back door, her hair sculpted in the direction of the blowing wind. She leans over to catch her breath. The others come from all corners of the house to greet her.

"We need to go to the lighthouse," Violet says, still leaning over. "Old Sally says we're in danger here. The lighthouse is where we'll be safe."

"We should go, right?" Rose says, looking at Max.

"I'm not going to some dirty lighthouse," Heather says, standing straighter.

Everyone turns to look at her, as though suddenly noticing the stranger in the room.

"Well, I'm not," she says. "That old lady probably has dementia."

"I trust Old Sally with my life," Rose says to her. If Rose were one of their dogs, her hackles might raise. "If she says we should go to the lighthouse, then we should go."

Violet agrees.

Max and Jack debate logistics. One truck. Twelve people and various animals. Can it be done? They challenge each other to think creatively.

Meanwhile, Rose goes to check on Katie and Angela, who have no idea what is happening. Their room is upstairs, the other side of the house from Queenie's. Rose knocks on the door and finds Katie lying on her left side, a recommendation from her doctor a month ago when her blood pressure was creeping up. Angela coaches her to breathe deeply; the smell of unearthed live oak fills the hallway like meditation incense.

"Sorry to interrupt," Rose says, "but we need to go to the lighthouse, the house isn't safe."

Katie sits up and holds her stomach. Where Rose expected panic, there is calm.

"The lighthouse?" Angela asks.

"Old Sally says to. We need to keep you and the baby safe."

"Then we should go," Katie says.

Angela looks at Katie, then at Rose, as if the calmness is a surprise to her, too. Rose and Angela help Katie stand and cover her shoulders with the light blanket on the bed. One thought reassures Rose. If this baby comes during a once-in-a-century hurricane, then they are better off with Old Sally than without her. As always.

CHAPTER FORTY-FOUR

Violet

The wind fights against Violet as she puts the food and water in the back of Max's truck, the only vehicle spared by the capsizing of the giant live oak. In the car are Katie and Angela, along with Lucy, Ethel, and Harpo. A cat carrier with Angela's two cats inside—Zelda and Gertrude—sits at Katie's feet, and Angela holds a terrarium containing Tia and Leisha's turtle, Jake. Lives are seldom set up with an evacuation in mind. They have animals. Too many possessions. But at least they have a destination that should keep them safe.

Queenie starts the truck, revving the engine, and then waves goodbye to Violet like she is off for part two of her honeymoon, instead of evacuating from a hurricane for the second time. Provided it is still passable, she will take the old gravel road to the back entrance of the lighthouse. The rest of them will walk through the dunes and up the beach to the same destination.

Standing on the back patio, where the wind is less intense,

Jack and Max secure a rope around everyone's waists and attach them, allowing six feet between each person. Violet wonders if this is necessary, but when they step away from the shelter of the house and into the dunes, everyone immediately stumbles backward. For several seconds they struggle as a group to stand upright again.

Violet is willing to be tethered if it will get them all there safely. Max leads. By way of the beach, it is a simple ten-minute walk. At least any other day it is. By road, it is half that, but the storm is fast approaching, and they don't have time to make multiple trips. It is still over an hour or so before the storm is due to hit, but someone needs to tell the wind that. It is already intense.

Like passenger cars attached to a train, they follow the person in front of them. Rose follows Max, followed by Heather and then Jack. Violet is next. Behind her is Tia, then Leisha, and then Spud as the caboose. Despite Heather's insistence, Rose wouldn't let her stay at the house alone, which Violet thinks is a good idea, and not only for safety reasons.

They shuffle toward the lighthouse, their human locomotion severely limited in comparison to the storm. Hurricane Iris pushes and pulls against them. Violet's cheeks stretch like they've become elastic. She lowers her head to get the short, shallow breaths the wind will allow.

Meanwhile, sheets of rain begin to fall, hitting them from every direction like thousands of tiny bee stings hitting their exposed skin. The steady roar of the wind makes Violet's ears ache. Periodically she looks back at Tia and Leisha, beaming courage in their direction. The storm of 2002 will be something they tell their children and grandchildren about.

Provided we survive, Violet thinks, and then tells herself to not even hold that result as a possibility. Her doubts create an opening to question the wisdom of their decision to walk up the beach. The lighthouse now feels like an impossible distance to cover with the intense rain and wind. But they are all tied together. If anyone falters, the rest of the group will pull them forward. Whatever happens, they will have to do it together.

Perhaps that occurs with whoever we attach ourselves to in life, she thinks. *Family and friends.*

The waves crash closer. How many times has she walked up this beach and seen only its beauty? Now she witnesses the sea's dark side. Its ominous presence feels as dangerous as the wind. Old Sally is right about the lighthouse. It is built for storms like this. Solid concrete. Their house is only wood. Wood may be too vulnerable to withstand the storm surge promised to come.

They follow the curve of the land and Violet spots light up ahead. Someone must have figured out how to turn on the beacon. How is that possible? It hasn't been turned on in twenty years. A surge of hope fills her. Violet jerks on the rope to get everyone's attention and points ahead to the light. Their rope line stops. Then they rock the line in celebration like a spectator wave in a football stadium. Every few seconds the beacon rotates in their direction. A rush of adrenaline pushes away Violet's tiredness. Her great-grandfather helped to build this lighthouse. In a way, it is like her ancestor helped construct this shelter for them years ahead of time, all the while knowing that they might need it someday.

The rain comes again, pinging against her raincoat. They turn inland toward the light. As before, walking is difficult in the soft sand of the dunes until they reach the concrete steps that lead up to the lighthouse. They're going to make it. She's sure of it now. Only a few more yards to get to the lighthouse.

With each step, the wind vibrates the ropes ahead of and behind her.

In the next instant, Violet remembers the missing railing where an hour or so before she almost fell into the dunes. If one person goes down, the others will, too, including her. She stops and yells to warn the others. The wind silences her. Violet pulls hard on the rope and Heather stumbles toward her. Violet helps her up, and everyone finally stops and looks around to see what has stopped their forward motion.

"Danger up ahead!" Violet yells to Heather, pointing to the handrail.

The look in Heather's eyes reminds Violet of how young she is. Only a little older than Tia and Leisha. The message gets passed up the line. They move more slowly now, and each person points out the danger as they pass the missing railing. She just hopes everyone can keep their balance. Now is not the time for clumsiness. Meanwhile, the beacon radiates light 360 degrees above their heads. A literal beacon of hope.

Finally, at the top of the cement stairs, the human chain stops again. Bodies huddle together at the entrance while Max pounds on the door. Slowly, the heavy metal door opens. They shuffle their way inside and turn as one body to push the door closed and latch it. Queenie, Old Sally, Katie, Angela, and all the animals await them.

Wild hair, bloodshot eyes, and red chapped skin tell the story of their escape. They are not only windblown but beaten up. Violet's ears ring, and she can barely hear. Tia begins to cry, and Violet comforts her, while Jack goes to Leisha. Everyone talks louder than usual. Perhaps their ears are ringing, too. Lucy and Ethel greet them, licking faces, while Angela's cats let out cautious meows.

It takes several minutes for Violet's hearing to return to normal. "Most definitely a bad hair day, Mom," Leisha says.

Both daughters laugh, and Leisha helps Violet unzip her rain jacket. The look they exchange has a new dimension. Is that appreciation she sees in her daughter's eyes? A new level of maturity?

The storm continues to rage outside, but it is now a muffled rage. Muffled through layers of concrete that make up the lighthouse. The constant fight with the wind to stay upright has made Violet numb. When the numbness begins to wear off her skin tingles to the point of pain.

The metal door rattles from the wind but holds secure. The lighthouse has the faint smell of wet dogs and an old musty attic. Yet, it is relatively dry considering how close it sits to the sea. The lighthouse, wide at the bottom and narrow at the top, has a set of metal stairs in the middle that spiral upward to a small section with just enough space to walk around the beacon. Small windows dot the walls all the way up to the top, where that smallness expands to a panoramic view of land and sea. The beacon bathes them in a dull, golden glow. Below the beacon, an old generator emits a continuous, almost comforting hum.

Violet thinks about what a shame it is that the lighthouse has been abandoned, as many have been over time. Given advances in sonar instruments on ships and on land, people are kept safe by other means. Now lighthouses have become symbols more than anything. Reminders of how things used to be, and a belief that something manmade might have the power to dispel darkness and bring hope and safety.

Jack and Max untie the ropes between them, and they begin to settle. Once free, Violet walks over to Old Sally, who embraces her.

"You did it," Old Sally says. "Thank you for bringing everyone here."

"You're welcome," Violet says. "Who turned on the beacon?"

"Angela," Katie says, sitting nearby on the cot, Harpo in her arms.

Violet turns and smiles at Angela, as word passes through the small space. The others thank her, too, and Angela takes a quick bow before returning to Katie's side.

Violet sits and rests her back against a cool wall. Suitcases are piled under the spiral metal stairs to give them room to walk around a little. If everyone in the lighthouse stood shoulder to shoulder they would reach the entire way across, with maybe a little room to spare.

Violet turns to see Rose watching her.

You okay? Rose's expression asks.

Violet nods, asking her the same.

Rose nods, too.

Violet thinks of the unspoken conversations she used to have with Queenie at the dinner table when Miss Temple ate. Now Violet has unspoken mysterious discussions with Old Sally, too. So much communication happens when she doesn't even realize it. Body language. Facial expressions. She looks at Rose again. She sometimes forgets that they are not only best friends but also half sisters, given what Miss Temple's will revealed about Violet being Mister Oscar's child.

They exchange a secret Sea Gypsy look. When they were girls, they played in this abandoned lighthouse. A secret hideaway. A prominent NO TRESPASSING sign was posted next to the door, so they were not supposed to be here. By accident, they discovered where the old lighthouse keeper had hidden a spare key in a dried-out old paint bucket under a rusted-out wheelbarrow on the north side.

As girls, when they let themselves inside, Violet and Rose would climb the steep metal stairs to the beacon. Looking out over the ocean, they made up stories and pretended ships at sea relied on them to find their way. Using a conch shell as a radio, they sent messages warning the ships of gales and storms, offering anyone in trouble safe harbor. Never imagining, of course, that someday the lighthouse might be a safe harbor for them, too.

They exchange a smile, as though remembering the same things, before Rose turns back to check on Katie.

"How are you holding up?" Jack asks Violet, taking her hand while the girls doze.

She shrugs. Truth is, she won't be entirely okay until this storm is over.

Jack leaves to help Max investigate their current haven.

While she rests, Violet begins to tremble from their harrowing walk to the lighthouse. It reminds her of the tiny birds that sometimes hit the front picture window. Stunned at first, they then begin to shake and let the trauma pass. It always takes longer than Violet thinks it will before they fly away again.

It is the middle of the night, and she hasn't slept. The only light, besides the diffused light coming from the beacon, comes from two battery-operated camp lanterns.

The beacon sends its rhythmic, sweeping light out into the darkness. If there are any ships at sea, they are in for a rough ride. Violet's thoughts drone on like the wind. She remembers a story Old Sally told her about an entire crew on a Civil War ship that sunk in a storm off the coast and ended up somewhere at the bottom of the ocean. It was near the end of the war and they carried much-needed supplies. Some say the ship's sinking helped seal the fate of the war for the South. She imagines a ghost ship somewhere at the bottom of the Atlantic, complete with skeletons and fish swimming amongst them. A vessel never found. All those men and supplies buried at sea.

In the distance, the surf pounds the land. Is it her imagination or is it even louder than minutes before? The life raft of safety Violet clings to disappears when she remembers what the weather forecasters said in the last report before the power went out. The storm surge is easily the most destructive part of the storm, its severity based on where the hurricane comes ashore.

Jack comes to check on her and the girls again, who are still dozing, as are several of the others. Violet lowers her voice and asks him about the storm surge.

"There's no way of knowing," he whispers back.

"But haven't we been getting the full force of the hurricane?"

"I wouldn't doubt it," he says.

"Then we'll also get the full force of the storm surge, right?"

"I don't know, sweetheart, but let's not panic."

Violet nods, repeating his words to herself, *Let's not panic.*

Getting everyone afraid will do no good, especially while they are so exhausted. However, shouldn't everyone be warned about the possibility? Just in case there is some way they can prepare for it?

According to Violet's watch, it is now 2:30. Everyone is either sleeping or sitting in silence listening to the storm. The small window to the left of the door reveals a dark and colorless world. A predator lurks outside in the form of a hurricane.

Trees snap and crash in the distance. Violet half expects them to moan with pain. If this part of the shoreline is supposed to be more protected, what is happening in the *un*protected areas? She imagines the dunes being beaten down with every wave of the unrelenting surf. Without the dunes, there will be nothing to stop the ocean from crashing into the lighthouse, as well as their home down the beach.

Ropes, raincoats, backpacks, and various supplies are piled on the floor nearby. Rose's two dogs lie together, their backs touching. They pant and salivate like they do whenever they go to the vet, their ears following the sounds of the storm. Hurricane Iris rages outside. The only thing left to do is wait.

CHAPTER FORTY-FIVE

Queenie

When Spud entered the lighthouse after his harrowing walk up the beach with the others, Queenie rushed to his side. Every strand of his thin, gray hair stood straight up like a geriatric rapper, unable to withstand the teasing of Iris. If she had known the walk would be so perilous, she would have tied Spud to the top of the truck.

Even now, Queenie attempts to tame his hair. "You sure you're all right?" she whispers to him while the others sleep.

"I'm fine, pumpkin spice."

She tires of his continuous search for a sweet nickname, but he could say anything right now and she would feel nothing but gratitude.

Earlier, while waiting for the others, Queenie and Angela clanked their way up the metal steps to the top of the lighthouse—Queenie holding onto the railing with a death grip, as she has never liked heights—to see if they could get that fool light on. Thanks to Angela's handiness, their multiple efforts, and giant-sized luck, they were able to get the generator going with the help of the spare canister of gasoline Max always keeps in the truck. Seconds later, with the flip of a switch, the old beacon groaned to life.

Nice to know that even an abandoned old lighthouse can still have some life to it, Queenie thinks.

Now they don't have to wait on this fool storm to be over in total darkness. It's even kind of romantic as the soft, throbbing light cascades down the stairs. Queenie thinks again of her aborted honeymoon and smiles with the thought that everyone she cares about is in this massive concrete phallic symbol.

In the meantime, a hurricane named Iris is huffing and puffing and threatening to blow the door down.

The human Iris was a blowhard, too. Not giving a hoot what anybody else had to say about anything. A big, bad wolf in pearls.

Queenie isn't sure how anyone can sleep with a hurricane right outside the door. Instead of whispering, she wants to yell: *What's wrong with you people?*

But instead, she is quiet and holds Spud close. To her surprise she finds herself dozing off, too. Something about the constant wind outside is like a white noise machine. Her shoulders relax. A dream peeks around the corner of her awareness. Then Katie lets out a moan that grows into a scream. Everyone, including Queenie, startles awake. It seems Katie's baby isn't that fond of hurricanes, either, and wants to vacate the premises, pronto. Although, in Queenie's opinion, it would be much smarter to stay put where it is for a while.

Rose rushes over to Katie and takes the free hand that Angela isn't holding. She says the things that mothers say to kids who are about to panic. Things like *Everything is going to be okay,* and *I'm here,* and *breathe, sweetheart.* Angela rubs Katie's back like she is helping the words sink in.

"Sweet Jesus," Queenie whispers to Spud. "What if this baby comes right here in this lighthouse in the middle of a hurricane?"

"Then he or she will have a great story to tell every year on their birthday," Spud says. "Don't worry, sugarplum."

Queenie gives him a look that now is not the time to bring up the *Nutcracker Suite* and sugarplum fairies. Not unless he wants his own nuts cracked. He offers a quick apology as if aware of the risk.

Though the sounds are muffled in the metal building, Iris's ferocity is growing. If this were the human Iris, Queenie would call this a great big hissy fit. Iris's hissy fits were infamous all over Savannah. They happened whenever a downtown chef didn't get her order just right. Or when someone at the Junior League or the Daughters of the American Revolution meetings didn't pay Iris what she deemed was adequate respect.

Katie lies on the cot with Harpo by her side, and Old Sally sits next to Katie on the only chair in the room. Angela is nearby. Both focus on what Old Sally is saying. The part Queenie overhears has to do with trusting the process. Old Sally reassures Katie that this baby knows exactly what to do even if she doesn't. Katie nods her agreement.

If Queenie were the one giving birth during a hurricane, she would probably already be cussing a blue streak, whatever a blue streak is. Her pain tolerance is practically nonexistent. She hates any type of pain, from small discomforts—like the pain in her knees after she stands too long at Violet's Tea Shop —to the pinched nerve she gets in her back sometimes. Her foremost intolerance is for stupid people. But thankfully, she manages to avoid them for the most part.

Old Sally tells Katie to be patient and breathe. Queenie must admit she barely has the patience to wait for toast to pop out of the toaster, much less breathe deeply.

In the meantime, Rose is focused on Katie. Becoming a grandmother appears to be nothing short of a holy experience. Queenie became a grandmother twice, though she didn't get to claim it at the time. Keeping that secret robbed her and Violet of the closeness Rose and Katie have now. The worst kind of disappointment is when she disappoints herself, and Queenie never wants to feel that again.

Tia and Leisha are awake now and take turns braiding each other's hair. They periodically look over to see what is happening on the cot. Violet looks tired. Queenie makes a point to catch her eye and smile at her. Violet returns the smile. No more secrets.

Queenie looks around at those waiting out the storm. Heather sits alone near the door, looking like a young Iris who doesn't want to get her hands dirty, first in line to leave once the storm is over.

"What are you thinking about?" Spud whispers to Queenie.

"About how Heather is a great big nothing burger," Queenie whispers back.

"A nothing burger?" Spud shakes his head, as though never knowing what his new wife will come up with next.

"It's like she's not even here," Queenie whispers again.

"Maybe she's afraid," Spud says.

Queenie nods with the knowledge that she is afraid, too. Perhaps Queenie would be more compassionate if Heather didn't look like someone who tried to make every day of her life miserable.

Meanwhile, Max and Jack speak in hushed tones near a large footlocker underneath the spiraling metal stairs. Whatever is in the footlocker is guarded by a rather large lock. Queenie wonders what they are talking about. Whatever it is, they look concerned. Except for Heather, it seems everyone else has been drawn closer together by this experience.

Iris rattles the windows, reminding Queenie who is in charge.

You are such an attention hound, Queenie tells her. *I'm onto you, even if nobody else is.*

Iris was at her brightest and most content whenever the newspaper photographer from the society section showed up at one of her philanthropic forays. For years, one of Queenie's jobs as Iris's companion was to clip these photographs and any write-ups that appeared in the newspaper and put them in a monogrammed album with the gold Temple name on the cover. A collection Iris kept in the sunroom to remind her of her importance. Something she could flip through after reading the newspaper and having her morning tea. Queenie, of course, was not in any of the photographs in the scrapbook, except for an occasional brown arm in the corner next to a sea of white people—the rest of her cropped out because Queenie wasn't a *true* Temple, only an imitation.

Queenie shakes her head. She can't wait until this damn storm is over and Iris is out of her life for good.

Before the power went out at the house, the weather reports predicted where the storm might make landfall. The highest storm surge totals would happen north of wherever the storm comes ashore. That would also be the area with the most significant destruction. Queenie remembers the arrows pointing to Dolphin Island. In a way, it is like those adventures where a damsel is tied to the railroad tracks with a locomotive coming straight for her. The storm increasingly sounds like a train engine, too.

Katie lets out another moan. A wave of tension vibrates through the lighthouse. Iris is right on top of them. The lighthouse is one of the highest spots on the island, the other being the cemetery. A ten-foot storm surge has been predicted. Are they ten feet up from the sea? Is a lighthouse waterproof? Queenie wishes now she had worn her pink flip-flops instead of her sneakers, which are already squishy wet. But her complaints are hiding a more pressing issue.

"Why are you so quiet?" Spud takes her hand, waiting for an answer.

"Well, the truth is . . ."

Queenie whisks a tear away.

"Tell me," Spud says, looking into her eyes with so much tenderness she looks away.

"I'm scared," Queenie confesses. "I've never been in a hurricane before."

Standing, Spud pulls her into his arms, which isn't as effortless as she would like. Queenie is taller by at least an inch, though Spud insists they are the same height. But she is happy to give him an inch if he needs it.

"We're all frightened," he says, his words soft. "I truly believe we are in the safest place on this island we could possibly be."

Every inch of Queenie's full-figured body wants to believe this. Yet, her knees are quivering and remind her that there were times in her life when she has been a weakling. She is not proud of those times. They were mainly in the past and had to do with keeping secrets for way too long. Storms are a different matter. With storms, she has absolutely no control.

Katie lets out another moan.

For a moment Queenie flashes back to the night she gave birth to Violet. It was also summertime, and every window of the house was open. Old Sally had been by Queenie's side, just like she is with Katie now. That night, Old Sally was equally calm and reassuring. Old Sally knows what she is doing. She has done this before. Queenie breathes deeply for the first time since the storm began and wants to cue a Bette Midler song. Not to sound too hokey about it, but Old Sally is the wind beneath Queenie's wings. Her light through every storm. A beacon lighting the path her entire life.

CHAPTER FORTY-SIX

Old Sally

Old Sally closes her eyes. She hears the faint music of a violin playing in her memories. The man with the violin would have been her husband if fate had been kinder. It was here in this lighthouse that she experienced the most profound love she has ever known—an attraction to last a lifetime, even an unusually long one.

Because of how well he played the violin, he was nicknamed Fiddle. He played for her here in this lighthouse, the rich sound echoing against the concrete walls. Old Sally hears the haunting melody that captured her imagination so many years ago.

Memory, like so many things in life, can be both a blessing and a curse. Memories like this one haunt Old Sally, while at the same time uplift her. To remember him is to know who she is. To remember her ancestors is to understand why she is here.

Old Sally opens her eyes to see Max trying to unlock the

rusty metal footlocker underneath the stairway with a small pocketknife. Old Sally remembers when that old footlocker first arrived. Until the 1980s, when it was abandoned, this lighthouse was never locked.

Old Sally gives Katie's hand a reassuring pat and tells her she will be right back. Her back and legs are stiff with pain when she walks over to Max and Jack.

"Please pull the footlocker away from the wall," Old Sally tells him.

He pauses and then does as she asks.

Old Sally leans behind the box and pulls out the key from where it was left decades before. She hands it to Max, who grins.

Opening the footlocker is like opening a forgotten time capsule. First-aid supplies are there from back in the days of World War II. Including three army surplus wool blankets. They pass two out to the others, and Old Sally keeps one for Katie.

Jack pulls out two small hurricane lamps—aptly named—and gets them going with some old but dry matches in a metal box. He wasn't sure if the oil would still be usable, but it is. The smell of lamp oil and sulfur mixes with the musty, salty air. Everyone comes over to investigate the metal trunk, even Lucy and Ethel, who both sneeze when exploring the contents. The lighthouse fills with chatter and light and feels almost homey.

Old Sally sits in the chair again and leans back, listening to the storm. Its dull roar has become familiar now. When she closes her eyes, she hears her grandmother singing in a long-ago kitchen. A song from a faraway home before she came to this new world. A new world where their lives were not their own. At least not at first. She hums along with the melody, wishing her grandmother were here.

In the next moment, the sounds outside change. The raging wind stops. Old Sally opens her eyes. No one moves. It is as if the world is holding its breath to see what will happen next.

Following the steady chaotic roar of the wind, the silence is almost painful. With caution, Max opens the door of the lighthouse as if Iris might lurch out at him if given a chance.

It is the eye of the storm.

To Old Sally, it feels like they have landed by spaceship onto a new planet. In a matter of seconds, their nightmare has become a paradise of stillness. Yet, evidence of the ordeal is everywhere. Trees down. Battered shoreline. Dead things spit up by the sea. The rain has stopped. Total calm surrounds them. Overhead, the clouds open and reveal a deep blue sky. The moon and stars, visible hours before, appear again. It is a glimpse of heaven. Iris has revealed a side of herself Old Sally didn't expect. After showing no mercy, the hurricane has presented a moment of grace.

Old Sally stands a few feet from the door, mesmerized by this strange, dark world. Her eyes continue to adapt to the darkness, and goose flesh crawls up her arms from the fresh, damp air. In the distance is the steady sound of the surf. A promise that never stops. No matter how still the earth becomes. The strong smell of salt and sea mixes in with broken trees—the odor of Christmas trees dipped in the ocean, decorated with seaweed.

An unexpected gift is found in the center of the storm. Old Sally puts a hand over her heart. Pledging allegiance to all that is good, real, and true. In some ways, it feels like she has been waiting her entire life for this scene to be revealed to her. A perfect chaos. Light inside darkness. Good inside evil.

Tears pool in her eyes. If this were her last moment on earth, all would be well. It is almost time. She can feel it in her bones. She clings to this promise. But there is at least one more thing she must do.

One more thing, Old Sally repeats.

She turns to look at Katie sleeping on the cot, lovingly holding her belly. She knows what it is like to rest up for a big transition.

The beacon rotates, offering periodic glimpses of the shoreline. A vast sea stretches where the dunes and beach used to be. A graveyard of debris litters the adjacent land. A door here. A bathtub there. Pink building insulation is spun into the limbs of trees like cotton candy.

All are silent as they step into the moonlight to witness this new world. Part of the walkway is missing. Pieces of porches and docks are everywhere, making it difficult to walk even a few inches. A large chunk of twisted metal, a boat before Iris got to it, blocks the stairway.

One by one, they venture farther out into the dark eye of the storm. Max cautions them not to wander too far. The eye won't last for long.

Tia and Leisha stay close to their dad, and Rose and Violet are arm in arm. Max goes out back to check on the truck, while Queenie and Spud stay close to Old Sally. Heather stands just inside the lighthouse, all alone. A trickster without a trick, and still someone not to be trusted.

"You okay, Mama?" Queenie asks.

"Yes, baby," Old Sally says. A mama can still call her children "baby" even if her children are in their sixties. No harm in that.

They stand inside the eye of the hurricane, and for the first time in her long life, Old Sally understands what it means for time to stand still.

THE WIND BEGINS to blow again. Slowly at first. Softly. And then the clouds gather again to cover the moon. With the same quickness that the eye came, the second half of the storm begins. The eye is only the halfway point. From the weather reports they heard, it is the second half of the storm that is the most destructive because the wind reverses itself. Yet, how can anything be more destructive than what Iris has delivered so far?

They quickly gather inside the lighthouse again. At that moment Old Sally remembers that humans are both a resilient and a fragile species. A young species. Governed by the laws of nature. A species that needs guidance. The others look at Old Sally as though needing something only she can deliver.

At first, she thought that building the courage fires meant getting the beacon going. But it seems that more is required of her. She hesitates, wondering what might be helpful. When nothing comes, she calls on her grandmother. Old Sally waits, but she doesn't appear.

Not the best time for you to disappear, she says to her grandmother.

Again, no answer.

But Old Sally knows what she must do.

She closes her eyes, drawing her words from somewhere deep inside herself, where all her people reside.

"We must be strong for one another," Old Sally says, opening her eyes again. "We each hold a spark of courage. It may not feel like enough when you are alone, but together it will be enough," she continues. "Together all those sparks build a fire. A fire of courage."

Outside, the wind and rain quickly surpass where the storm left off before the eye. Nobody talks about the storm surge that is destined to come. At the top of the lighthouse stairs, Old Sally's vision returns, and her grandmother nods her approval. The courage fires have been prepared for whatever is to come.

CHAPTER FORTY-SEVEN

Rose

K atie's contractions have sped up along with the storm. What they had hoped were fake have proven themselves real. Rose doesn't let her daughter see how frightened she is that this grandbaby is almost ready to come with no hospital, telephone, or any way to communicate with the outside world.

Rose pulls the charm from her pocket that Old Sally gave her and holds it in her left hand. She feels the roundness of the pearl, along with the gnarled root. Along with her prayers to God for protection, Rose calls on the charm to keep them from harm. She will take whatever help she can get. She opens her hand to show Old Sally what she is holding, who nods her encouragement.

Angela rubs Katie's back to help her relax before the next labor pain. Rose regrets now her harsh judgments of Angela when they first met. It turns out that she is everything Rose would want Katie to have in a mate. Kind, respectful, and unwavering in her care for Katie.

Old Sally told them they each have a spark of courage and together they make a fire. Rose returns the small sack to her pocket, and Katie squeezes Rose's hand, the sign that the next labor pain is coming. Like Katie's grip, the storm outside isn't letting up. Angela and Rose exchange a look that contains the spark. They take turns comforting and reassuring Katie. They must stay calm. Together, Rose and Angela have enough courage for the three of them.

Between pains, Katie becomes talkative, something she did as a girl whenever she was afraid and needed a distraction. Katie motions her head toward Heather, asking Rose what she intends to do.

"Not sure," Rose says, which is the truth. Heather is the least of her worries now.

Needing her own distraction, Rose glances over at her purse across from the cot. Inside is the first faded ledger. Every hour or so she checks to make sure it is still there. She can't imagine what is in that old book that Edward would have been looking for before the fire, and she can't help but wonder if that is why Heather is hanging around, too. Rose doesn't believe that she only wants to get to know who her father is. They could do that over the phone. She is apparently searching for something else. Like Edward was searching for something else other than the secrets.

Rose remembers what Heather told her earlier in the day about her mother's job when she worked for Edward. She had been hired to research and compile the history of the Temple family for a possible book. Was Heather's mother given access to either of the ledgers in the bank vault? Doubtful. But she might have found something out through other means. And would she have shared that *something* on her deathbed with her daughter?

Rose looks around at the menagerie of people and animals gathered. Talking is sporadic. It is like a makeshift Noah's Ark. Katie and Angela are on the cot, Harpo at Katie's feet. Max and Jack speak near the stairway. Max's two dogs stand nearby. Queenie and Spud lean into each other while sitting on the metal stairs. Tia and Leisha and Violet rest against the wall. Old Sally and Rose are near the cot. Heather is at the door like someone whose adventure took an unexpected turn, and she no longer knows who she is in this new setting. For the first time since they met, Rose feels compassion for her. Like her mother, Heather is all alone and doesn't know how to connect.

Rose leans back, looking at the building towering over them. She hasn't been inside this lighthouse since she was a girl. When she takes walks on the beach, it always looks lonely sitting back from the ocean, overlooking everything. Solitary. Unapproachable. But she doubts it is lonely now.

Old Sally rocks her body while sitting in the gray desk chair. She hums something that is barely audible.

"How did you know we should all come here?" Rose asks Old Sally.

Old Sally pauses. "Do you remember the night of the fire at the mansion?" she asks.

"Yes, of course," Rose says. "Max and I had just driven across the country."

"That night I had a dream that Queenie was in danger, and the dream told me to get Queenie and you and Max out of that house, so I telephoned until Queenie finally answered."

"I never knew that," Rose says. "Or if I did, I'd forgotten."

Many times, Rose has thought about what might have happened if Queenie hadn't rushed into their room and told them to get out. She saved their lives. What Rose didn't know was that Old Sally had saved all of them.

"Earlier today, I had another dream," Old Sally begins again. "This one told me to get everyone to the lighthouse."

"Oh my," Rose says, wondering if she has had dreams she ignored and shouldn't have. She guesses everybody does.

"I guess I've lived long enough to know that when a dream gives me explicit directions, I follow them," Old Sally says.

"Thank goodness," Rose says. "I might not even be here if you hadn't listened."

Rose remembers the dream she had recently of her mother hiding her paints. Storm or no storm, Rose is tired of being distracted from what feels necessary to her. When the storm is over, she will start to paint again. She promises herself this.

In the meantime, Rose trusts Old Sally with her life and the life of her family. She helped Rose survive her childhood. If getting them to this old lighthouse is what Old Sally's dream told her to do, this is precisely where they should be.

CHAPTER FORTY-EIGHT

Violet

The hurricane's peaceful eye had almost lulled Violet into believing the worst was over. But what's true is that they hold front-row seats to a drama that has only reached intermission.

Violet's throat tightens as she sits against the wall with Tia and Leisha. She tells them not to worry. However, there appears to be plenty to worry about.

The storm crescendos. Hurricane Iris is outdoing herself. The more Violet tells herself that they are safe, the more the hurricane begs to differ. The question remains: Will this lighthouse protect them from a wall of water? An alarm pounds its warning into her left shoulder with such intensity it brings tears to her eyes. A fear she can't verbalize, or it might scare the people she loves.

In the meantime, Old Sally sits calmly next to the cot as though awaiting a special guest. Violet can hear her humming and tries to discern the melody. She finally recognizes

"Amazing Grace." She begins to hum along, the tune vibrating in her throat. On the second round, Rose starts to hum, too, as do the girls. Queenie and Spud join in, as well as Jack and Max, who add a bass line to the hum. Only Heather is quiet.

In the distance, Hurricane Iris pounds the shore like a boxer poised to win the heavyweight championship of the world. Waves crest closer to the lighthouse, and the winds grow in volume yet again. Violet has heard eyewitness accounts of tornados and hurricanes where it's said that the wind sounds like a locomotive barreling down the tracks. She can hear the train coming now.

They continue to hum as the lighthouse vibrates with each crashing wave. The storm has its own song. Nothing stands between them and the ocean, except this lighthouse. If not for this structure they would already be lost, perhaps never to be found again.

A low rumble grows in the distance, and everyone stops humming to listen. At first, it sounds like a stomach growling. A huge stomach. Violet can feel the vibration deep inside her.

Jack yells that the storm surge is coming. Everyone is to get up the stairs as fast as they can. At the bottom of the spiral steps, Max and Jack remind everyone to move quickly and stay calm, an impossible feat. One by one they climb the winding metal staircase toward the beacon of light, their shoes echoing against the metal stairs. Violet's legs feel like she is attempting to run in pluff mud.

Jack yells for them to stay away from the glass around the beacon of the lighthouse. Queenie and Spud are first up and they stop at the top of the stairs. Tia and Leisha and Violet pack in closely behind her, followed by Old Sally, Rose, Katie, and Angela, who holds Harpo. All of them help Katie climb the stairs. Max tells them to move closer together, while Jack grabs dogs, a cat carrier, and a turtle in a terrarium and passes them up the steps. He holds out his hand to Heather, who is still sitting on the floor. The look on her face is terror, her body frozen, unable to move.

Violet cannot remember a time her heart has beat this wildly. She yells at Jack to not do anything heroic and get himself hurt. She and the girls need him. But he isn't listening. When he takes Heather's arm, she slaps him away with her backpack, causing the faded ledger to fall out onto the floor, several of the pages falling loose. Like a game when someone yells "Unfreeze," Heather scrambles for the pages. Violet looks at Rose, who is searching in her purse for what is now on the floor of the lighthouse.

"Get up the stairs!" Jack yells at Heather.

The hairs prickle on Violet's arms. The storm surge is growing. Electricity is in the air, the energy building and moving toward release.

Heather is on her hands and knees gathering up the pages.

Violet screams at Jack to come on. To leave Heather if he must. The low rumble grows louder, and Violet's entire body involuntarily shakes. Beyond the small windows, the sea swells. Finally, Jack picks up Heather while she is leaning over to get the remaining ledger pages and carries her up the metal steps.

Through a small window near the top of the lighthouse, all Violet can see is water. The wave crests. She feels like one of the minnows she and Rose collected in her plastic beach bucket when they were Sea Gypsies. Like the minnows, they are about to be sacrificed to the sea.

"Hold onto the railing as tight as you can!" Violet yells to Tia and Leisha. The roar of the wave swallows her voice. She secures both girls between her and the metal bars and turns to see Queenie and Spud doing the same with Old Sally.

The big wave hits its apex and prepares to fall. Violet tells Tia and Leisha that she loves them with all her heart. She feels her lips move, unable to hear the words.

The giant wave crashes against the lighthouse. Windows around the beacon shatter above them. The door crashes open, swept off its hinges. For a few seconds the lighthouse seems to rock backward but then holds firm. Freezing water pours down the stairway and takes Violet's breath away. She coughs and gasps to get it back. Old Sally said the ocean was warm for this time of year, but to her, it feels freezing cold. It pours from overhead, forming a steadily rising pool of water in the bottom of the lighthouse. The generator flickers on and off several times and mercifully stays on. Without the beacon, they would be in total darkness.

Violet holds onto her girls so tightly she can barely feel her hands. She refuses to let them be washed away into the dark, freezing water. Her teeth chatter, her body longing for sunlight and warmth. For an instant, she imagines sitting with Old Sally on the porch when Violet was a girl. A sunny, warm day stretching out in front of them.

Like someone filling a glass of water from a giant faucet, the frigid water fills the lighthouse frighteningly fast. It rises a third of the way, and then halfway up the wall. In seconds it is below Jack and Heather's feet, who cling to the railings like everybody else. They are all stacked like sardines in a metal tin on the top half of the steps.

In the next instant, Violet loses her grip on the railing, and the force of the water pulls Tia away from her. Tia screams and is washed down to the step below. Spud grabs her and pulls her between him and Queenie. One by one they inch themselves higher up the steps to get away from the rising water. Finally, Violet and Leisha are at the top of the lighthouse stairs looking down. If they go as far as the landing they will have nothing to hold onto. The cat carrier, along with the turtle terrarium, are passed up the steps to keep them safe from the rising water. Lucy and Ethel and Harpo stay with their owners.

The papers Heather had in her purse float on the top of the water, a swirl of off-white pages. Rose grabs as many as she can and stuffs them in the pocket of her raincoat before the rest of the faded ledger floats away. Along with the pages are their suitcases, rising from under the staircase. They swirl like part of an oceanic baggage claim area. Violet gasps, seeing her suitcase begin to swirl on a conveyor belt she cannot get close enough to claim. She thinks of all the photographs she crammed into her one suitcase, the special ones she would be the most bereft at losing. But she has no time to grieve her losses now. The sea threatens to swallow them whole.

Time slows, perhaps the last seconds of her life ticking away. Thankfulness fills her like the water filling the light-house. She thinks of how much she loves Jack and the girls. How much she loves her makeshift family and the home they built together. How much she appreciates finally getting to open her dream tea shop. Her shop may be underwater, too. But she can't think about that now. If she is lucky enough to survive, she will deal with whatever the aftermath brings. Grateful for the chance.

The storm surge finally slows and stops rising.

Seconds later Queenie begins to giggle. Adrenaline releasing, no doubt. Before long they all are laughing, tears in their eyes. Giddy with relief that they have survived the most dangerous part of the storm, couples kiss. Family members hug. Friends embrace and pat each other on the back. All except Heather. But then Violet notices that Old Sally isn't laughing, either. In the next second, she realizes what Old Sally already knows. All waves—big or small—must return to the sea. The storm surge is only half over. This awareness passes to the others. The wall of water is on its way back out. If there is worse news, Violet can't imagine it.

A new surge of water rushes in, coming from the other direction. The water swirls its wildness and starts to rise again. It makes Violet dizzy to watch it.

Along with the tons of ocean water comes tons of debris into the lighthouse. Fish, some floating dead and others frantically trying to stay alive, swirl in the water with pieces of trees and houses. Things living and dead churn together in the crucible of the lighthouse. Drowning is no longer their primary concern. They must also avoid being crushed by debris.

The water edges its way up the walls again, surpassing the high-water mark from moments before. It leaves Jack and Heather halfway underwater.

Violet prays to the lighthouse to keep them safe. The beacon light flickers again as if wanting to offer them hope on such a dark night. It groans and clanks. The water forces them even higher, edging them toward the beacon. Broken glass litters the way and crunches underneath Violet's shoes. No longer is there a danger of water coming in from the top, it is now on its way out. The new threat comes from below, the threat of being pulled out of the lighthouse with the receding floodwater.

From Violet's new vantage point, the intermittent beacon illuminates a horrifying sight. The land has disappeared entirely. The ocean is everywhere. As a girl, the sea had been her playmate, but now that playmate has turned dark and has come to claim her.

From now on, Violet and her family and friends may be part of a tragic story on the island, like the family that lost their lives because they captured a mermaid. They will be the unfortunate people who fled to a lighthouse during a hurricane and didn't survive. But Violet doesn't want her story to end this way. She refuses to end up as fish food.

The sea lunges forward one last time. Violet isn't sure how much time passes before the water starts to recede like water draining from a bathtub. Eventually, the wind also ceases to rage. Then, slowly, Iris begins to leave.

CHAPTER FORTY-NINE

Queenie

The orange-and-yellow sunrise filters in through the top of the lighthouse. They have remained crouched on the steps for what feels like hours and Queenie's sciatica is giving her fits. Wet, shaken, but alive, they wait for the water to recede. Spud holds Queenie in his arms and tells her the worst is over.

"That had better be true, Mister Grainger." Queenie is weary from having not slept and is so hungry if she had a way to fry these fish thrashing around she would have some breakfast.

Katie shrieks with the labor pains that are coming with growing frequency. Everyone wearing a wristwatch checks the time. The pains are only a minute apart now. It is all Queenie can do to not shriek with her. One of those primal screams like she used to do when driving over the Talmadge Bridge from Savannah on the way to Dolphin Island.

Old Sally, Violet, Rose, and Angela are now with Katie at

the top of the lighthouse, by far the driest place they could be. Queenie likes that it also gives Katie a little privacy. Anticipating the storm surge, Max and Jack created a spot near the beacon for Katie to give birth, the floor padded with army blankets. They also brought the first-aid kit from the old footlocker. It is not ideal, since everything is wet, but it is better than nothing.

At least a foot of water still stands in the lighthouse and keeps them from venturing down the metal stairs. A baby shark thrashes around in the low water, trapped inside as the wave went out. Max and Jack grab two boards and stand on each side of the baby shark to help guide it through the doorway. But the shark is frightened and swims into the darkened corners of the lighthouse.

A metal trash can lid floats in. Queenie fishes it out and bangs it against the metal stairs to discourage the shark from swimming near them. It works. Their unwelcome guest finally finds its way outside and into the small river of water returning to the sea. Given the shark's example, one by one they carefully wade through the debris.

In stark contrast to the dark eye of Iris, the sunrise is so bright that Queenie has to cover her eyes. A new day greets them. A perfect summer day, from the looks of it. However, this day isn't at all typical. Even though the wind and rain have stopped, the morning light reveals a chaotic scene that reminds her of 9/11.

Queenie remembers that awful day last fall. They had only been living on the island for a few months when they sat around the television in the living room watching those towers go down, all of them disbelieving that this horrific event could happen here in the United States. Old Sally went silent for days, as did Spud. No one knew what to do. Life seemed suddenly dangerous and unpredictable, just like now. All distractions fell away. A few weeks later, Spud proposed to Queenie. And Katie got pregnant again after miscarrying a few months before. The most essential elements of life seemed clear. Humans aren't meant to be isolated and alone. We are destined to be together and create community. No matter what that might look like. And together they became survivors in a way, just like now.

"I have something I need to say to you," Queenie says to Spud. "But I don't want to hurt your feelings."

"Go on," Spud says, a look of concern in his eyes.

Queenie pauses. She isn't someone who usually needs the courage to speak her mind.

"I want to keep my old name," she says.

"Yes?" Spud says, waiting for her to say more.

"That's it," she says. "Just that one thing."

"Of course, gingersnap." Spud gives her a relieved smile, as though much more concerned that he was about to be asked to find new homes for his bow ties.

"You don't mind?" Queenie asks.

"Not one bit," he says. "You'll still be my wife, and that's all I really want."

Now it is Queenie's turn to look relieved.

Spud helps Queenie leave the lighthouse.

"Careful, sweetheart," he says, wading through the water in front of her. "Watch your step."

Queenie watches every step and then some. She has no intention of falling into what smells like the inside of a dumpster at Red Lobster.

Outside, water continues to make its way back to the sea, cutting jagged ruts deep into the soft earth. Large puddles create a natural obstacle course. Queenie hangs onto Spud's arm. It seems years have passed since they made their way to the lighthouse last evening.

Live oak trees, once majestic and beautiful along the shoreline, lie wounded on their sides, their roots exposed like the one that now rests in Queenie's bedroom. The ones that have not entirely fallen over lean in unison in the direction Iris came, like witnesses pointing out a murderer in a courtroom.

In addition to the fallen oaks, pine trees are snapped halfway up, as if Iris took a giant ax and knocked all the trees down with one blow. Queenie feels oddly satisfied. Iris has thrown a massive temper tantrum for everyone to see, not just Queenie. A hissy fit of hurricane proportions.

A butterfly crosses in front of them, following a jagged flight pattern, drunk from the storm or perhaps disoriented by its surroundings. A visible mark graces the outside of the lighthouse about fourteen feet up. Is it possible that the storm surge was this high?

Max reports that his truck is nowhere to be seen. Washed away by the storm surge.

Spud squeezes Queenie's hand. "I hope we still have a home."

Queenie hasn't thought that far ahead. When the Temple mansion burned down, she felt displaced for months. But once they moved to the beach, she felt like she was finally home.

Sweet God in heaven, Queenie thinks, *please don't ask me to start over again.*

But from the looks of things that seems entirely possible. She reminds herself that houses don't make homes, but the love and the people in them do. It seems trite to even think that way, but she will settle for any comfort she can find.

With Spud nearby, Queenie takes in the scene of the chaos on their island. When they were outside during the eye of the storm, Queenie would have never thought the destruction could get any worse. Unfortunately, it did. The dunes are gone. Debris is everywhere, dotting the beach. Vast rivers of water return to the sea. The one-lane road to the lighthouse has been washed away, water still standing everywhere. They have no way of letting anyone know where they are.

Unexpected things have traveled on the wind or washed up with the swollen tide. Next to the lighthouse are a variety of displaced objects: a rake, an unopened bag of diapers, the gate of a white picket fence, a yellow rain boot, a container of mint-flavored dental floss, and a pink toilet seat that Queenie hopes no one was sitting on.

The concrete steps leading from the beach to the lighthouse have disappeared, along with the railing. There is some question of how they will get home. Heather sits on an overturned tree a few yards away. The storm seems to have taken away all her rough edges. She still looks like a younger version of Iris in this light, but also like someone who is lost (like in "Amazing Grace") and not yet found.

During their time at the lighthouse, Heather made no effort to connect with any of them. Hard times usually bring people together. But not Heather. If anything, it seems to have reminded her of how separate she is.

The sunny, humid day feels more like late August instead of June. However, the sky is the bluest Queenie has ever seen it. If not for the astounding physical evidence around them, no one would believe a hurricane had hit a few hours before.

Isolated at the lighthouse, she has no idea how far the damage extends. For all she knows, Iris may have devastated not only Dolphin Island but Savannah, as well. It is the not knowing that is the worst.

In the distance, Queenie hears what sounds like Iris returning. But then they realize it is a rescue helicopter flying along the coast. Excited, everyone gathers near the lighthouse and waves as it hovers nearby.

A man on the helicopter uses a bullhorn to ask how many of them there are, promising to return with help soon. They look at each other, counting, yelling different numbers until Queenie finally gets it right: "Almost thirteen!"

In the aftermath of Hurricane Iris, the most devastating event Queenie has ever witnessed, it seems that the most significant development is happening now, as Katie pushes a new life into their world. Lucky number thirteen.

CHAPTER FIFTY

Old Sally

Old Sally hasn't delivered a baby in years, but Violet is a great help, and of course, Katie and the baby know through pure instinct what to do. Overhead, helicopter sounds drown out Katie's efforts for a time, before it moves away. With the final push, Old Sally catches a perfect baby girl in her arms.

After the cord is cut and the mother and baby are resting, Old Sally takes out a thimble she put in her pocket right before she came to the lighthouse.

"What are you doing?" Violet asks.

"The first water taken by a new mother must be sipped from a thimble," Old Sally says. "This will ease the baby's first tooth."

Violet helps Old Sally pour a tiny bit of bottled water into the thimble before giving it to Katie. Then Rose and Violet help Old Sally finally stand. She has been on the floor for over an hour, with only a soggy folded army blanket underneath her knees. She is wobbly, at best, yet also exhilarated to have helped a new life come into this world.

"What's this?" Rose asks, picking up a small glass container filled with what looks like dirty sand.

"Oh, that be mine, too," Old Sally says, returning the small bottle to her pocket along with the thimble. "Childbirth be a dangerous time," she continues. "Mother and baby are vulnerable to spirits who may wish them harm. But I brought along some graveyard dirt to protect them."

Violet and Rose exchange a look of surprise.

A warm, salty breeze drifts through the broken windows at the top of the lighthouse. Old Sally looks out over the island. Her island. The island of her Gullah ancestors. The last time she stood in this spot was the night she and Fiddle stayed here. On that night, so long ago, it was romantic to look out over the island because she was so much in love. Her knees were wobbly then, too.

The baby cries and Rose helps Katie place her new daughter at Katie's breast to feed.

"Birth be such a hopeful process," Old Sally says. *As is death,* she wants to say, looking out over the eternal sea.

"Do you have a name yet?" Violet asks.

Angela and Katie exchange a look, and Katie nods, giving Angela permission to say it.

"Sally Rose."

Old Sally lets out a short laugh, and tears rush to her eyes. Rose takes Old Sally's hand.

"What an honor," Old Sally says to them.

"Truly," adds Rose, who is a mixture of tears and smiles.

This lighthouse holds a vibrant part of her history. From now on, Sally Rose will have a history here, too, just like Old Sally, and everyone who survived the storm. Someday, Sally

Rose may even run down the beach and play here. A descendant of the light.

DOLPHIN ISLAND EXPERIENCED the full force of the storm. Not only were the winds devastating, but most of the island was underwater. It turns out that the lighthouse was the safest place they could have been.

While most people experienced the storm sitting in long lines on the interstate, those who stayed on the island sought refuge on the second floors of their houses or in their attics. After the storm, there were stories of resilience everywhere. Stories of people climbing into live oaks in their backyards to try to outrun the sea—rescue workers found them the next day, clinging to limbs, battered and bruised. Stories of people coming from all over the United States to help the residents of Dolphin Island with the aftermath of the storm. Helpers who brought bottled water, food, supplies, and generators because they were told it would be months before the power would be restored. Miraculously, only one person died on the island, an elderly gentleman who had a heart attack while hammering up plywood before the storm.

The winter after Hurricane Iris, bulldozers droned up the beach, rebuilding the fragile dunes that were destroyed by the storm surge. Like the helicopter that found them, the sound of the bulldozers reminded Old Sally and the others of Iris's roar. Iris changed everything on Dolphin Island. Even now the ocean spits out reminders of the storm. Pieces of houses. Pieces of people's lives.

When they returned to their home after the storm, two feet of water was still in the house, but it had been much higher. The high-water mark stopped right below Queenie and Spud's wedding presents in the top of Queenie's closet. A fact that made Queenie cackle, as well as cry. While most of their things were destroyed, the structure and foundation of the house stayed strong. Old Sally attributes this to the graveyard dirt she used to surround the house. Dirt she gathered at midnight, the night before the storm hit, from her grandmother's grave. Midnight being when the graveyard dirt is the most potent.

Like everybody else on the island after the storm, they started a massive cleanup that took months to complete, and then they began rebuilding. Like the pains of childbirth that most mothers forget, Old Sally has mostly forgotten the pains of starting over. What matters most is that Katie and her baby are healthy, and they all survived.

ON THE ONE-YEAR anniversary of the hurricane, Old Sally sits facing the sea in her favorite rocking chair. Life has a habit of keeping on. She has lived on this same piece of land her entire life. A rare occurrence these days. In extreme contrast to Iris's storm surge, waves break gently along the shoreline. Now that things are starting to return to normal, there are some days she can fool herself into thinking that the storm didn't happen at all.

There will always be storms. Storms of the heart and mind, and storms on land. Storms that have a beginning, a middle, and an end, and storms that seemingly last forever.

Where the old live oak once stood, a new oak is rising. An upstart, as we all are upstarts in one way or another, with the clear purpose of sinking roots where its ancestor once stood.

Without speaking, Old Sally sends Violet a message to join her. She has a final ritual to share with her, and then the passing on of the Gullah secrets will be complete.

Violet has seemed different since the storm, somehow lighter, but also more purposeful. Her tea shop suffered no damage. But it is more than that. She is growing into her wisdom.

We're getting good at this, Violet says to Old Sally when she steps outside.

Old Sally agrees.

"Have you seen the painting Rose is working on?" Violet asks, speaking aloud this time. "I just saw it." Her eyes dance with pleasure.

"She showed it to me last night," Old Sally says. "She told me it be the first portrait she's ever done. It's for sure the first portrait of me to ever exist."

"She did a wonderful job," Violet says. "It's a great likeness of you. And we've already decided where we want to put it in the living room."

"Oh my." Old Sally's face warms.

"The one she wants to work on next has all of us standing in front of the lighthouse," Violet says.

Old Sally remembers the storm and thanks her ancestors for helping them stay safe. A sudden awareness reminds her that her work is finished. She has done enough.

"I be so glad Rose is painting again," Old Sally says. "How are things at the tea shop?"

"Queenie and Spud are covering the breakfast crowd this morning," she says. "How are you feeling? Still a bit dizzy?"

"I have moments. But nothing to worry about."

Old Sally sleeps more than she is awake these days, her world full of dreams. When she isn't sleeping, she is here in her rocking chair overlooking the sea. Or telling Gullah stories to Katie and Sally Rose. Her walks on the beach with Rose are now short ones. She can no longer make it to the lighthouse. Yet, its purpose in her life has been fulfilled.

"Just a reminder that Rose is in Savannah today to handle the court issue," Violet says.

"Did you tell me about this before? I can't remember what it was about," Old Sally says. She has very little interest in worldly things these days. Not the news or the weather or anything that doesn't have to do with this island and her place on it.

Violet sits in the rocker next to Old Sally and reminds her about the ledger pages that Rose rescued from the rising water in the lighthouse. It seems they contained a manifest for that old Civil War ship that sank off the coast. It turns out that the boat didn't have soldiers on it, but gold to subsidize the war.

"It was a Temple ship," Violet concludes.

Old Sally chuckles. "Too bad Iris didn't live to see that. She would have been tickled pink. But why does Rose have to go to court?"

"Heather says the ledger was in her possession and belonged to her father. She's suing Rose for the contents of that old ship," Violet says.

"Oh my," Old Sally says again.

"Rose and I have been trying to put all the pieces together," Violet begins again, "and it looks like Heather and her half brother planned the whole thing based on information their mother gave them before she died last year. Heather's brother goes to college in Savannah, and Rose and I saw them in my tea shop one day."

"Fascinating," Old Sally says, always amazed by the drive of humans to amass money when true riches are never—ever —tangible.

"Years ago, their mother was researching the Temples and

found an old newspaper article that told about the ship," Violet continues. "Then she must have heard about those secrets being released in the Savannah newspaper and put two and two together."

"You know, I saw Heather take that old book from Rose's purse when we were outside during the eye of the hurricane." Old Sally rocks gently in her rocking chair.

"You did?"

Old Sally nods. "It's a good thing that the storm surge took most of it. All those secrets needed to finally be buried at sea. And all those Temple ghosts finally put to rest."

"Rose said something very similar," Violet says. "The attorney seems to think it's an open-and-shut case. Heather doesn't really have any rights in this situation. But we'll see. In the meantime, there are no plans on locating the ship yet," Violet continues. "I guess they have to figure out who has rights to it first."

"And just as that old Temple ledger be buried at sea, the Gullah Book of Secrets be born."

Violet holds up her notebook, held together with a sturdy rubber band, and filled with everything Old Sally has told her over the last two years.

"I be relieved it wasn't lost in the storm," Old Sally says.

Violet agrees. "I had it stuck in my shirt, as close to my heart as I could get it," she says.

"That be very smart," Old Sally says. "You want to finish up our lesson out here?"

Violet pulls a pen from her pocket and opens her book to take notes. Old Sally notices that it is near the end of the book, and Old Sally is at the end of what she needs to share.

"Ready?" she asks Violet.

Violet nods, her book open, pen in hand.

Old Sally pauses again, gathering her thoughts. She tells Violet how very few people remember the funeral rituals used when Old Sally was a girl in the early 1900s. In those days it was believed that if a dead person didn't have a proper funeral, their spirit would be unable to join the ancestors and be doomed to wander around and cause trouble as ghosts. In the Temple mansion, this unfortunate dilemma played out all the time.

"I remember that dilemma quite well," Violet says. The two of them exchange a smile.

"When I be four years old," Old Sally begins again, "I be passed over the open grave of my Grandpa Joe at the cemetery. Several times, in fact."

Violet's expression is one of disbelief, but Old Sally crosses her heart that it is true.

Violet shivers. "What if they had dropped you?"

"That happened to one of my cousins once, but thankfully not to me."

"But why would they pass you over an open grave?"

Old Sally pauses again, remembering how her grandmother explained it to her.

"I be his favorite grandchild," Old Sally begins. "There was a worry that our attachment was so strong that he might pull me into the spirit world and that I would die, too. Passing me over the coffin was the Gullah way of cutting our connection to each other so that he could go to the ancestors, and I could stay here and finish out my time on earth."

Violet writes swiftly to capture every word.

"Children can hear the voices of the dead, you know," Old Sally begins again. "Even more if they are close to the person who died. I remember my Grandpa Joe talking to me long after he was buried."

Violet gasps but doesn't let it deter her from writing. The sound of Violet's pen flowing across the paper, documenting her words, gives Old Sally a sense of deep satisfaction. A written record will exist now, instead of only a spoken one. As a girl, she was proud of herself for learning to read and has read books her entire life. She was the first in her family to learn to read, and after her everybody did.

"Rituals were part of everything, especially deaths," Old Sally continues. "The night before he died, my Grandpa Joe had a 'sit up.' A vigil that goes on all night. Relatives and friends sang and shouted over him."

"They shouted?" Violet's eyes widen.

"You bet they did," Old Sally says. "My grandmother told me the reasoning behind it all later, but with Grandpa Joe I was old enough to see it with my own eyes."

Old Sally remembers how hot it was that night. It was high summer.

"First they said prayers to strengthen him as he passed by death's door," she continues. "Then the instant he died everyone in the room shrieked and shouted to scare off the spirits of hell that always roam the earth and search for a soul to claim."

"Oh my," Violet says, still writing. "What happened next?"

"After the shouting, there was all this sobbing and grieving from everybody there," Old Sally says. "I remember sitting in my grandmother's lap, who cried so much my little dress was soaked straight through."

Old Sally waits for Violet's ballpoint pen to slow and then finally stop.

"This is fascinating." Violet smiles and looks at Old Sally as if receiving an unexpected gift.

"That's not all," Old Sally begins again. "After that, several women came to our house to wash and dress Grandpa Joe and prepare his body. Coffee was placed under his arms, legs, and open spaces, then his body was dressed and kept for three days." Old Sally pictures it as she describes it, remembering more of the ritual. "They used water in an earthen pot to clean him, and they made a big deal about how the water inside must never touch the ground. The water was sacred. Later, the pot and remaining water would be placed on the top of the grave."

Like her dreams these days, the scene she describes is so real Old Sally can almost smell the coffee grounds. She waits again for Violet's pen to stop and gives her a moment to rest. Violet nods when she is ready to begin again.

"Some of his favorite things were placed on his grave," Old Sally continues. "The knife he used his entire life. His favorite coffee cup. His plate and silverware. A deck of cards in a wooden box—the box he had carved himself. A layer of white seashells was created on top of the grave to look like the ocean. The ocean that brought him here and the ocean that would return him to the ancestors."

This morning, Old Sally visited the graveyard. Jack drove her over there first thing. Several markers had washed away when Iris came ashore, but last winter Violet hired someone to return it to how it looked when Sally was a girl.

Space is saved for Old Sally, overlooking the ocean, under the live oak in the back that survived Hurricane Iris. She will be next to her husband, who died in the war, and both her parents and her beloved grandmother on the other side of the tree. Close enough to hold hands if they wanted to. This morning when Old Sally walked among the simple graves, she was aware that she wouldn't exist if not for the people who came before her. To those people she owes everything.

"I don't expect you to do all that for me, Violet, but when

the times comes, hopefully very soon, Sally Rose must be passed over my grave. And you must put this on my grave." Old Sally hands her the piece of cloth with her baby's embroidered A.

Tears spring to Violet's eyes, and Old Sally reaches over and takes her hand.

"Please don't be sad, sweet girl. It be a celebration."

"But, I'm going to miss you so much."

"I know you will," Old Sally says, squeezing Violet's hand. "But we can still talk to each other. And when it's your time, I'll be right there to help prepare the way."

Old Sally thinks how lucky they are to get to say goodbye. Not everyone does.

Violet leaves the rocking chair and gets down on her knees in front of Old Sally. She puts her head on her lap, her tears making Old Sally's dress wet. Salty tears by the salty sea. Old Sally caresses Violet's face and wipes her tears like she used to do when Violet was a little girl.

"I know a lot about grief," Old Sally tells her, her voice soft. "When someone you love dies, grief comes like a hurricane and threatens to destroy you. But grief isn't bad," she continues. "Grief means you've loved someone with your whole heart. Love and grief go hand in hand. There's no other way."

Old Sally was right to pass the mantle of Gullah secrets to Violet, and perhaps Tia or Leisha will be the next to carry the secrets. Or maybe even Sally Rose. Everyone else has died off. Families have left the island. But it is important to remember the history. We stand on the shoulders of our ancestors. Those known to us and those unknown. Some we can be proud of and others we would like to forget. But all are important. And our job is to always try to do better.

"Last night, I dreamed of my grandmother again," Old Sally says to Violet.

"You've been doing that a lot." Violet takes a tissue from her pocket and blows her nose before returning to her own rocking chair.

"Would you like to hear the dream?" Old Sally asks.

Violet nods.

"My grandmother was walking down the beach toward this house," Old Sally begins. "She was as real as anything, and she was wearing the indigo-colored dress she wore whenever she had reason to celebrate. She was buried in that dress."

Before the hurricane, Old Sally still had indigo plants out behind the cottage that her grandmother had cultivated to make dye. But since the storm, those plants are gone.

"In the dream, I realized how much I had missed her," Old Sally says.

"I wish I could have known her," Violet says.

"You'll know her someday," Old Sally says. "When it's your turn to celebrate."

Violet retakes her hand. "I need to tell you something."

"Yes?" Old Sally says, looking into Violet's eyes.

"It has been a great honor to learn the Gullah secrets from you."

Now it is Old Sally's turn to use a tissue. "It has been my great pleasure to teach them to you."

For several seconds they sit together in silence. A moment of grace by the sea. Then Violet glances at her watch and apologizes for having to get to the tea shop.

"I can send Katie and Sally Rose to sit with you if you'd like," she says to Old Sally.

"No, no, I'm fine. I like sitting out here alone sometimes.

Did you know that I was born almost exactly in this same spot? It was back when babies were born at home."

"I never knew that," Violet says. "But come to think of it, I was born in this spot, too."

"You were indeed," Old Sally says.

A Gullah person wants to die in their place of birth. Even if they move away, many want to come back home to die and be buried there if they can. Old Sally is lucky that she never had to leave.

I love you, Violet, Old Sally says in their unspoken way of conversing.

I love you, too, Violet answers. She leans over and kisses Old Sally on the cheek before walking away. *Can we talk more when I get home?* she asks.

Of course, Old Sally says, knowing how important this will be.

ALONE AGAIN, Old Sally overlooks the vast ocean. Waves rise and fall and break gently on the shore. After months of staying away after the storm, dolphins have finally returned to the inlet. One swims now in the distance, its fin gracing the surface of the water, and then it is joined by another. The sky is a vibrant blue. It reminds her of the bluebird singing on the porch before the storm. A sign of company coming.

The June day feels somehow new. It reminds Old Sally of the eye of the storm and the feeling of absolute calm that came over her on that dark night. All the chaos ceased. Millions of stars embraced her, along with a full moon, and she felt part of the entire universe.

Violin music begins to play. A lilting, floating melody. Fiddle, her love from long ago, stands in the dunes. It reminds her of Queenie's wedding. Sweet Queenie. Old Sally is so glad she finally found love. Her daughter will be fine now. As will the others. They will continue on as we all do, risking love and risking grief.

Meanwhile, Fiddle looks the same age as the night she last saw him. His smile makes her feel young again.

A sense of deep joy washes over her like a gentle tide. Seconds later, her grandmother approaches, wearing her indigo dress. The one reserved for celebrations. Old Sally takes her grandmother's hand as she leaves her old body behind. She always knew it would be her grandmother who came for her.

THE END

~

Dear Reader,

Even before I began writing this sequel to *Temple Secrets*, I knew that *Gullah Secrets* would end with Old Sally's death and that the character wouldn't fear it, but welcome it. Perhaps I wanted to believe that it is possible to leave this life—as we all must—with gratitude and a sense of completion.

I began writing *Gullah Secrets* in 2016. Since then several hurricanes have impacted the United States, most recently Hurricane Florence which devastated the eastern part of my state of North Carolina. My heart goes out to everyone who has suffered in those storms. In 1989 I was living with my two young daughters in Charleston, SC when Hurricane Hugo hit the area. My experiences in that storm greatly informed *Gullah Secrets*.

I am grateful to you, dear reader, for taking the time to read this book and others that I have written. It is an honor to create stories for you. I love hearing from readers, and I welcome your emails. Feel free to let me know what you think of *Gullah Secrets*.

Next, I will be writing the third book in the *Temple Secrets Series*. if you would like to be notified when it is published, please sign up here: susangabriel.com/new-books.

Thank you again for spending time with me and these characters I create. I hope this story somehow helps you keep your courage fires burning.

With every good wish.

Susan Gabriel

P.S. If you enjoyed *Gullah Secrets*, I am always grateful for reviews. It helps new readers discover my books.

ACKNOWLEDGMENTS

Gullah Secrets came into being because the readers of *Temple Secrets* asked for more from the characters they had grown to love—Old Sally, Queenie, Rose and Violet. Thankfully, I loved these characters, too, and was happy to spend more time with them and continue their story. So, first of all, thank you to my endearing readers. A writer is nothing without her readers.

Of great help to me on *Gullah Secrets* was my daughter, Krista Lunsford, whose love of history and research talents made her the perfect person to gather information on Gullah spells and traditions. Anything you found interesting in this book is surely a result of her input. Also, of monumental importance to my writing life is my business manager, Anne Alexander, who skillfully completes all the marketing and technical things that are so absolutely foreign to my writer skill set. And if that isn't enough, she also talks me down from the cliff whenever my confidence wanes.

The first readers of this book were incredibly helpful in

offering their feedback: Nancy Purcell, Cheryl Groeneveld, Susan Burnside and Maureen McGough. Susan Burnside also does an amazing job as project manager for the audiobook versions of all my books. Thanks to Laura Dragonette for her excellent copy editing and Lizzie Gardiner, who created the wonderful cover.

Gratitude to all of these members of my writing team who have been an enormous help in getting *Gullah Secrets* out into the world and into the hands of readers.

ABOUT THE AUTHOR

Susan Gabriel is an Amazon & Nook #1 bestselling author who lives in the mountains of North Carolina. Her novel, *The Secret Sense of Wildflower*, earned a starred review ("for books of remarkable merit") from Kirkus Reviews and was selected as one of their Best Books of 2012.

She is also the author of *Temple Secrets, Trueluck Summer, Lily's Song, Grace, Grits and Ghosts: Southern Short Stories* and other books. Discover more about Susan at SusanGabriel.com.

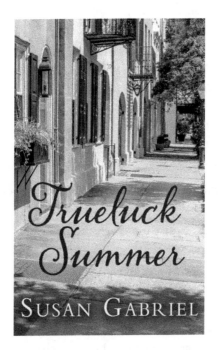

A hopeful grandmother. A sassy young girl. Their audacious summer stunt could change their southern town forever.

Charleston, 1964. Ida Trueluck is still adjusting to life on her own. Moving into her son's house creates a few family conflicts, but the widow's saving grace is her whipsmart granddaughter Trudy. Ida makes it her top priority to give the girl a summer she'll never forget.

When a runaway truck nearly takes her life, Trudy makes fast friends with the boy who saves her. But since Paris is black, the racism they encounter inspires Trudy's surprising summer mission: to take down the Confederate flag from the South Carolina Statehouse. And she knows she can't do it without the help of her beloved grandmother.

With all of Southern society conspiring against them, can Trudy, Ida, and their friends pull off the impossible?

Trueluck Summer is a Southern historical women's fiction novel set in a time of great cultural change. If you like courageous characters, heartwarming humor, and inspirational acts, then you'll love Susan Gabriel's captivating tale.

Buy *Trueluck Summer* to live the courage of youth today!

Available in print, ebook and audiobook.

Praise for *Trueluck Summer*

"Having read three previous captivating books by this author I was afraid this book may disappoint. In the first chapter I knew I was in for a treat. Once again, I fell in love with the richly drawn characters. I could not wait to find the time to read this treasure. The courage shown by these characters portrays how real change evolves. It is a book you will not forget!" – Cheryl Quinn

"*Trueluck Summer* is a thoughtful, excellently written adventure. I am a big fan of Susan Gabriel's books and this one may just be one of her best. She brought Charleston and the characters to life. I felt like I laughed and cried with Trudy, Ida and Paris. Was scared with them and proud of them. I will reread." – Molly

"WOW what a book. Even though it is written about what was going on in the southern states in the late 1950's, unfortunately it still exists. I have read several books by this fantastic writer, and thought each one was the best, until I read the next one. It is truly a book worth reading and then look forward for her next book. Great job Susan Gabriel....this historical fiction really shows what it was like in that time period." – Ro

"Just finished *Trueluck Summer* and I loved it. Such an important message for these troubled times…Not only was the subject matter of the story poignantly written, the aura brought back so many good memories from my childhood during this era."

– Joan Meyerhoefer Roddy

"Simply fantastic!! The emotions of this story are as relevant today as in the timeframe in which the story was written. I didn't want it to end and hope there may be a sequel in the future that will continue the fascinating story of the characters."– Mary

"This is a coming of age story, for all ages. A story of the 60's when not only people in that era had difficult choices to make, but of a country, stretching and becoming more, finding its footing as much as any adolescent. If you didn't live through the sixties, then this book will speak to you of things on a large scale, and on smaller ones. It shows you the sweeping changes, and the fear that people battled as they dealt with all the volatile situations. The book has heart. And soul." – Loretta Wheeler

Available in print, ebook and audiobook.

"A quietly powerful story, at times harrowing,

but ultimately a joy to read."

—Kirkus Reviews, starred review

(for books of remarkable merit)

Named to Kirkus Reviews' Best Books of 2012.

Small southern towns have few secrets. But when a grieving daughter confronts the local bad boy, she exposes a dark history.

Appalachia, 1941. Thirteen-year-old Louisa May "Wildflower" McAllister's heart still aches for her father. A year after her dad's tragic sawmill accident, she relies on her strength of spirit and her heightened intuition to deal with a critical mother and cope with the aftermath.

But when she's targeted by the town's teenage bully, she may need more than her "secret sense" to survive.

Despite these hardships, Wildflower has a resilience that is forged with humor, a love of the land, and an endless supply of questions to God.

But after an affront to her father's memory, she lets her anger get the better of her and unwittingly triggers a series of traumatic events that will change her life forever.

Will Wildflower fall to another tragedy or will her faith in her family and herself be enough to carry her through?

With prose as lush and colorful as the American south, *The Secret Sense of Wildflower* is powerful and poignant, brimming with energy and angst, humor and hope.

Available in print, ebook and audiobook.

Praise for *The Secret Sense of Wildflower*

"Louisa May immerses us in her world with astute observations and wonderfully turned phrases, with nary a cliché to be found. She could be an adolescent Scout Finch, had Scout's father died unexpectedly and her life taken a bad turn...By necessity, Louisa May grows up quickly, but by her secret sense, she also under-stands forgiveness. A quietly powerful story, at times harrowing but ultimately a joy to read." – Kirkus Reviews

"A soulful narrative to keep the reader emotionally charged and invested. *The Secret Sense of Wildflower* is eloquent and moving tale chock-filled with themes of inner strength, family and love."
– Maya Fleischmann, indiereader.com

"I've never read a story as dramatically understated that sings so powerfully and honestly about the sense of life that stands in tribute to bravery as Susan Gabriel's *The Secret Sense of Wildflower*...When fiction sings, we must applaud."
– T. T. Thomas, author of *A Delicate Refusal*

"The story is powerful, very powerful. Excellent visuals, good drama. I raced to get to the conclusion...but didn't really want to read the last few pages because then it would be over! I look forward to Gabriel's next offering." – Nancy Purcell, Author

"Just finished this with tears streaming down my face. Beautifully written with memorable characters who show resilience in the face of tragedy. I couldn't put this down and will seek Susan Gabriel's other works. This is truly one of the best books I've read in a very long time." – A.C.

"An interesting story enhanced by great writing, this book was a page turner. It captures life in the Tennessee mountains truthfully but not harshly. I would recommend this book to anyone who enjoys historical fiction." – E. Jones

"I don't even know how to tell you what I love about this book --- the incredible narrator? The heartbreaking and inspiring storyline? The messages about hope, wisdom, family and strength? All of those!! Everything about it!" – K. Peck

"Lovely, soul stirring novel. I absolutely could not put it down! Beautifully descriptive, evocative story told in the voice of Wildflower, a young girl of the mountains, set in a wild yet beautiful 1940's mountain town, holds you captive from the start. I had to wait to write my review, as I was crying too hard to see!" – V.C.

"I write novels, too, but this writer is fantastic. The story is authentic and gripping. Her voice through the child, Wildflower, is captivating. This story would make a great movie. I love stories that portray life changing tragedy and pain coupled with power of the human spirit to survive and continue to love and forgive. Bravo! Susan. Please write more and more." – Judi D.

"This is a wonderful story that will make you laugh, cry, and cheer." – T.B. Markinson

"I was pretty blown away by how good this book is. I didn't read it with any expectations, hadn't heard anything about it really, so when I read it, I realized from page one that it is a well written, powerful book." – Quixotic Magpie

"If you liked *Little Women* or if you love historical fiction and coming-of-age novels, this is the book for you. Definitely add The Secret Sense of Wildflower to your TBR pile; you won't regret it."
– PandaReads

"Bottom line: A great story about a strong character!"
– Meg, A Bookish Affair

Available in print, ebook and audiobook.

BOOKS BY SUSAN GABRIEL

Fiction

Temple Secret Series:
Temple Secrets
Gullah Secrets

The Wildflower Trilogy:
The Secret Sense of Wildflower
(a Best Book of 2012 – Kirkus Reviews)
Lily's Song
Daisy's Fortune

Trueluck Summer
Grace, Grits and Ghosts: Southern Short Stories
Seeking Sara Summers
Circle of the Ancestors
Quentin & the Cave Boy

Nonfiction

Fearless Writing for Women:
Extreme Encouragement & Writing Inspiration

CPSIA information can be obtained
at www.ICGtesting.com
Printed in the USA
LVHW021715160321
681694LV00005B/1169